GREEN EYES

GREEN EYES

By JEAN NIELSEN

Decorations by
MIMI KORACH

NEW YORK   FUNK & WAGNALLS COMPANY

1955

For Elmer

6

Green Eyes

CHAPTER 1

Special Assembly

IN FOUR HOURS and fifteen minutes the big news would be officially announced, and by evening, small towns being what they were, everyone would know about her.

Ever since yesterday afternoon, when she had appeared before the school council to receive her appointment, Jan Morgan had been in a half-thrilled-half-afraid-to-believe-it daze. Editor of the school paper—the goal of three years of high school and many more years of wanting to write. But it wouldn't seem real until it was officially announced, and in four hours and fifteen minutes the assembly bell would ring at Mountain View High and all the students would spill out of their classrooms, study halls, and labs and crowd into the auditorium. Then, when the band finished playing "The Stars and Stripes Forever," Mr. Larsen would take his glasses from his vest pocket, brush them quickly with his handkerchief, put them on, and read out the names of the newly chosen student-body officers.

Jan's hands were clumsy with excitement as she reached in the closet for her new dress, the dress that had caused such a family row because she wanted to save all her baby-sitting money to buy a typewriter and her mother had insisted that she needed something new for special occasions. An occasion just couldn't be any more special than this, Jan thought as she slipped it over her head.

But zipping it up and facing herself in the mirror, she grimaced. Special occasion or not, there didn't seem to be

1

much point in having a new dress that was modishly styled
and the green of new apple leaves when it hung on her like a
sack. She didn't any more fill it up than a ten-year-old.

With a sigh she smoothed it down and grabbed a hair-
brush. Nothing glamourous on the upper story, either. Just
straight and brown. Permanents didn't take on her hair, so
after one disastrous try she'd worn pigtails until a few weeks
ago when she had decided that any girl aspiring to be editor
of the *Argus* should look a little older. Over her mother's
protests she had unbraided her hair and, since she couldn't
think of anything else to do, tied a ribbon around it and let
it hang long and lank behind her.

Oh, well, it was her brains the school needed to edit the
Argus, not what covered them—though for some mysterious
and stupid reason the girls with pretty coverings on their
brains seemed to make a bigger splash in life than the plain
Janes or plain Jans.

"Janice!" Her mother's voice, harsh with early morning
hurry, interrupted her thoughts. "Janice, if you don't hurry
you won't have time for breakfast."

Jan quickly put down the brush, grabbed her sweater, and
clattered down stairs. Why, there were only three hours and
forty-five minutes left now!

Seeing Jan come in wearing the new dress, her mother
turned away from the stove with an approving smile. "Janice, that's very becoming. I'm so glad you decided on green.
Is something special happening today?"

"Why—why, I felt like spring," Jan evaded. Then as she sat
crumbling a piece of toast, much too excited to eat, she re-
considered. Mr. Larsen had said that she could tell her family, that they could come to the assembly, and Mother
sounded as if she really wanted to know; she sounded friendly,
almost gay, the way she used to be. "Mother," she began
shyly, "uh, Mother, are you going to be busy today?"

"So there *is* something special," her mother concluded.

"Well, you know what Friday is like with all the week-end shopping and baking to do and the house to be cleaned so it will look nice when your father comes home. But if there's something you need—"

"Not exactly," Jan interrupted nervously. "There's going to be a special assembly at school today and some of the parents are coming and I wondered . . ."

Her half-hearted words trailed off into uneasy silence. She had known all along that the word "assembly" would change her mother's mood from pleased expectation to anger. It always had the last few years. Why should she expect today to be different?

"Don't expect me to go to another of those affairs where they hand out honor pins for good grades," she said crossly. "You know I feel it isn't fair to judge a child's intelligence that way. Some of the most successful people in the world didn't get good grades in school."

Listening to her mother, watching her face get that special tight-lipped irritated look, Jan had a sense of uncertainty, as if she were not at home at all but cast up on a strange planet where no one spoke her language. Her parents had been so proud of her scholastic record once—she remembered their faces alight with pride as they bent over her report cards. They had given her a nickel for each A.

Any way you looked at it the reason for the change was Andrew. For her younger brother was a total creep scholastically. Here she was fifteen-and-a-half and finishing her junior year in high school, while Andrew at twelve was in the fifth grade.

Of course it wasn't all his fault. He had been as studious as most boys, which wasn't saying much, until the year he was eight when he had been skating and had fallen through the ice. He hadn't been in any danger of drowning—what the boys grandly called a pond was only a puddle—but by the time he dragged himself home his clothes were stiff and he had a cold that turned into an ear infection which in turn brought on a bout of rheumatic fever.

Andrew had spent most of the next year in bed. Jan didn't like to think about those months. They had been very unpleasant for everyone—especially her. Mother, who had been a friend and a companion, disappeared completely, leaving in her place a tired, worried woman who noticed her daughter only to scold her.

Andrew was back in school now, leading what the doctor called a "moderately active life," but his mother still hovered over him constantly, had no time for anyone else, and obviously felt that if he didn't get good grades, grades should be abolished.

"Honor pins aren't till next month," Jan reminded her. "This is different."

"The grading system isn't fair," her mother said. "Anyone who understands children can see that Andrew in his own way has as much ability as you. And think of all the poor boy has to overcome."

Jan pushed away her uneaten breakfast and stood up rebelliously. "Do you think it's fair for Andrew to have curly hair and a dimple in his chin while I'm all straight hair and bones? No one would know I was alive if I didn't win honors and get good grades. You aren't being fair when you pick on me just because I'm smart."

"Why, Janice, what a thing to say," her mother protested. "Naturally we're glad you get good grades. But you should realize there are other things in life, too. You've been getting more and more immersed in your studies and losing contact with the world. You don't seem to have any friends or any fun any more, and you used to be such a happy, sweet child. As for looks, you could be pretty if you wanted to be. You seem to *want* to sulk around looking sloppy. You don't try to bring out your best features."

"My mind is my best feature," Jan retorted.

"That's enough, Janice. I'm not going to argue with you," and her mother turned her back and began stacking the dishes.

Jan blinked back angry tears and thought wistfully about her father. He was always nice to her and interested in what she was doing, but that was small comfort when he was home only on week-ends. "If Dad were here instead of in the lumber camp, he would go," she said.

"I wish he lived at home, too, Janice, but you must remember that even the fathers who live at home and work here in town hardly ever go to school affairs in the middle of the morning."

Jan put on her sweater, gathered her books, and opened the door. Then she turned back and said, "That assembly is just the most important thing that ever happened to me and you don't care at all."

She slammed the door behind her and started the long walk to school. Alone, of course. There were other high school students strolling along in chattering groups, but Jan avoided them. They were silly, and besides they didn't like her. She was younger than the rest of the juniors and much too smart for most of them.

Usually she enjoyed her walk through town. First down the hill to River Road and along its tree-shaded length, with a furtive glance at the staring windows of the vacant house on the bluff. Then over the bridge, across the railroad tracks, and along the length of Main Street. From Main Street she climbed another hill to where Mountain View High School stood backed up against one of the Cascades while its front windows looked across the little valley to the ring of mountains on the other side.

In wintertime the deep snows made Cascadeville look like a ski resort advertisement, but now it was the last week of April and the foothills were every shade of green. As she crossed the bridge she took a quick automatic look at the river straining at its banks with the spring run-off from the mountains, too busy wondering—why she out of all the world had a family who didn't like her—to get any pleasure out of the sight. Presently Andrew rode by on his bicycle shouting, "Janny's mad and I'm glad . . ."

She stared after him somberly. What a terrible thing it was to dislike your own brother, but how could she help it when all he lived for was to tease her and turn her parents against her? Some of the other girls complained about brothers, too. Melanie Conners kept saying she was going to swipe some chloroform from her grandfather's office and fix that brat good and proper next time he heckled her friends, but she laughed and gave freckle-faced Jim an affectionate squeeze when she said it. Melanie wasn't really mad. Jan was.

Everything Andrew did was unfair. Whining till he got a bicycle, for instance, when his school wasn't half as far away as hers. Of course she didn't want a bicycle herself. She just wanted to be treated like a member of the family, not like an orphan left in a basket on the doorstep. Condensed, clarified, and flashing in her mind like a neon sign was the reason she couldn't stand Andrew: He had pushed her out of the family circle. Only you'd think that having demoted her to a second-class citizen he would let her alone instead of buzzing around like a mosquito trying to sting where it would hurt the most.

Well there was one thing about Andrew that was certain, he would never be editor of the *Argus*. He'd be lucky to get to high school at all. She rushed the rest of the way to school and looked up at the clock tower. Only two hours and thirty-five minutes now.

Morning classes had never been longer and duller, but finally it was assembly time and Jan sat twisting clammy fingers in her lap as she looked up at the stage. The officers standing there in self-conscious importance had been elected by their fellows. The editor was appointed by a joint student-faculty committee. It didn't matter too much if the student body elected a grinning moron as president—and sometimes they did—but the editor had to be able to write a coherent sentence.

She wrote a very coherent sentence, Jan reflected as she glanced down at the honor pin shining on her dress. In addition to turning in news and feature stories for the *Argus* that were the best in the journalism class, she had spent all her free time this year doing the unglamourous jobs on the paper —like proofreading and headline writing and running errands.

Considering her record, she wouldn't have thought the newspaper committee would even need a formal meeting to vote her into office. Yet her appointment was anything but a cinch. There had been bitter opposition.

She had felt the tension the minute she stepped into the room to face the committee. There was a feeling of disapproval, especially from Miss Layton, the Dracula of an English teacher, who had spent at least a thousand years teaching literature in the dullest possible manner and searching for grammatical errors in compositions with the joyous ferocity of a bloodhound.

"Immaturity" was the word Miss Layton tossed emphatically across the room. "Janice, do you honestly feel you are mature enough?" she queried. "We all know you do the best writing in the class, there is no question about that. But are you mature enough to organize the editorial work, make assignments and see they are carried through, oversee the advertising and all? Editorial work is very exacting," Miss Layton warned.

"I've tried to work on each department of the paper so I would know all about it," Jan had replied. "I feel I'm qualified."

"So do I," Budge Nichols, the retiring editor, had affirmed warmly. "Jan has been a real girl Friday."

As she left the room she heard someone say, "Now about Cassie Warrenton . . ."

Heavens above, Cassie Warrenton! Jan thought she might collapse. Why, everyone knew that although Cassie had a gift for catchy phrases she giggled constantly and rarely met a deadline on the nose. If they wanted to send the *Argus* into complete confusion Cassie was just the girl to do it.

A few minutes later—it was only a few minutes according to the ponderous grandfather clock in Mr. Larsen's office, though it seemed a lifetime to Jan—they had called her back to offer her the post of editor-in-chief. On trial, that was. It hurt a little that she couldn't have their unqualified approval, but she was not afraid. She knew she could edit the paper. The committee would sing in a different key after they had seen her in action.

At last her long morning of suspense was over. From the platform Mr. Larsen gave her an encouraging smile as he announced, "Editor-in-chief of the *Mountain View Monthly Argus*—Janice Morgan."

She would have to get to work right away on Mr. Larsen to convince him that her name on the masthead should be Jan, not Janice. Some of the kids called her Jan without prompting, and Budge usually remembered, because she had once awkwardly mentioned it to him, but everyone else kept on calling her Janice, which sounded like the ruffled-petticoats sort of girl her mother would like and not a bit like an experienced newspaper woman.

In the meantime, buoyant with happiness, she walked to the platform. There was a polite spatter of applause, not like the acclamation given the elected officers. By now everybody was probably anxious for lunch, and anyway most of the students didn't much care who edited the paper as long as it came out once a month. Jan faced them with a feeling of joyous confidence. She had her chance now and she could prove by her work what she couldn't with her personality— that she had something worthwhile to give to the world. She shook hands with Mr. Larsen and he pointed her towards the microphone. That was right, she would have to say something. The others had made short, modest speeches.

"Thank you," she said hesitantly and recoiled from the harsh crackle of her voice in the microphone. "Editing the *Argus* is a privilege, but following in Budge's footsteps is a chore and I just hope I'll do half as well." This time the applause was more genuine.

The band played a last number as the assembly was dismissed and the students headed for the cafeteria. On the stage the new officers were shaking hands and congratulating one another. Jan found her hand seized and pumped by genial red-headed Ben Barton, the new president. "Glad to have you on the team," he said warmly.

"Thank you," she replied shyly, and before she could think of anything else to say Ben was replaced by Dotty Graham, the new recording secretary, who gripped her arm and looked earnestly into her eyes.

"I'm so glad it's you," Dotty said. "I was just shuddering for fear they would make Cassie editor. She's my dearest friend on earth but she simply won't coordinate her talents, as she'd be the first to admit. The *Argus* needs a strong personality who'll make it really reflect the student body. I'm counting on you."

"I'll try," Jan replied, rather nonplused. Then she smiled, remembering that Dotty had gone all out for dramatics the same way she herself had gone all out for journalism. Dotty would undoubtedly be class-play lead next year and was always more or less in rehearsal for the big scene.

"Off to lunch while there's still something to eat," Mr. Larsen said, coming up to them. "And save a bite for Janice. I want a last word with her."

Away they went, their excited laughter permeating the air behind them. The principal looked down at her kindly. "I just wanted to say that I hope you aren't feeling bad about the committee members who thought you were too young. I know you aren't. I know you're going to maintain the high standard of journalism we've always had at Mountain View."

"Oh, thank you, Mr. Larsen." The warmth of his belief in her made her feel older and more capable already.

"I won't keep you from your lunch any longer." He picked up his papers and started to leave. "Just wanted you to know you can count on me all the way. Did any of your family come today? They must be very proud of you."

Somewhere in Jan a switch flipped and the joy and light vanished. "No," she said bluntly, "nobody in my family came. Well, thanks, Mr. Larsen."

She left the auditorium quickly and walked into the noise and confusion of the cafeteria. As she took her tray and started down the line several students called congratulations, but she smiled and replied absent-mindedly, for the pleasure of her achievement had melted away considerably when she faced the fact that no one in her family knew and furthermore Mother and Andrew wouldn't be impressed when they did. Only if it happened to Andrew would there be a hullaballoo, and it never would because he was so dumb he didn't know a comma from a coma.

She had started for her usual table in the corner when Budge Nichols, leaning lazily against a post surveying his kingdom, reached out a long arm and halted her. "Whoa there, Madam Editor," he drawled. "Drop the body here and we'll talk shop."

Jan sat down awkwardly, that fleeting touch-and-go happiness back again because even aside from being editor Budge Nichols was the most outstanding senior at Mountain View, and to share his table for a few minutes . . . "How are you feeling?" he asked with a smile as he sat down facing her.

She gulped and blurted out the truth. "More thrilled than I've ever been in my life—and scared stiff."

"You won't be once you know the ropes. Come down to the shop this afternoon with me. Pete will be making up the pages, so we can read the page proofs right there and put most of the old *Argie* to bed."

"Oh, dear, I'd forgotten all about that horrible old Pete," Jan said with dismay. "How will I ever manage him every month? Whenever I bring down copy or stop in to pick up proofs he snarls and practically throws a lead bar at me."

Budge laughed. "Oh, he just treats the slaves that way. Once you get on the upper half of the masthead he's grand. You'll like him."

Jan was skeptical. "I hope so," she said. "But honestly, Budge, he's a horrible grouch. He would never let me come behind the counter and all the while I was so anxious to see the shop and all his equipment."

"You'll see all you want from now on," Budge assured her. "In fact if you aren't careful you'll find Pete not only running your paper for you but taking over your whole life. He may treat the reporters like fleas in his beard, but he really takes an interest in the editors."

Cassie, returning her tray to the counter, saw them and came over. "Nice going, gal," she said brightly. "You really deserved the job. I'll be glad to help with the features or any other spot where you can use me."

Jan started to thank her but Budge interrupted. "Oh, no,"

he groaned. "The help shortage can't be that critical."

Cassie snapped her fingers in his face. "To heck with your opinions, Grandpa. You're all through and washed up. Isn't he, Melanie?"

They turned around to greet Melanie Connors, Budge's long-time steady, a dainty, dimpled senior with a sparkling personality that made her the most popular Tulip Festival Queen the school had had for many a year.

All queens should be like Melanie, Jan thought, assured yet sweetly modest. She wondered how Melanie had felt when she faced her student-faculty committee a few weeks ago. Melanie's ordeal must have been far worse than an editor's, because the candidates, nominated by the various school organizations, were subjected to a rigorous weeding out by the committee and the three finalists were then presented to the student body for their votes.

It must have been soul-tearing, but Melanie had shown smiling poise in every situation. She smiled now as she rolled down her sleeves. "We are now officially through dishing it up, so I hope you had enough to eat. Congratulations, Jan," she continued. "I missed the assembly, but Budge confided that you were going to be it. I know you must be thrilled."

Before Jan could reply Cassie snorted. "No thrill to being editor," she said. "It's nothing but a lot of hard work . . ."

"And a lot of being on time," Budge said wickedly.

"For thrills I'll take being Tulip Queen. You can hand me your crown any time," Cassie went on, unperturbed by Budge's criticism.

They all laughed—Jan a little sadly because she suspected that was the way most of the world felt. It's nice to be editor, but I'll take vanilla.

"It's sweet of you to say that," Melanie replied. "Cassie, I wouldn't be at all surprised if you did get to be Tulip Queen next year, but I know it's a thrill to be editor, too, and I'm very happy for Jan."

"Yakity, yakity, yak," Budge said holding his hands over his ears. "How did I ever get surrounded by so many women? Come on, Melanie, let's get out of this airlock. As for you, kid," he instructed Jan, "get excused from study hall and go out the side door. I'll bring my hundred weary horses around."

"Such service," Jan replied. "When I was running copy back and forth I always walked."

"You're in the upper brackets now," Budge said modestly. "I'll be seeing you later."

"How do you like that?" Cassie queried. "You're off to spend the afternoon with her true love and Melanie doesn't wrinkle an eyelash. I guess Queenie isn't worried about editorial competition."

The words hung ominously in the air. Cassie looked appalled and fumblingly tried to apologize. "Oh, golly, I didn't mean that to sound the way it did."

Jan managed a small smile as she stood up and started back to the counter with her tray. "Never mind, Cassie. You don't need to draw a diagram. Why should Melanie worry? I'm going to be editor for a year, but she'll always be a queen."

CHAPTER 2

The Print Shop

AFTER THE BRIGHTNESS of the spring afternoon the print shop seemed cave-like in its gloom. Jan sniffed the permeating smells of ink, dust, and melting lead happily. "It's nice in here, isn't it? I like the smell."

Budge chuckled appreciatively. "To heck with Chanel Number 5, give the lady Print Shop Number 6. But I know what you mean," he continued. "I'll miss this next year. University freshmen are probably lucky to be allowed to carry stacks of copy paper from desk to desk. I'm sure I won't get to hang around the works like this.

"But allow me." Budge stepped forward, gave the gate by the counter a mighty swing, and bowed ceremoniously. "The gates of the sanctum sanctorum are open. Walk right in."

Although Jan laughed, she was truly thrilled to be on the other side of the wall, face to face with all the fascinating machinery. Face to face with Pete also. He stepped up from the back of the shop carrying a bunch of handbills for the supermarket sale. "Pete, meet your new boss," Budge said. "Janice, or rather Jan Morgan. I'm turning the old rag over to her."

Pete's hand was callused, his shoulders stooped, and his clothes mussed and ink-stained. But his bright blue eyes shining behind steel-framed glasses were warm with welcome. "Glad to see you, Jan," he said. "Bet myself a quarter you'd be the one."

She nearly rocked on her heels with surprise while Budge

said gleefully, "Didn't I tell you? Pete may snarl at all the kids but he really knows what's cooking."

"But, Pete, why are you always so cross?" Jan asked.

"Self-defense," he explained. "The average journalism student is an uninhibited demon who would tear my shop apart at the slightest opportunity, so I make 'em keep their distance. The good ones get behind the scenes anyhow, and the others don't count."

"Pete, you're a hard man," Budge said with a laugh.

"Me? Hard?" Pete asked in amazement. "You have the nerve to say that after the way I've pampered your literary genius along?" He turned to Jan with a smile. "It's going to be nice to get rid of Mr. Bossy Know-Nothing and have a pretty girl around."

Jan had been admiring Pete more and more each minute, but now she stiffened and gave him a disgusted look. She wasn't a pretty girl and they all knew it, and if what he wanted was a pretty girl she wasn't going to like him after all.

Pete evidently read her look correctly, for he laughed softly and said out of the corner of his mouth, "Being literary-minded you'd call it a cliché, but pretty is as pretty does and don't you forget it."

Before Jan could recover her wits enough to comment, Budge laughed and said, "I warned her about you. Good advice every hour on the half hour."

"It hasn't hurt you a bit, has it, sonny?" Pete asked. "Come on now, Miss Editor, I'll show you your new domain."

Quickly forgetting her annoyance, Jan trailed after Pete. She watched the presses, fascinated by their mechanism, and smudged her fingers marveling at the sight of page one of the *Argus* cast in lead and locked into frames of steel. When they came to the gargantuan miracle of the linotype she was speechless.

"Just a minute," Pete said with a grin. He picked up a block of lead and put it into the pot of molten metal at the top of the machine. The linotype rumbled ominously. "Jan is what you want to be called?" Pete asked.

"Yes," she said firmly.

"Jan Morgan," Pete typed, his blunt fingers tapping the keyboard lightly.

While Jan watched, little pieces of brass came clicking down the length of the machine. When they were all in place Pete pushed a lever and the linotype seemed ready to leap from its bed of cement as it clacked and shuddered and its monstrous arm went back and forth. Pete reached into the galley and pulled out the finished slug with her name on it.

"Thanks," Jan said, shifting it from hand to hand to cool it.

Here was her name set in raised letters on a block of lead and all she would have to do would be to put on ink and she could print Jan Morgan on anything, over and over again! A hundred years from now when she was dead and no one wanted to print Jan Morgan any more the slug could be tossed back into the pot and melted and made into a new slug and that slug could be melted and used again and again and again. The next time those giggling six-year-olds in her Sunday school class asked what eternity was she would tell them about the linotype. It was the most wonderful thing she had ever seen.

"I wish I could be a printer," she said fervently.

Budge and Pete exchanged amused glances. "I knew you'd like it," Budge said. "I knew you and Pete would click. But say, kid"—his smile elongated and his eyes danced—"there's something you still haven't seen. You'd better let me show you the type lice."

"Type lice?" Jan asked in surprise. "Do you mean there are bugs in the type?"

"Sure are," Budge assured her, while Pete let out a noise somewhere between a snort and a moan and walked away.

"Did we hurt his feelings talking about bugs in the type?"

Jan asked, concerned. "Is he embarrassed because his shop isn't very clean?"

"No, no," Budge assured her. "Nothing like that at all."

He guided her over to page one of the *Argus,* unlocked the frames, and spread apart some of the slugs. Jan watched him anxiously. "I still don't see how there can be lice in lead," she worried. "Bugs have to feed on something."

"You'll see," Budge replied. He reached for a bottle of green ink but Pete suddenly appeared beside him.

"No ink, you sadist," Pete said sternly. "Water is bad enough for your infantile tricks."

Crestfallen, Budge put away the ink and poured water between the slugs. "Get your head down close," he instructed. "You have to look carefully to see them."

"Why did Pete call you a sadist?" Jan asked as she scrooched down close to the form. "Does the ink hurt the type lice too much?"

"Doesn't hurt *them,*" Budge replied, then abruptly slammed the slugs back together, forcing a geyser of water into Jan's astonished face.

"What happened?" she shrieked as she jumped back. "I didn't see any type lice. . . ." Then with the water wiped from her face she saw Budge leaning against the wall doubled over with laughter while Pete dug a finger behind his glasses and wiped away a mirthful tear.

"Oh, you were just kidding me," Jan said as realization came to her. Budge laughed harder than ever.

Jan felt her cheeks grows hot, but she wasn't really angry. It was rather fun to be teased by Budge. "I've been wanting to do that to someone all year," he confessed happily. "It was better than I'd hoped to find you were born yesterday and not in the know about type lice."

"Now I'll have to find some moron to hoax," Jan said, but she knew it didn't sound very convincing. Suddenly she understood a little of what her mother had meant when she said there were other ways of being smart besides earning good grades. Andrew wouldn't have been fooled by anything that obvious, and certainly Cassie Warrenton would have hooted and pushed Budge's face in the type if he had tried it on her.

"Are you kids having a party or did you by any chance intend to read proof?" Pete asked caustically.

"Coming right up," Budge assured him.

When the proofs were read, the corrections made, and the forms locked up ready to be run off early next week, Pete said to Budge, "Now I've left some space on page three for those last-minute stories you're always dreaming up. Be sure to see that they fit."

"Yes sir, Mr. Legree," Budge replied with a wink at Jan. "Boy, I'm glad I'm graduating and getting out of this uranium mine."

"Not quite yet," Jan reminded him. "I'm only supposed to assist you next month. I don't start battling on my own with Pete till fall."

Jan took a last look at the *Argus*. On the front page was a cut of Melanie in the robes she would wear at the Tulip Festival. Even in the black and gray monotone of a lead block she looked radiant and vital.

"That's how all good little papers go to bed," Budge said happily as he rubbed up a lather with the gray, gritty soap Pete kept on hand for eradicating ink stains—even though he never seemed to use it on himself. "Strenuous exertion like this uses up lots of calories. I suggest we adjourn to the drugstore and contemplate two super-special black-and-white sundaes."

A minute ago he'd been boss and co-worker and Jan had been perfectly at ease with him, but when he suddenly turned into a genial host she felt self-conscious and confused. "Oh, no, Budge," she said.

He looked so surprised that she fumbled on, trying to explain and sounding to herself more and more inadequate. "I mean, thanks a lot, but I have to get home. It was swell of you to bring me down here and show me the ropes, but you mustn't bother any more."

"Oh, sure," Budge said seriously. "I didn't stop to think of the time. I have a few chores myself. My dad comes home Friday nights too and we always try to have things extra-special for him."

"You're so right. I should have been home helping mother with dinner but I just couldn't pass up a chance to come down here."

"There speaks the true newspaper hound. I'll drive you home soon as I comb my hair. Right now I'd frighten the gophers back into their holes."

Budge walked to the back of the shop, where a small, dis-colored mirror hung aslant against the wall. While he was busy scowling at his reflection Pete ambled over to Jan and said, "Look sis, it's all right for some kinds of chickens to bristle their feathers, but it wasn't meant for you."

That was the limit. Being editor wasn't going to be so wonderful after all if Pete was going to question and criticize every statement she made. Goodness knows she got enough bossing at home. "You know perfectly well he doesn't want to buy me a sundae," Jan replied sulkily. "He's just being polite. He goes steady with the prettiest girl in school."

"The Tulip Queen, huh!" Pete affirmed. "Yes, she's prettier than most. But you're a cute little character, espe-cially when you're happy. We can't all be tulips. Some of us have to be marigolds, too."

"Oh, you sound just like mother," Jan said with sharp dis-appointment. "She's always nagging at me to bring out some non-existent good points. I thought you knew how to judge people by their internals, not their externals."

"Don't be upset, Jan," Pete said. "If I sound nosy it's be-cause I like you and I want you to be successful editorially and personally both. And you know something—if your mother heckles you it's probably because she wants you to be happy, too. Think it over sometime."

"Coming, Jan?" Budge interrupted. "Let's get the show on the road."

Jan gave Pete a last baffled look as they left. He was a weird character, sure enough. Although until today he hadn't spoken a civil word to her he had known all about her and hoped she would be editor. His unqualified "I like you" warmed her heart. Evidently he meant well.

As Jan and Budge came out of the shop they heard a shrill whistling drifting down from the mountain tops. Then it came again louder and nearer. Instantly the children playing in the streets and vacant lots dropped their marbles, bats, scooters, and doll buggies and started racing for the railroad tracks. "They're coming," they shouted to one another. "The speeder's coming, we'll see Daddy. . . ." Some of them tripped and fell in their headlong rush but they got right up and went racing on towards the railroad station.

Jan and Budge looked at each other with sheepish grins. "Time for the speeder," she said. "Oh, my, we spent the whole afternoon with Pete."

"We're too late to help much at home now," Budge said with a shrug. "We might as well do a thorough job of going AWOL. How about it?" he asked, nodding his head towards the tracks. "Shall we join the reception committee?"

The whistle shrieked out just beyond the bend. "Let's do," Jan agreed.

"Come on then." Budge gave her a tug and they ran down the bank to the tracks and stood near the children, who were dancing wildly around.

"Good old Shorewood," Budge commented with a grin as the mill whistle blew an answer to the speeder's blast. "Between the mill and offices in town and the logging camp back in the woods they about keep this town going."

"Yes, and how I wish Dad worked in the office here instead of camp," Jan sighed. "Having just a week-end father isn't so sharp."

"True enough, but I'm afraid the camp would fold up without your Dad. When I worked in the mess hall last summer I saw what a job he did keeping the time cards straight and the supplies in hand and all the paper work like that. The guys call him Johnny Inkslinger after Paul Bunyan's helper."

"They do?" Jan asked in surprise, pleased by Budge's words of praise and intrigued by this glimpse of the life her father led when he was away from them.

When the speeder pulling two trailer cars came in sight of the station the waiting children yelled and whistled while the men yelled back. Looking at the bug-like open-air machine, the leather benches at each side of it, now loaded with husky lumberjacks in bright plaid mackinaws, Jan sighed and said, "I can remember when it was the biggest thrill of my life to ride from the yard limit to the station in the speeder."

"Remember!" Budge said. "I still get a bang out of it. Though there's nothing much to running one—it's just a little put-put gasoline engine. I like to hear the old-timers tell about how they used to have nothing but a hand car, and by the time they pushed it back up the mountains on Monday morning they weren't good for much logging."

Before the speeder could come to a full stop the men were all piling off while the waiting children ran up and dived at their pockets, for it was a tradition with the lumberjacks that they came home loaded with candy from the camp canteen.

Mr. Morgan smiled at the group and, not noticing Budge and Jan, started up the hill. Jan said a hurried good-by to Budge and took off after him. "Hello, Dad," she said shyly, slipping her arm through his and falling into step with him.

"Why, Janice." His face lit up with pleasure and surprise. "I certainly wasn't expecting you. I thought you and Andrew were too grown-up to come meet me any more."

"I was downtown when I heard the whistle so I waited," she explained. "I was at the print shop with Budge Nichols because . . ." She stopped. No, much as she wanted to tell him now, it would be best to wait till the whole family was together and then drop her bomb on them.

Budge and his father came by in the jalopy and offered them a ride but they both shook their heads. It wasn't far and it was a nice afternoon for a walk.

"It's good to see you," Mr. Morgan said heartily, "but I fell down on the job. Don't have any candy in my pockets."

"I don't want any candy, thanks. It's nearly dinnertime. I just hope mother doesn't take my head off for being so late."

"So that's the ticket," her father said with a laugh. "You want me for moral support."

Jan laughed too, and squeezed his arm. How she wished he could come home every night instead of just week-ends!

Jan counted a dozen bicycles in their yard as they came up the walk. "Looks like all the kids in town," Mr. Morgan commented. "Television again, I suppose."

"Mother will send them home as soon as you come in," Jan assured him.

"Oh, I don't mind the kids. Makes me quite a plutocrat to

be one of the few lumberjacks in town with a television set. It's awful to have to spend so much money on a machine like that, plus all those adapter gadgets for fringe areas."

Jan agreed with him. She thought it would be much better to spend the money on a typewriter for her, or to put it aside to help her go to college. But she sighed and said, "It's good for Andrew. Keeps him from running around too much and getting sick again."

"I suppose so," her father agreed.

The house was full of noise. In the living-room Andrew and his friends sprawled over the floor eating popcorn and watching Howdy Doody. In the kitchen her mother was cooking dinner amid steam and confusion.

"Sorry I'm late," Jan said, snatching her apron from its hook in the broom closet. "What shall I do first? Set the table or make the salad?"

"I've already made the salad," her mother replied. She straightened up from the stove where she was furiously mashing potatoes, sighed, and brushed the hair back from her face. She looked terribly tired and nervous and Jan felt guilty about having such a gay afternoon when she should have been helping.

"I was counting on you to help," her mother said coldly. "At least you should phone if you aren't coming home, so I'll know how to plan my work."

Jan's guilt hardened into the same old sense of frustration. "Andrew could have helped a little. Setting the table wouldn't hurt his heart."

She took the pottery plates from the shelf and slapped them down on the table. She clashed the silver into place and went to the cooler for the cream pitcher. They didn't have an electric refrigerator to keep things cold and sweet, she reflected, and her mother still cooked on the hot, wood-burning stove that had been in the house ever since it was built. But Andrew had a television set to keep him amused.

Mr. Morgan came back in from washing up and stood

looking around happily. "My, but it's good to be home. When do we eat?"

Mrs. Morgan dashed into the living-room to turn off the television and send the other boys home. Jan put the dinner on the table, sat down at her place, unfolded her napkin, and waited for them to notice her again. Finally, after the edge was off their hunger, she said, "Budge Nichols took me to the print shop after school to introduce me to Pete and show me how the paper functions. I'm the new editor."

The effect was as good as she had hoped. Her parents stopped eating and stared at her in amazement. Andrew scowled.

"Editor of the high school paper," her father said with a pleased smile. "That's wonderful, Janice. So that scribbling you do really amounts to something."

"Yes, it really does," Jan replied proudly. "I'm the youngest editor ever appointed on the *Argus*."

"Yes, you're too young," her mother said, missing the point completely. "I've been thinking of that ever since this morning. We were wrong to let you skip those grades and get ahead of the others your age. You keep up with the school work all right, but the emotional strain is too great."

Jan was tempted to retort, "It isn't school that strains my emotions," but a minute later she was glad she didn't.

"So that's what your assembly was about," her mother continued. "I tried to get there, Janice. I was all dressed to go when Mrs. Parsons called, and you know how she is. She wouldn't leave even when I told her I was planning to go out."

"That's a shame," Jan said with genuine sympathy. Old Mrs. Parsons had only one regular activity and that was complicating people's lives. Jan's spirits lifted. Mother had intended to come.

"I'm glad you're going to have an important position for your senior year," her mother said. "Senior year should be fun, but you're so young. . . . We'll have to look around and find some new clothes for you—something to make you look a little older."

"A lot of good new clothes would do her," Andrew interrupted scornfully. "Might as well put gunny sacks on a broomstick."

"Andrew!" his father said sternly.

"Now, son, that's no way to talk," his mother said more mildly.

But Jan, feeling the truth in the remark and stinging from its hurt, replied, "Actually what I wear won't make any difference at all. That's one job where brains count the most," and flicked her eyes at Andrew angrily.

Andrew pushed back his chair, his face flushed and his voice ragged. "It's a good thing they wanted your master mind. If they'd gone by looks they would have picked Lena the Hyena before you. Go peddle your silly paper, old sourpuss."

"Enough of that," their father commanded. "If you two can't be civil, you may be excused."

Andrew had already stomped into the living-room. Jan muttered, "I didn't say anything wrong," and stubbornly stayed at the table.

Her father drummed his fingers on the table, his brows contracted and his face troubled. "I don't like coming home every week-end and finding the children at each other's throats. What's wrong with them, Alice?"

I could tell you plenty that's wrong, Jan reflected, but she realized she wouldn't get a chance.

"I wish I knew," her mother said with a sigh. "I know Andrew gets upset because he can't do everything the other boys do, even though we try to make it up to him with the television set and all. I can understand that. But I don't understand what's wrong with Janice. She's so cross and sassy to me and so mean to Andrew. Between them I'm about ready to give up."

Me cross! Sassy! Mean! Jan could feel her cheeks flame. It

wasn't true. She wanted to cry out and defend herself but the words lay heavy within her.

"Well," her father said uncertainly. "We'd better talk about it later when we all aren't so tired."

He rose and started to leave the room. "You haven't had dessert," his wife protested. "It's lemon pie."

"I'm not hungry," he said shortly.

Jan got up and started to clear the table. She always had to do the dishes while the rest of them enjoyed the television. Doing dishes wasn't hard work, it wouldn't hurt anyone's poor, frail heart, but of course Andrew never had to help her.

"I hope you're satisfied at ruining your father's dinner," her mother said as she got up to go into the living-room.

"Andrew started it," Jan protested hotly. "All I did was stand up for myself. Nobody else around here will. You know perfectly well Andrew started it."

"Yes, but you're older and you should have self-control enough not to indulge in these childish quarrels. If you're old enough to be editor of your paper you should be old enough to deal reasonably with a sick little brother."

Sick little brother . . . Sick stupid ox . . . Jan turned on the water taps full force and shook in the soap flakes. She wouldn't always be doing dishes for other people.

When fall came and she was editor she would be so busy she wouldn't have time to be home much and when that year was over she would be ready to go away. And she would make something of herself, too, because she had brains and willpower. If you didn't have brains all the curly hair and television sets in the world wouldn't give them to you, either.

Only she did wish her mother liked her and approved of what she was. It was such a lonesome feeling being disapproved of all the time; it made a wall between her and the family. Today she had found the gate and passed through the wall between herself and the print shop. If only someday she could find the gate in this other wall.

CHAPTER 3

Tulip Queens of Then and Now

THE PHONE RANG while Jan was finishing the dishes. "It's Mrs. Preston," her mother called. "She wants you to baby-sit."

"Swell," Jan agreed. "Tell her I'll be right over." She loved to go there. Mrs. Preston was glamourous, the house new and modern, and eight-month-old Johnny a love of a baby. "I want to earn all the money I can from now on," she added.

"Yes, indeed," Mrs. Morgan agreed. "Senior year is expensive and there's no reason why you shouldn't help pay for your own clothes. Lots of girls do."

Jan shrugged. After tonight's dinner-table discussion she didn't care if she never had any new clothes. Her new dress had felt crisp and pert this morning, but now it hung limply and her spirits sagged along with it. Besides, now that she was editor she really needed a typewriter of her own and this summer she would have to earn enough money to get one. Her parents could have bought one for her long ago if they had cared at all about what she wanted, if they weren't always concentrating on Andrew.

From past experience Jan knew that the best procedure at the Prestons' was to ring the bell and go on in. Sure enough,

Mrs. Preston in a frilly peignoir peered out of her bedroom and called, "That you, Jan? Come on in."

First Jan stopped by Johnny's play pen in the corner of the dining-room. He let out a crow of delight and pulled himself up on the bars. "Oh, you grow so fast, you old stinker, you," she said kissing his fat neck and listening to his laugh. "I'll be back for you soon," she promised as she put him down.

In the big bedroom Jan sat down on the chintz slipper chair and watched the ever-fascinating process of Mrs. Preston's party preparations. She was doing her face—picking up one jar after another, rubbing with tissues and patting with cotton. "John has been out of town on business so much lately that I have cabin fever," she explained. "I decided I'd better go some place even if the only event in town is our Mountain Maids Alumni Club."

"Oh, did you graduate from Mountain View?" Jan asked.

"Goodness, yes. Ten years ago."

"We don't have a Mountain Maids Club now," Jan said, "but I'm sure I've heard of it before."

"Ancient history, that's us," Mrs. Preston said with a laugh. "We were a girls' service club—cheerleaders, ushers, interior decorators, and that sort of thing. A year or so after I graduated the group combined with the Live Wires, the boys' group, to form the Mountaineers. I'm sure the mixed group is more fun. Anyhow, the old Mountain Maids—though we're mostly mountain matrons now—get together occasionally for food and fun. I've been looking through my yearbook to get in the proper spirit."

"May I see it?" Jan took up the book. She'd been a shy, lanky first-grader when Mrs. Preston was a senior. She leafed through the pages, then exclaimed in surprise, "Why, Mrs. Preston, you were Tulip Queen!"

Mrs. Preston leaned over Jan's shoulder and chuckled at the sight of herself in the royal robes. "Yes, that was the biggest event of my seventeen years. Graduation was strictly secondary."

"It must have been wonderful," Jan said earnestly. "Any girl glamourous enough to be a tulip queen is sure to have a fabulous life and be adored by everyone."

Mrs. Preston, coming out of the closet in a sheath-like black dress, stopped in surprise. "What a nice idea," she said with a little laugh. "Too bad it isn't true."

"But look at you," Jan persisted. "You have everything."

"It's sweet of you to think so," Mrs. Preston said as she clipped pearl earrings on her ears and fastened a pearl choker around her neck. "I do have a nice life but it's nothing spectacular. Being Tulip Queen is wonderful when you're seventeen, but it isn't the biggest thrill in the world by any means, and it certainly doesn't guarantee a rosy future."

Mrs. Preston picked up the yearbook again and flipped the pages. "Here's what I mean. Take Elsie Abbott—" she pointed to the picture of a mousy-looking girl—"when she was in school she was a total creep—president of the Honor Society, most wholesome member of the Girls' League, teacher's pet all around, and I doubt if a boy ever looked sideways at her the whole time she was at Mountain View."

"That doesn't sound like much fun," Jan commented. How well she knew that it wasn't.

"Ah, but that isn't the whole story," Mrs. Preston went on dramatically. "After we graduated she joined the WAC and got to see a good part of the world as secretary to this VIP, Colonel Abbott. Then if he didn't marry her and retire from the army! Now they live in a beautiful house in Madrona Park and have three little girls. That's where I'm going tonight."

"Wow," Jan said with a long-drawn-out sigh. After a day spent envying Melanie and the other tulip queens news like that was jarring. Homely girls like herself and Elsie Abbott got good grades and then worked all their lives at dull but responsible jobs. They didn't marry important men or have adventures—or did they?

Mrs. Preston nodded as if she had heard the unspoken question. "Yes, I'm sure that most of the girls I'll see at the alumni meeting have done as well as the Tulip Queen."

After Mrs. Preston left, Jan prepared Johnny for the night, gave him his bottle, and tidied up the room in a very thoughtful mood. Then she took the yearbook out to the living room, turned on a lamp, and looked again at the picture of Mrs. Preston, so eager and happy, at her coronation. She started wondering about the other girls who had worn this crown so briefly. Suddenly she caught her breath with excitement and called Budge's number. "Hello, you old retired and pensioned-off editor," she said happily.

"Do I detect the faint aroma of disrespect from my inferiors?" he retorted.

"Not exactly. But I did get an idea about how to fill in that empty space in the *Argus*."

At the other end of the line Budge went through a series of noises intended to convey disbelief.

"Listen," she said earnestly. "I'm over at the Prestons' bratting and she had out her old yearbook and it turns out she was Tulip Queen and I thought we might run a story about all the tulip queens for about ten years back and tell what they are doing now and if being queen is their happiest memory and so forth. We could close the story with a paragraph on Melanie's hopes for the future."

"Hey, kid, that's cool. I'm going to pick up Melanie in a few minutes. We're going skating but there's no rush about it. We'll stop by to see you first and take a look at that yearbook."

Jan was uncertain. "Do you think you ought to come here? After all, I'm supposed to be working."

"Oh, I don't think she'd care. Phone and ask if you like, but I often go with Melanie when she sits. We'll be by in ten minutes. If you want to start writing the lead you have my permission."

"You're too too kind," Jan said as she put down the phone.

She did sit down with a pencil and notebook but she was so excited that the words just wouldn't come. The ten minutes had lengthened to half an hour before Budge came, but finally she heard his car sputter to a stop outside. She opened the door quickly and he and Melanie came in laughing and carrying stacks of old Mountain View annuals.

"They must go back to the Civil War," Budge said as he dumped them on the floor. "We stopped at Mr. Larsen's to pick them up, and when I told him what was percolating he was really tickled. Said he guessed you'd show those characters who didn't think you had the stuff for the job."

Jan warmed with pleasure, but all she said was, "We'd better sit down and get to work. Do you think we should just take the last ten years?"

"I'm afraid so," Budge said with a sigh. "I don't imagine we could talk Pete into giving us an extra four or five pages this time."

"I'm getting all excited," Melanie said as she picked up some of the newer annuals and started to list the names of the past queens. "I thought working on the paper was mostly trouble and inkstains, but it must be fun if you do this sort of thing very often."

"The best fun in the world," Jan assured her.

"Look at those pictures. Oh, some of the girls are so attractive," Melanie said.

Peering over her shoulder, Jan said with sudden generosity, "I don't see a one of them as pretty as you." The minute the words were out of her mouth she wondered what on earth had come over her. She didn't approve of paying compliments to girls who seldom heard anything else, but right now she was so happy at the prospect of being editor and so interested in her story that she hadn't thought to be jealous of pretty girls.

"Why, thanks, Jan," Melanie said happily. "You're wrong, though. Your Mrs. Preston is more than pretty. She has class."

"Jan's never wrong. She's too smart," Budge said. He sounded pleased, and Jan realized that her impulsive words had bound the three of them together in friendship. The feeling was so good she stopped working for a minute just to soak in this unaccustomed glow. Could be she should try it more often.

Suddenly Budge snapped his fingers. "Hey, how about those Mountain Maids? They ought to be loaded with tulip queens. If we could get hold of them tonight and interview them en masse it would save a lot of running around. We don't have too much time to get this little opus whipped into shape."

"It would help a lot to get them all together," Jan admitted. "But I don't have nerve enough to barge in on them. It's bad enough for me to be doing this story on Mrs. Preston's time."

Budge shook his head. "Miss Morgan, there's one thing you'll have to learn. A good newspaperman or woman has nerve enough for anything." He reached for the phone. "What's the Abbotts' number?"

The rest of the evening was so hectic that Jan didn't know how she would ever get it sorted out in her mind. Inspired by Budge's phone call, the Mountain Maids had packed up— hostess, guests, and refreshments—and driven over to the Prestons' for the mass interview.

Melanie thoughtfully looked after Johnny, who objected to all the noise, while Jan and Budge took notes as fast as they could scribble about the life, times, and vital statistics of every tulip queen anyone could remember. Jan smiled to herself as she noticed that the ladies were dredging forth information with as much giggling and confusion as any of her own contemporaries. She and Budge made phone calls to check details on the girls who no longer lived in Cascadeville and soon had full notebooks.

In the midst of her note-taking Jan couldn't help stopping for a few quick looks at Elsie Abbott. In spite of the fact that her party had been lifted right out of her living-room and turned into a meet-the-press session she was kind, cheerful, and helpful about remembering the names and places they needed.

She wore glasses—not personality rims, just plain glasses—didn't have much chin, and instead of being too skinny the way she was in her yearbook picture, she was now too plump. Still, she looked serene and contented. I'll bet she's a more interesting story than all these queens put together, Jan thought. But she didn't suppose she'd ever get to write that one.

"I know this is going to be a wonderful story," Budge said, trying to shake the writer's cramp out of his hand. "And if you four queens who still live in Cascadeville will come to school Monday morning and pose for a picture with this year's queen I'd be mighty obliged. It would make a superb layout."

"Us old abdicated queens will be there," Mrs. Preston said, and the others agreed enthusiastically.

Jan said good night to Mrs. Preston, refusing payment for the evening on the grounds that Johnny had been neglected in favor of journalism, and Budge and Melanie insisted on driving her home.

"Can you come down to the shop tomorrow?" Budge asked as he stopped at her door. "Pete's temper is going to be hotter than his lead pot when he sees what we're doing to the paper. This story is lots bigger than the space we've got left and I don't want to cut it any."

"We can just throw out those stories about the Latin Club

having a picnic and the cafeteria saving money," Jan suggested.

"Sure, that's what we'll do. You're a gal after my own heart. Well, I'll see you tomorrow. Watch out for those type lice."

"Scallions to you. 'Night, Melanie," Jan called after them.

As she came through the door she found her mother peering over the stairwell. "Who brought you home?" she asked.

"Budge Nichols. He was over at the Prestons' too."

"What!" Mrs. Morgan was incredulous. "Did he go over there to see you?"

Suddenly Jan was so tired she just sighed and sank down on the bottom stair. It had been a long, bursting-with-emotion day. "Strictly business," she explained. "We're working on a special article." She told her mother about the tulip queen feature.

Mrs. Morgan listened intently. "How about the queens?" she asked. "Didn't any of them turn out exceptionally well?"

"No, not really," Jan said very thoughtfully. "Linda Evans, 1946, won a screen test and went to Hollywood. She's still there but she's a receptionist in an office instead of a star, and the others are just plain nice people and not a bit ahead of Mrs. Abbott."

"Elsie Abbott?" her mother asked in surprise. Then she nodded. "Yes, I see what you mean."

"Oh, do you know her?" Jan asked with interest.

"Yes, I went to a Sewing Circle meeting at her home once. It's a beautiful place. Well, you'd better get to bed, Janice. You've had a long day."

Jan agreed with a sigh and began to climb the stairs. As her mother turned back to her room Jan heard her say softly, "The apple-blossom queens haven't done so well, either."

Jan stopped in surprise. "Why, Mother," she blurted, "were you an apple-blossom queen?"

"Why, yes, you know that. I'm sure you do, you've just forgotten. When you were younger you used to love looking at the festival pictures in my album and once in a while opening the old cedar chest to admire my royal costume."

"I do remember now," Jan admitted. Questions raced through her mind. "Was that the biggest thrill of your life?" she thought of asking. "Is it harder for an apple-blossom queen to settle down to hardships than it is for someone who wasn't expecting much anyhow?" But she didn't ask the questions. She didn't want to think about her mother having dreams and aspirations of her own.

Her hand on the doorknob, Mrs. Morgan hesitated a minute and to Jan's surprise looked a little embarrassed. "Your father and I had a talk tonight after you left, and we decided that we had all been so upset by Andrew's illness we've forgotten how to live together as a family. We're going to try to do more things together and see if we can't develop more unity and harmony. Don't you think that would be a good idea?"

Right now Jan couldn't think of anything she wanted less than doing things with her family, but seeing the sadness in her mother's eyes she said quietly, "Well, we can try."

On graduation night Jan walked over to school alone, found an inconspicuous seat in the balcony, and watched with a heavy heart while her friends wound up their high school careers.

The band, in bright uniform, played harmoniously. Parents and friends watched proudly as the graduates paraded across the stage in their academic gowns. Pete, mighty uncomfortable in his ancient suit and stringy necktie, scribbled hasty notes. If only she had thought she could have offered to cover the event for him. She must train herself to be more news-minded.

In the front row, hearing-aid turned on full tilt, sat that character Mrs. Parsons. She didn't have any relatives in the group but the ceremony was probably something to relieve the monotony of her life.

From her seat Jan had a good view of Budge, who was trying not to look bored as the Senator made his speech. Watching him, Jan felt a strange new pain in her heart. They had had such a wonderful month working together. The special tulip queen story was so popular that although Pete balked and grumbled he had printed enough extras for the students to send copies to friends and relatives who had moved away. Their special senior edition was well done, too. Budge had been generous with help and advice and Jan was deferential and eager to learn from him.

Now Budge was graduating and going off to work in the woods for the summer and then to college. Melanie would be going, too. And Jan knew she wasn't really jealous of Melanie; she didn't want the kind of relationship Budge had with her. She only wanted the luxury of a friend who liked her just as she was.

After the last graduate had been congratulated and the band broke into the recessional, Jan slipped quietly down the aisle and walked home ahead of the crowd so she wouldn't have to say polite nothings to anyone. Budge was gone as she had known he was going to be. Nothing for her to do now but work hard all summer, making the best of things, and be ready to take over the *Argus* in the fall. The summer days would be long, but fall would come.

CHAPTER 4

Unity and Harmony

EXPECTING THREE MONTHS of acute boredom, Jan was surprised to find the first part of her vacation almost too hectic. The school doors had hardly slammed shut before the June day camp for the younger girls got underway in the park adjoining the school playfield, and Jan was shyly pleased when the camp committee asked her to help. Specifically her jobs were to see to publicity, keep records, and help handle supplies, but not being able to endure idleness, she also helped the handiwork classes with their woven baskets, beaded bracelets, and other projects. It was lots of fun.

One happy result of day camp was coming to know Cassie and Dotty and to appreciate their talents. Cassie was a natural at leading song fests and thinking up games for rainy days. Dotty, as director and producer of the closing-day pageant, bullied and cajoled her cast of amateurs into a remarkable performance.

Both girls were very friendly to Jan and treated her like one of the gang. Sometimes she thought cynically that it was because she now had the power of the press, but mostly she knew they would have been just as nice long ago if she hadn't shut herself up in a Deep Freeze. Anyway, she was looking forward to working with them at school this fall.

In the meantime her mother, who had not forgotten her intention to promote family unity and harmony, made plans for a camping trip. She and Jan and Andrew were to go to the Forest Service campsite near the Shorewood logging camp and Mr. Morgan would be able to spend his evenings with them. Jan was appalled at the idea, and not only because she would have to leave friendships that had begun at day camp. If her family was disagreeable here in town where there were other activities, what on earth would they be like all alone in the mountains? But she kept silent about her objections. Andrew, however, announced that if he couldn't go to Scout camp he didn't want to go anywhere, but even that did not deter their mother.

"We look like immigrants on a steerage boat," was Jan's opinion, as in their camping clothes, with bundles and boxes piled around them, they stood in the bus depot waiting for the little bus (hardly more than an oversized station wagon) that meandered through the foothills and backwoods.

"It's silly to go on a trip when we don't have a car," Andrew sulked.

"Son, there may be many times in your life when you don't have everything you want," Mrs. Morgan tried to explain. "You must improvise and make do or you'll miss a lot of good times."

"I miss out on everything I want," Andrew insisted, but his words didn't sting too much since they were partially lost in the bustle as the little bus arrived just in time to meet the cross-state express to Seattle. I wish I were going that way, Jan thought enviously as she helped load their equipment.

But going anywhere at all was fun, she decided, as they bounced and jogged along the rough road. When they arrived at the general-store-gas-station post office town that was their destination, Jan decided that a change of scene might be diverting after all, for there was her father waiting for them in the company jeep.

"This is wonderful," her mother said, her face aglow with more brightness and enthusiasm than Jan had seen for many a day. "I hadn't dared think how we would get our stuff to the camp."

"The boss insisted I get my family settled in style," he replied happily. "It's going to be grand having you all here."

In a few minutes they arrived at the camp ground and found a large wall tent already pitched for them in a pleasant clearing. "Wish I could stay to help you get settled," Mr. Morgan said as he hurriedly unloaded. "I'll be back as soon as I can."

He left and his family turned their attention to the unpacking. "It's been a long time since I've been camping," Mrs. Morgan said. "I hope I haven't forgotten anything vital."

A fire was laid in a circle of stones in the clearing, and she lighted it as she spoke. "We have our gasoline stove, but we'll need this fire, too," she explained. "We'll need it to heat water and to keep warm. You'll be surprised how cold it can get at night in the mountains. Now I think I'll set up the cots first thing. Janice, did you notice that faucet down the road? Would you take these two buckets and get us some water? Then when you're finished bring some more firewood over. We'll need a lot."

Jan was sitting on a stump enjoying the feel of the quiet and the smells of evergreen trees and wood smoke. She looked up rebelliously. "Why can't Andrew do that?" she asked. "Isn't he supposed to be a boy?"

"Yeah," Andrew agreed eagerly. He had been crawling around under the trees picking up pine and fir cones, but he got up, dusted off his hands, and reached for the buckets. "Let me do that."

"No, Andrew, you mustn't." She got the wrinkle in the middle of her forehead that both her children recognized as her especially worried look. "Heavy lifting might be too great a strain on your heart."

"You're always saying that," Andrew complained. "Any time I want to do anything you're afraid it's going to be a strain on my heart. And why? I don't ever have any pains."

"I know your heart doesn't pain you now," his mother said patiently. "But if it is damaged now it might hamper you when you grow up—keep you from working and living a normal life. It could even shorten your life. I know it's the hardest thing in the world for a boy your age to understand that you should curtail your fun now so that you can do more in the future."

"I don't care," Andrew replied, trying to force back angry tears. "I don't care at all. I don't want to live for years and years if I can't ever have any fun."

There were tears in his mother's eyes, too. She bit her lip hard, grabbed the buckets, and stalked down to the faucet.

For a minute Jan was tempted to run after her and say she was sorry. But what good was being sorry? She had managed to touch off a quarrel that made everyone thoroughly unhappy and didn't accomplish a thing. Very chastened, she went to the wood pile and gathered all they would need for the evening and stacked it neatly by the tent.

By the time Mr. Morgan returned they were all in a good mood again and enjoyed their dinner around the fire. He laid a stack of paper-bound books beside Jan. "Janice, my little bookworm, I suspect you won't want to spend all your time bird-watching or nature-hiking so I brought these along. The classics are for you and the who-done-its for your mother."

"Oh, Dad, thanks," Jan said with enthusiasm. "I brought my notebook and some knitting, but I didn't have much to read. But look at these—Shakespeare and historical books in a lumber camp, yet."

"You'll find all kinds of people in a lumber camp as well as anywhere else," he told her.

As the lingering darkness came, Jan and Andrew roasted marshmallows in the campfire while their parents sat and talked. Catching glimpses of her mother's face in the soft, flickering firelight, Jan was surprised at how peaceful she looked. Come to think of it, when did Mother ever get a vacation or even much help with her work? And she didn't have Dad around to help boss or entertain the family. It was enough to make anyone unfair and crabby, and Jan resolved to try to be more understanding about her mother's problems.

The next afternoon Jan took a book, a blanket, and a candy bar to a half-sunny, half-shady spot under one of the big trees in the camp ground and prepared to be lazy in luxury. She had just sat down when she heard a shout that brought her to her feet in astonished delight. Striding across the camp towards her was Budge Nichols.

"The kitchen crew works a split shift," he explained to Jan and her mother, "so I'm at leisure a few hours most afternoons. I thought I'd come over and see if Jan and Andrew would like to hike up the Ridge. The going isn't too rough and the view at the top is wonderful."

Jan assented with delight. It was such a grand surprise to see Budge and such a joyous prospect to spend some time with him that she didn't even mind the idea of having Andrew along. Budge seemed handsomer than ever in his rough work clothes.

"That's ever so nice of you," Mrs. Morgan said warmly. "I don't think Andrew had better go, however. Thank goodness he isn't here right now or he'd give me quite an argument. But you see, Budge, that climb to the Ridge is straight up and high altitude can be hard on the heart."

"That's too bad," Budge said. "You're probably right. A person does get to breathing hard on that climb."

"It's such a problem knowing what to do," she confided. "I want him to have a good time, but it seems all I do is scold him for exerting himself too much. What I should have done, but I didn't think of it in time, was have Dr. Conners check him again and tell us exactly what he could and couldn't do on a camping trip like this. Right now he's in the woods looking for nature specimens. You two had better be gone before he gets back."

Jan was ashamed of herself for being so glad that Andrew couldn't go. She would always remember the afternoon—the muscle-pulling climb up the steep trail and the wonderful view of layer after layer of mountains when they reached the top. They sat on a boulder and shared her candy while Budge talked about his work at the camp.

"I like all this so much," he said with a wide sweep of his arm. "Life in the open, hard work. I could be a good lumberjack. But I want to be a newspaperman, too. And of course that's what Melanie wants for me."

"You have to go on with your newspaper work," Jan said seriously. "Maybe some day you could free-lance for the lumber or forestry trade journals or the sports magazines and get a slice of outdoor life along with your writing."

Budge looked at her with admiration and astonishment. "Why, that's just what I could do. I don't know why an idea like that hadn't ever penetrated my lame brain. Jan, I always said you were the smartest girl in town. Golly, that would be a wonderful life."

It was a wonderful life right here and now in Jan's opinion, sitting in the sun talking to Budge and seeing the look of respect he gave her. He glanced at his watch and sighed. "Time for the K.P.'s to hit the trail."

On their way down to camp again Budge said, "Tell Andrew I'll be over tomorrow and help him with his specimens. When I was in the Scouts I learned all sorts of things to make out of pine cones and stuff. Handwork is good for kids. Keeps 'em quiet and happy."

So Budge adopted himself into the Morgan family and contributed materially towards making a wonderful vacation for them. He showed Andrew how to gild pine cones, make winter corsages, fashion decorations from cat-tails and weave grass baskets.

He took Jan on hikes and took both her and Andrew over to the Shorewood camp to show them the bunkhouses, mess hall, and offices. They watched the colorful, difficult work of the logging crews and heard the long-drawn-out call, "Tiiimmmmmberrrr" before one of the giant trees crashed. One day they visited the tree farm, where logged-off land instead of being left bare and ugly as it had been in the old logging days was now scientifically planted to preserve the forests and eventually yield another crop of lumber.

Budge would always be very special to her, Jan thought to herself. She didn't really like boys the way most of her classmates did. They were forever giggling and talking about them and having dates, and Jan knew her mother was disappointed because she didn't have dates, too. But she really didn't want to—it seemed like such a waste of time being pleasant to some dull boy just to say you had been out with him.

Besides, she didn't have many opportunities. She supposed the boys could tell that she didn't like them. Maybe if Andrew were different she wouldn't have such an antagonism towards all boys, but anyhow, it didn't matter. Two weeks of friendly companionship with Budge was worth a year of dates with someone ordinary.

Shortly after they were back in town Jan happened to come out on the porch just in time to watch a parade of Scouts, packs on their backs, marching down the road on their way out of town. Spotting Andrew on the lawn, they yelled to him and waved. Although he waved back cheerfully, Jan thought she could detect a look of envy in his face.

Andrew had just become a Cub Scout at the time of his illness. Jan remembered how as soon as he could have visitors at all the den mother and cubmaster had come and pre-

sented him with his bobcat pin. At other times groups of
Cubs had visited. But although the cubmaster had urged
Andrew to work on his achievements, explaining to Mrs.
Morgan that he could substitute something else for the active
"Feats of Skill," she had discouraged the idea, saying that she
was afraid a group of Cub Scouts, even one engaged in
"quiet" handwork, was too active for Andrew.

Suddenly very sorry for him, Jan went over and patted his
shoulder. "Someday you'll be able to go with them," she said.

He shoved her hand away. "Leave me alone," he said angrily.

Jan shrugged her shoulders and turned away. After all, it
took more than one person to promote family unity and harmony. But she did feel sorry for Andrew, anyway.

CHAPTER 5

Summer Employment

AFTER THE LAST Fourth of July firecracker sizzled away, most organized activities suspended for a while and the summer settled down to a procession of hot, quiet days. Jan decided it was time to get going with her project of earning money.

Naturally the first step was a visit to Pete, whom she hadn't seen since day camp, when she had written publicity stories for his Cascadeville *Courier*. He put the weekly out alone except for the dubious contributions of a few country correspondents. The paper needed help and she needed a job, so what could be more logical than for them to get together?

Jan walked slowly along the street to the shop, feeling as relaxed as the leaves hanging limply from the alders, as sluggish as the river at low ebb with hardly a trickle between the rocks. It was the sort of day to be spent in a hammock thinking about working on newspapers; but thinking didn't buy typewriters, so Jan set her jaw with determination and began to walk a little faster.

The door to the print shop was open in case a stray breeze should slip between the mountains and fan down to cool the valley. Pete was at the linotype working rapidly, pausing only to wipe his face with a dusty handkerchief. Jan sat down quietly. He finished the copy he had set up, lifted the long rows of type, and carried them over to the table where a form was waiting.

When he groped around for some space bars to tighten the

column Jan handed them to him. He winked at her but didn't stop his work until the form was finished and locked. Then he wiped his hands on his apron, smiled, and said, "Howdy, stranger. Thought you must be off to the big city by now."

"Oh, Pete, don't be coy," Jan protested. "You know perfectly well what I've been doing. You don't miss one thing that goes on here in town."

Pete didn't deny this. He merely queried, "Well, what's on your mind now? Getting more and more fancy ideas for the *Argus*, no doubt."

"No, I'll worry about the *Argus* come fall. Right now I'm thinking about your *Courier*. You need help, Pete. The country correspondents are getting terribly sloppy."

"Now look here, young lady," Pete said in genuine alarm. "My country correspondents have been sloppy for thirty-four years and they aren't about to change now. You peddle your papers and I'll peddle mine."

"But, Pete, I could do some features that would be much more interesting than all those columns full of 'Mr. and Mrs. Jones motored to Seattle last Tuesday' and 'Joey Smith celebrated his birthday with a weiner roast at Barren Mountain.' "

"I'm sure your features would be more interesting, Jan," Pete replied. "That is they would be more interesting to everybody but the Smiths and the Joneses. They are the ones who subscribe to the *Courier*. They want to see their names in the paper and they want to see their neighbors' names in the paper. So that's out. Any further suggestions?"

"You might at least spell the names right," Jan snapped, sulky and hurt that her big idea had gone over with such a thud.

"Now you're talking sense," Pete agreed. "My correspondents are mostly housewives with a little spare time. Only in the middle of the summer they go places or have company or can raspberries and either call in their copy and I get the names wrong over the phone, or else they send in a bunch of scribbles that a State Department code expert couldn't unravel. It's really a headache.

"Tell you what," Pete said, snapping his fingers in sudden decision. "It would be a big help if you would take over the getting-the-names-spelled-right department."

"What duties would that include?" Jan wanted to know.

"You can talk to the ones who call up and get hold of the copy mailed in and check each name. When the items sound too vague to be news, try to get the complete story. Then type up the whole shebang so it's readable. It will make my typesetting much easier."

"O.K.," Jan agreed. "I'll do that. But I still think I should write some feature stories. Sometimes you don't have enough news to fill your space and you put in one of those boilerplates the Department of Agriculture sends out about how to raise barley in Minnesota, and believe me, the Smiths and Joneses in Washington don't care how they raise barley in Minnesota."

Pete winced. "Guess I know when I'm overruled. All right, kid, you can write a few features about this area—parks, schools, county officials, traditions—you know the sort of thing."

"I certainly do," Jan said, her eyes sparkling. "I already have some of them outlined."

"I'm sure you do," Pete said limply. "Well, get over to the desk and start plowing through today's mail."

"Pete, before I start, I want to tell you about one more idea," Jan said hesitantly.

Pete sighed, then he sat down and lit his pipe. "Something tells me I'm going to be a tired old man before your year is over. All right, what's this one more idea? I guess I can stand anything except a poetry column about the mountains at sunset."

"I don't write poetry," Jan said disdainfully. "I thought you ought to publish a high school column every week next year. Since the *Argus* only comes out once a month we don't get complete coverage on all our school events."

"That isn't a bad idea at all," Pete decided. "It would save Mr. Larsen and me both a lot of bother. Having all the school news in one spot would be handy, too. I suppose the resourceful Miss Morgan would do the column."

"Naturally," Jan agreed. "Now I'll get to work on your mail."

Mostly it was pure joy to Jan to come down to the hot, dusty office and wrestle with the misspellings and grammatical errors of the correspondents. But she went at the corrections in such a brisk and efficient fashion that several of the women complained to Pete about her snippy ways. He teasingly reprimanded her, softening the scolding with a little praise, saying that after all not many people had her enthusiasm and all-out interest in the paper.

So Jan worked at curbing her tongue and being polite. She spent some time on her feature stories, too. The first one was about Barren Mountain, the stark, treeless hill that stood just behind Cascadeville, a crag-like contrast to the heavily firred mountains all around. The Indians had considered it the home of evil spirits and given it a wide berth. By the same token the early pioneers had considered it a symbol of good luck. Pete insisted that it was just a displaced Rocky Mountain dropped off on one of Paul Bunyan's journeys and unable to find its way home.

Into her story about the mountain Jan skillfully wove facts and legends. She told all about the ski festival held every January on Barren Mountain and closed the article with details and descriptions of the state park and campsite. She found a picture of the mountain in the morgue, dusted it off, gave it a bright new caption, and dumped the whole works on Pete's desk.

Pete made no comment on the story, though Jan knew it was obvious that she was fretting and fuming to the explosion point. After several days of this incommunicado situation, she headed for the shop one afternoon grimly determined to hear Pete's opinion of her story if she had to hit him over the head with one of his own lead bars.

She found the old printer sitting at his desk, long streams of galley proofs flapping feebly in the breeze of the electric fan. "Come here, kid," he ordered. "I need your advice on a problem."

Her story was in front of him and he tapped it with his big black pencil. Her heart sank. Could she have made an error on one of her statistics? "An editor should always avoid starting any community brawls," Pete explained, "so you see I'm really in a spot. If I give you a by-line as Jan Morgan your mother will blow her stack and if I make it Janice you'll undoubtedly quit."

Emotions warred in Jan. She wanted to sing, shout, and turn somersaults at the thought of getting a by-line in the *Courier*. Sloppy old weekly that it was, it had a wide circulation both in town and back in the hills. But she wanted her own name, too. "I'm Jan," she said firmly. "Janice is for some namby-pamby lavender-and-lace girl, not for me. Mother will just have to face it."

"Janice is a very pretty name," Pete scolded. "However, I agree that Jan suits your particular personality better. What's your middle name?"

"Marie," she replied sadly. "Janice Marie. Honestly, how frilly can you get?"

"Hey, that's O.K.," Pete said, coming out of his slump. "I'm putting you down as Jan Marie Morgan. I like that name." He wrote it firmly above the story.

"Jan Marie Morgan." She said it slowly, liking the sound of it.

"If you want a formal christening I could always dump some ink on you," Pete offered.

"Cola would be better," Jan laughed. "And in me, not on me. Hold the fort and I'll get two—with limes."

She wanted to skip down the road, but it wouldn't be dignified for Jan Marie Morgan, foreign correspondent . . . Jan Marie Morgan, executive editor . . . She threw back her head, laughed, and skipped anyway.

Although Jan's formal hours of duty were from two to five each afternoon, to learn all she could she managed to hang around most of the day and help Pete with all the different phases of newspaper publishing and job-printing. Then several evenings a week she worked as a baby-sitter, mostly for Mrs. Preston, who didn't miss any opportunities for summer entertainment.

Sometimes the Prestons even drove the seventy-two miles to Seattle for a special dinner or theater party. On these occasions Jan spent the night and got up with Johnny in the morning while his mother slept till noon or thereabouts.

Mrs. Preston always woke up happy and relaxed those after-party mornings, but before long with Johnny demanding attention and housework confronting her, her pretty face would take on a bored, sulky look. Sometimes Jan wondered why anyone as lucky as Mrs. Preston should seem so discontented, but she didn't often take time to worry about other people's problems.

Jan's mother complained that she was never home except to eat and sleep, but really it was more peaceful for everyone when she wasn't at home complaining about Andrew and acting like such a smarty. Certainly there was nothing she could do to keep her mother from worrying and fretting over Andrew through the bright summer days.

The day her by-line story was published in the Cascadeville *Courier,* Jan brought the paper home and laid it casually on the kitchen table. She wasn't going to say a thing about it, just wait for the family to read it in their own time, and then—oh, well, it wouldn't matter if they didn't say anything. Really it wouldn't. She couldn't impress them with a by-line in the New York *Times.*

"Mrs. Preston called," her mother told her.

Jan pushed back her long, heavy hair with a tired hand. "Johnny's so full of mischief since he started to walk," she sighed. "I'm too weary to cope right now."

"You shouldn't work such long hours," her mother said fretfully. "I don't want your health ruined, too. Andrew is enough worry. I had such a time with him today. He sneaked down to the river bend and was swimming in that filthy pond by the mill. I know it must be contaminated. When I found him and made him come home he cried like a baby. Imagine, a boy his age! He's gone to bed with a bad headache now, and I certainly hope it isn't going to be anything worse than that."

"That's too bad," Jan said, feeling vaguely sorry for both Andrew and her mother, but mostly concerned with her own problems. "I ought to see what Mrs. Preston wants, anyhow," she went on as she reached for the phone.

Surprisingly enough, Mrs. Preston didn't want a baby-sitter this time. "I'm calling for my friend, Mrs. Abbott," she explained. "You met her the night you wrote your tulip queen story, if you remember."

"Yes, I remember," Jan said eagerly. Ever since that night she had been hoping that some day she'd find out more about the woman who was popular and happy even though she'd never been a tulip queen.

"Well, she's looking for someone to type postcards for our Community Club Bazaar and I suggested you. If you'd like the job give her a call."

Jan felt her weariness vanish in a surge of excitement as she asked for the Abbotts' number. Mrs. Abbott's voice was brisk and cheerful. "We have a hundred and fifty postcards. There's a message to be typed on each, the lot to be addressed, and a week to get it all done. Will five cents a card suit you?"

"Just fine," Jan replied, mentally computing the profits as she talked. "Would it be all right if I worked in the mornings so I could be at the *Courier* in the afternoon?"

"Certainly," Mrs. Abbott agreed. "I wouldn't want you to miss your time on the paper. I just read your article. It's very interesting and well written. It will give us all a new slant on our old mountain."

"Oh, thank you," Jan said happily as she replaced the phone.

She walked back to the kitchen, where her mother was sitting at the table having a cup of coffee and looking through the paper. "Have you read it yet?" she asked eagerly, forgetting her resolution not to mention it herself.

Her mother looked up absently. "I'm going to try this new recipe for peach preserves in the homemaker's column. It sounds wonderful. It would cut the time I have to stand over that hot stove by two-thirds. Someday you might tell Pete he's doing a good thing with that column."

"But my story—page one of the second section—the one with the picture. Haven't you seen it yet?"

Mrs. Morgan turned over the pages. "Oh, yes, I saw it. And I can't help but be unhappy that you insist on using a nickname in public. Long before you were born I had decided that if I ever had a little girl I would name her Janice because it sounded so sweet and pretty and gay. Why should you repudiate such a nice name?"

Jan was tempted to ask who was repudiating whom but she held her tongue. "Is that all you noticed about the story?" she asked. "Just my name?"

"I didn't read it all the way through. After all I've lived around Barren Mountain all my life and I'm not much interested in reading about it. I'll read it more thoroughly later when I have the time. Do you have a pencil handy? I want to take down this recipe before it gets lost."

Jan handed over the pencil and crept upstairs. In her room she flopped down on the bed and tried hard to keep from crying. Pete's kindness, Mrs. Abbott's words of praise—they were nothing, didn't mean a thing when her own mother wouldn't even read her story. "I'll go away," she whispered. "Soon as I'm old enough I'll go away."

But even as she dreamed about the future, she knew that no matter how much fame and fortune she won she would be incomplete if her own family didn't accept her talents.

Although the typing itself was monotonous, Jan thoroughly enjoyed working at the Abbotts'. Their house was as pretty as Jan expected, and Mrs. Abbott thoughtfully set up the typewriter and equipment in the patio and kept watch to see that her three little girls didn't intrude on Jan.

After the first few cards the work became almost automatic and Jan could let her mind and eyes wander a bit. She especially liked to watch Mrs. Abbott playing with the children in their own special yard equipped with a sandbox, swings, and a wading pool. She was gentle and gay with them, even when they were troublesome.

You didn't need a crystal ball to look into the future and know that Mrs. Abbott would encourage her daughters to be themselves. She wouldn't close her heart to them and try to force them into some stereotyped pattern. Jan felt a catch at her throat and turned abruptly back to her work.

One mid-morning Mrs. Abbott appeared with a glass of iced tea and instructions to rest her fingers awhile. She watched Jan push back her hair, frowned thoughtfully, and said, "Your hair is so long and shiny. Does it bother you much in hot weather?"

Taken off guard, Jan blurted out the truth. "I really don't

like it this way, but I'm too old to wear pigtails and a permanent just frizzles away. What else could I do?"

Mrs. Abbott laughed. "They say a rose is a rose is a rose, but believe me, a pigtail isn't necessarily a braid. Why, braids can be made into some of the most attractive hair-do's in the world. I saw some beauties in a magazine recently and I've been itching to find someone with long hair so I could try them out. Would you mind being my guinea pig?"

Surprised and a little apprehensive, Jan stammered out, "No, I wouldn't mind."

"Then come along," Mrs. Abbott commanded. "The typing can wait."

In a few minutes a still-bewildered Jan found herself sitting in front of a mirrored dressing table, the magazine in her lap. Mrs. Abbott went to work. "All you need are two braids," she instructed, "and you can do practically anything. You can put them on top of your head like a coronet, or coiled over your ears like an old-fashioned belle, wound in back in a chignon, but no, that would be too old for you. However, this would be good—looped up and tied with ribbons."

They tried them all. Jan's head began to ache, but she couldn't help being thrilled at the difference a neat, attractive topknot made in her appearance. It was cool and comfortable, too.

Finally they settled on the coronet braids for Jan to wear the rest of the day. "I do think it's very becoming," Mrs. Abbott said enthusiastically. "It's dignified, too. Wear it this fall when you want to put your cub reporters in their place or when you go out to interview the ambassador to something-or-other."

Jan laughed delightedly. She almost felt she was looking at someone else, and in a way she was. The chic young lady in the mirror was scarcely related to the Jan who woke up with the sulks and hardly bothered to brush her hair.

"Then some bright morning you'll oversleep and won't have time to make braids," Mrs. Abbott cautioned. "When that happens, pull your hair back and tie it in a pony tail. That would be cute on you, too."

"Take the magazine along," Mrs. Abbott insisted as Jan prepared to leave. "Make a game out of it from now on— change your braids to suit your moods. The other girls will really be taking notice, and the boys will be, too."

Walking down the hill to the shop, Jan stepped lightly. A weight had been lifted from her shoulders in more ways than one. As she walked in, head high and face bright, Pete glanced up quickly, took a second, longer look, and rose. "Good afternoon, Duchess," he intoned in a deep bass voice. "How's every little thing up at the castle."

"Never mind the performance, Pete," she said impatiently. "Do you like it or not?"

He didn't answer immediately. He sat down, leaned back in his chair, and looked thoughtful. "Time was when you could always pick a girl reporter out of the crowd," he said musingly. "She was the one with the sloppy clothes, shiny nose, scraggly hair, bad manners. Must have figured she was more dedicated to her job if she carried on like that."

He paused while Jan looked down at the floor guiltily. He knew perfectly well she had been operating on that theory.

"You girls are wrong," Pete said. "As a reporter you'll live a thousand lives. You'll feel your heart swell up with excitement over the good news you share and sometimes you'll think it's just going to kill you to have to write one more story about the tragedy and cruelty and wickedness in the world. But good or bad you'll be there, standing by when history is made, sizing up the captains and the kings and getting it in time for the next edition."

"Which people will skim through lightly and toss into the fireplace," Jan reminded him.

He gave her an understanding smile and finished his

speech. "You're privileged to be a reporter, Jan. And along with dedicating yourself to getting the story and getting it right you should dedicate yourself to looking your best, to being attractive and pleasant-mannered. Above all, you should be humbly aware of your responsibility to look into the heart of the human race and put it all down on paper. Yes, Jan, I like your hairdo. I like it very much."

For several minutes Jan couldn't say anything. She couldn't even look at Pete. She knew she would remember his words all her life and be a better reporter, indeed a better person for having heard them. She ought to tell him so, too, but somehow she just couldn't, and anyway he would know.

Finally she cleared her throat and said lightly, "That much philosophy out of a muggy August sky can only mean you forgot to eat lunch. Can I get you a milkshake or something?"

"Now there's an intelligent idea," Pete agreed, dredging up some coins from his pocket. "A chocolate milkshake would be fine for me. But tea and petits fours for you, Duchess. Got to keep the peasants in their places, you know."

Pete was being Pete again, not the Voice of Experience. Jan made a face at him and started down town, her coroneted head held proudly.

CHAPTER 6

The Mallorys Come to Town

AFTER AN AFTERNOON SPENT reading proof in the grimy heat of the shop, Jan was delighted to be out in the fragrant coolness of the summer evening, and in no hurry to go home. She was walking slowly along River Road when she was jolted out of her preoccupation by the sound of voices. "Why can't I have the sun porch for my room?" a boy's voice asked. "Nobody, but nobody uses sun porches any more—they have patios in back, and we could fix one up in no time."

"Meaning *I* could fix one up in no time," an older voice said with a laugh.

"And we could each have a room of our own!" "Oh, yes!" There were two girls' voices, high and chirping.

Jan stepped quietly behind the drooping branches of a willow tree and watched the scene across the street with interest. Several people were milling around the yard of the vacant house while Mr. Gwenn the realtor, happily tacked a SOLD sign against the wall. Her eyes sorted them out: middle-aged comfortable-looking parents, a boy about her age or a little older. About as tall as Budge he looked to be, but not as handsome. Two small girls chased each other around the lawn. A nice-looking, enthusiastic family. She was happy to see them there. The house needed someone.

Most new people in Cascadeville, and a lot of the old ones,

bought modern ranch houses in the Madrona Park subdivi-
sion, which was a beautiful, well-planned development
with winding roads, playgrounds, and natural landscaping.
But Jan had always had an affection for this old-fashioned
house with its wonderful view of the river and the mountains. She was glad it had a family to shelter again.

"The painters will be out tomorrow," Mr. Gwenn promised.

"And we'll move in in a week," the man agreed.

Jan was tempted to cross the street and introduce herself,
but they were heading for their car. Besides, a little skilful
questioning of Pete might reveal all there was to know about
why a strange family was moving to Cascadeville.

Sure enough, the next day Pete received a letter from the
public relations department of the Northern Railroad saying
that Mike Mallory of Seattle had been appointed foreman of
the railway repair shops at Cascadeville.

"They're the ones who're moving into the vacant house,"
Jan said delightedly. "I just know it."

"You do not just know it," Pete reproved her sternly.
"Since when do we print a newspaper full of wild conjectures and half-baked ideas?"

"I didn't tell you to print it," Jan replied huffily. "Before
I turn in anything for you to publish I'll find out what kind
of toothpaste they use and where their Great-Aunt Matilda
went to school, much less whether or not they bought the
house on River Road."

"See that you do," Pete replied, unperturbed by her sarcasm.

On the day the Mallorys were scheduled to move in Jan
planned to stop by and interview them on her way home. But
that afternoon the boy she had glimpsed the other evening
came into the shop. Seen close up he was dark-haired, smiling, alert and energetic. "Hello," he said. "This the Cascadeville *Courier?*"

"That's right," Pete said, swinging around in his chair. "What can I do for you? Classified ad?"

"No. I want a subscription. Mike Mallory, Box 146. I'm Danny Mallory. We just moved here from Seattle."

Jan laughed gleefully. "Who has wild conjectures and half-baked ideas now?" she asked. She took her pencil and notebook and walked up to the counter. "Would you mind telling us something about your family? We'd like a story about you in next week's paper."

"No kidding?" Danny asked. "You must be really hard up for news if you write up everybody who comes to town."

"Evidently you aren't familiar with small-town weeklies," Pete explained. "Nearly everybody in town takes a daily from Seattle to keep himself up on world events and the comics, and then we have our weekly *Courier* with all the local news about the Smiths and the Joneses and the Mallorys moving to town."

"Sounds great," Danny said thoughtfully. "The different communities in Seattle have weeklies, too, but they're mostly geared for the woman shoppers and I never paid much attention to them. Say, if you really want a piece about us why don't you let me write it? I'm an old hand at this who-what-when business." He laid a hand on the swinging gate by the counter and looked at Pete hopefully.

Pete looked him in the eye a minute, then nodded. "O.K., there's the typewriter. Make it about three inches."

Jan stood by nonplused while Danny sat down at the typewriter, put in some copy paper, and started the story with the unmistakable confidence brought about by long experience. In a few minutes he tapped out 30, pulled the paper from the machine, and handed it to Pete.

Pete read it over and nodded thoughtfully. "That's fine," he said. Then he turned to Jan. "Gonna need any help this fall? Better grab him."

"I'm editor of our school paper, the *Mountain View Monthly Argus*," she explained. "Are you going to school in Cascadeville or have you graduated?"

"No. I'll be a senior this year. I'm really glad to hear you have a school paper. I'd been wondering. If you can use me just whistle and I'll come a-running."

"We'll be glad to have you," Jan replied. "I wish now I hadn't been in such a rush to get the staff positions filled last spring. What position did you have at your school?"

Danny's happy look changed to one of melancholy. "I was supposed to be editor this fall, too. On the Bayside *Barnacle*. Ever hear of it? I had to give it all up when we moved."

"Oh that's awful," Jan sympathized. "I haven't seen the *Barnacle* because we only exchange with monthlies as a rule, but I've certainly heard of it. In fact I think it's one of the examples in our journalism book."

"It is," Danny confirmed.

"How terrible for you to have to leave," Jan said, shaking her head. "Be sure to come around when school starts. We'll find something for you to do."

"I'll be there," he promised. "I don't want to get rusty. I'm going to enroll in the School of Journalism at the University of Washington next fall. Are you?"

"I don't know," Jan said sadly. "That's a long ways away. I'll worry about it when the time comes."

"Well, suppose I'd better go," he said reluctantly. "Whenever I get near a newspaper I don't have sense enough to leave till I'm thrown out. I hope I can stop in again."

"Sure, come on down," Pete said hospitably. "I'm resigned to the fact that I can't keep you demon newshounds out from underfoot."

Danny, smiling again, winked at Jan. Evidently he understood Pete perfectly. "See you around," he said as he left.

After that Danny seemed to pop up everywhere. Jan found him in the drugstore having a root beer float and talking to the gang around the soda fountain as much at home as if he had been there for years.

He went to the young people's meeting at church on Sunday evening and talked himself onto the softball team in less time than it takes to swing a bat. He even came over to the Morgans' one night to watch the television, but Jan had to go out baby-sitting so she didn't have an opportunity to talk to him.

"How did you like Danny?" she asked Andrew the next day.

"He's swell! He went through a television studio once in Seattle. He's done lots of interesting things. I'm glad to know all newspaper writers aren't crumbs."

Jan glared at him and slammed out the door. She ought to know by now that it was a waste of time to be civil to Andrew.

Yes, Danny was fitting right into the life of the town and making a fine impression on everyone. She even saw him standing and listening to old sourpuss Miss Layton. Pete often told her it was part of her training in newspaper work to be nice to weird characters like Miss Layton, but training or not she drew the line at somebody who had tried that hard

to keep her from being editor, and she quickly scurried by
so they wouldn't notice her.

Later that afternoon Danny came to the office. "I've been
talking to Miss Layton," he announced.

"Yes, I know," Jan replied with a grimace.

He grinned. "She's a character, no doubt about it. Anyhow, she's going to attend a conference in Spokane this week
and I wondered . . ."

Jan jumped up from the desk. "The typewriter and Miss
Layton are all yours."

"Thanks, but it's all finished. I typed up a little story at
home just in case you could use it."

He pulled it from his pocket and handed it to Pete, who
read it and nodded approval.

"Do you have a typewriter?" Jan asked wistfully. She
hoped the envy she felt wasn't evidenced in her face.

"Yeah. A portable. At Bayside I used to take it along when
I covered athletic events or interschool conferences. It's
neat."

"Oh, it must be," Jan said. "I want to get one as soon as
possible."

"Good idea," Danny agreed.

Good idea! After Danny left she took a piece of scratch paper and tried to total her resources. There would be enough
if she didn't buy any new clothes this fall. And she wouldn't.
Why should she? New clothes weren't nearly as important as
a typewriter.

Besides, it would serve her mother right if she looked miserable and shabby. She didn't have to spend all their money
on Andrew. She directed a cold look at Pete, too, while he,
happily unaware of her, was working on the press. If he
thought an attractive appearance was so important to a newspaper reporter he ought to start with himself. He obviously
hadn't had anything new since President Roosevelt's inau-
gural ball—Teddy Roosevelt, that was.

After Miss Layton returned from the conference Danny wrote another story about her and she was delighted. Then he turned in an amusing feature about the softball game between the young people's church group and another group down the valley. Jan and Pete readily agreed that he deserved a by-line for it. Jan was especially glad to have him do sports stories, because she knew she didn't have the aptitude for athletics. Pete laughed and said his two eager-beaver apprentices were giving him a real vacation.

An easy comradeship quickly developed between Jan and Danny whenever they were in the shop together. In a way it was even better than her friendship with Budge, because she had always been a little in awe of him while she and Danny could meet as equals. She admired his gift for making friends and fitting into a new environment so quickly. There was no doubt that he would make a fine newspaperman someday

The last day of August was hazy with a hint of Indian summer. Only a week till school began. Jan was amazed that vacation could have gone so fast. Reviewing the past months in her mind, she dreamily rounded the corner by the bridge and banged smack into Dotty Graham.

"Yeow, take it easy," Dotty cautioned as she grabbed the bridge railing and stopped short. "Dramatic as I am, I have no desire to be bunted into a watery grave by an absent-minded keyhole peeper."

"Watery grave, forsooth," Jan laughed as she glanced down at the nearly dry summertime river.

"Jan, I was planning to get in touch with you today," Dotty said. "Not so literally, of course. I was wondering if we couldn't go to the school council meeting together."

Jan was so surprised that she too grabbed hold of the railing. "What school council meeting?" she asked.

"Why, the school council meeting tonight, of course, to

make plans for the opening of school. Honestly, how absent-minded can you get?"

"I'm not absent-minded," Jan protested. "I didn't know a thing about it. Pete hasn't had any notice either or he would have put it in this week's calendar."

"Really?" Dotty was incredulous. "Well, it's at Mr. Larsen's house at seven thirty—but imagine Miss Efficiency Layton slipping up on that one!"

"Miss Layton," Jan gasped. "Is she, that is, did she . . ."

"Why, yes. She sent out postcards all inscribed in her neat refined handwriting. Jan—"

"Thanks for telling me, Dotty," Jan interrupted. "Don't wait for me, though. I may be a little late. 'By now.'"

Leaving Dotty abruptly, she raced the rest of the way to the shop. Anger and an incredible suspicion were burning in her as she flew through the door and over to Pete's desk, scattering papers on her way. "Pete, Miss Layton is trying to pull a fast one on me," she said, and in a choked voice told him of her conversation with Dotty.

"It does sound bad," Pete admitted, "but it could have been an oversight. Everyone makes mistakes once in awhile. Call her up and find out."

"Call her up," Jan said, horrified. Then she nodded. "Yes, I must," she agreed and picked up the phone.

"Miss Layton, why didn't I receive a notice about the council meeting?" she asked abruptly as soon as she heard a voice at the other end of the line.

"Oh, it's Janice," Miss Layton said nervously. "I meant to call you about that but time has been so short. You see, the editor isn't actually a member of the council. In the past the editor usually attended meetings to get information for the school paper, but was never a voting member of the council."

"Oh!" Jan said in surprise.

"Yes," Miss Layton hurried on. "Now it has been suggested that the editor be given formal membership and that is one of the things we are going to discuss and vote upon to-night. Under the circumstances I thought you might not want to be present."

It all sounded perfectly logical but somehow Jan still felt suspicious. "Formal or informal membership doesn't bother me at all," she said. "You can discuss it all you please. The only thing I'm interested in is getting the news, and if it's customary for me to attend to get it then I'll attend."

"I really do not advise it," Miss Layton said sharply. "You had better not force yourself in where you aren't wanted."

"I wouldn't want to intrude," Jan said, mentally scorning the tradition that required students to be polite to their teachers even if they were unprincipled liars. "Since it troubles you, Miss Layton," she went on, thinking fast, "I'll just check with Mr. Larsen on whether or not I should attend."

"It's your responsibility," the lady snapped as she hung up her phone.

Jan spoke briefly to Mr. Larsen, who said cheerfully, "Of course, come along. The editor definitely should be a council member and I trust we'll take care of that business in short order tonight."

Jan put down the phone, still hurt and puzzled, and then suddenly the whole plot exploded in her mind, making all this strange behavior horribly clear. "She wants Danny to be editor!" Jan exclaimed. "She's never liked me—always bleating about how immature I am—and she thinks he's so wonderful because he wrote those stories about her. That's what she's planning for the council meeting—she wants to change editors."

"That would be the type of thing the old harpy would scheme up," Pete agreed. "I've had an itchy-nose feeling for several days that something nasty was going on around town. But don't blame Danny for this, Jan. He's a good, honest boy. He probably doesn't even know what she is doing."

"Rats. She isn't brainy enough to think about it by herself," Jan replied, her liking for Danny turning rapidly to hatred. "You've seen yourself how he's been flattering her and playing up to her."

"I have seen him being decently kind to her because he is a kind person," Pete said calmly. "He got news from her and it's a newspaper's job to print news. Now calm down, Jan, I'm not going to scold you. We have to get busy and draw up a plan of battle. In the first place, just why does Miss Layton consider you immature and unsuitable for the editorship when you've always been an outstanding English student?"

"Oh, we've been feuding ever since I was a freshman," Jan explained. "I proved that she had a sentence diagrammed incorrectly and she hasn't liked me ever since."

Pete groaned and pulled at his hair. "If that doesn't sound just like you. Will there be anyone else there tonight with a knife out for you?"

"Miss Travers the gym teacher doesn't like me, either," Jan said, a little ashamed. "I told her I wanted to be excused from gym so I could study, because only morons enjoyed exercise."

"Oh, brother!" Pete muttered. "How to win friends and influence people. Anyone else?"

"No. Mr. Larsen is my friend and Miss Johnson doesn't care one way or the other and there are only four faculty members on the council. The student officers have all met Danny and I'm sure they like him. But they're independent, Pete, and maybe they won't want anybody from out of town to be put ahead of one of their own members."

Pete nodded. "Now I'll tell you what to do," he dictated. "You go to the meeting wearing your best clothes, with your hair all fixed, and be more sweet and refined and deferential than you've ever been in your life. If you're above reproach in your conduct even Miss Layton will have a hard time getting rid of you."

"I don't think I could be above reproach," Jan said seriously. "I think I'd scream and howl and tear her hair out. Besides, I really don't know if I can go. I said I'd baby-sit for Mrs. Abbott tonight and she's so extra-nice that I couldn't just run out on her."

"Go explain the situation to her," Pete advised. "If she can't get anyone else, I'll baby-sit for her."

"Why, Pete!" Jan's heart flooded with affection for him. "Why, Pete, you're always talking about how much you hate children."

"Not nearly as much as I hate injustice," he replied gruffly. "Run along now, I have a little errand of my own." He reached for his mouse-colored, shapeless hat. "Larsen always gets his mail this time of day. Think I'll accidentally run into him and then just happen to drop a few remarks about my talented little helper. Won't do any harm."

Jan did run, literally, all the way to the Abbotts' and arrived trembling and breathless. As she talked to Mrs. Abbott she felt the humiliating sting of tears. "I'm not crying," she insisted with a mighty sniffle. "I'm just out of breath."

"Of course you don't have to come tonight," Mrs. Abbott said, tactfully looking the other way as Jan reached for her handkerchief. "We don't care much about going to the movie anyhow, so tell Pete his sacrifice won't be necessary. But, Jan, this is a bad business. I wish I could help you."

Jan sniffed back a last tear and squared her shoulders. "Pete says I have to be sweet and ladylike."

"Pete's right," Mrs. Abbott agreed. "And after it's all over, put it out of your mind and forget it ever happened."

"How could I possibly forget?" she asked in amazement. The hatred she felt for Danny and Miss Layton coursed through her with every beat of her heart.

"You must," Mrs. Abbott insisted. "Sooner or later a person has to fight against injustice, but you mustn't let it poison your enjoyment of the goodness of life."

It made sense, Jan reflected. Mrs. Abbott usually made sense. She was happy and adjusted to life. But she couldn't always have been adjusted, from what Jan remembered of the picture in the high school annual. "Can life really be good when you're shy and homely and in high school?" she asked bluntly.

"It can be if you're wise enough," Mrs. Abbott replied thoughtfully, not at all offended by Jan's searching question. "I was bitter and unhappy until I joined the WAC. Then doing for others made me happy and happiness is the greatest cosmetic in the world. Then I met the Colonel . . ."

Mrs. Abbott patted Jan's shoulder and changed the subject. "The minute I met you, Jan, it was like seeing myself over again—the same belligerence, carelessness, concentration on work while all the fun went past. I wish I could help you a little, steer you into paths that are pleasanter than mine were."

"You've already helped." Jan tried to smile at her. "I've thought about you a lot and you've really given me a new slant on life."

"Why, thank you, dear. That makes me feel most encouraged. I hope I can go on slanting things for you. Now take Pete's advice about wearing your best clothes, and fix your hair in the coronet braids very, very elegantly, and I just know that everything will come out all right for you at the meeting. And don't think of yourself as homely because you aren't. Your features are nice and regular and as you grow more self-confident you're going to be very attractive.

"Jan, there's one more thing," Mrs. Abbott said as they walked towards the door. "I want you to think about Miss Layton's position for a minute. No, now don't be upset—just try to get a picture of her.

"Think of her living in this small town all these years, must be fifteen or more, teaching English. She doesn't have any talent for making friends, so her life is incredibly dull.

Her students are only as polite as the law demands, they aren't really friendly. Is it any wonder that when Danny comes along friendly as a puppy and very talented that she should lose her sense of judgment and want him to be editor?"

"But it isn't right," Jan insisted stubbornly. Why did Mrs. Abbott and Pete have to keep stinging her with insinuations that she should have been nicer to Miss Layton?

"No, it isn't right and I'm quite sure she won't get away with it. I just want you to realize that she wouldn't be so mean if she weren't pretty thoroughly unhappy. She's not all bad. I know because she helped me once when I was down— and I mean way down. . . . Run along now, you have lots to do today. I'll be thinking about you."

Soothed and strengthened, Jan walked home. She knew she should think about all Mrs. Abbott had said, especially about seeing Miss Layton in a different light, but right now she had to consider her clothes. She just didn't have anything you could call a best outfit. Last spring's green dress had been through too many washings to be very special now.

That meant she had to buy some new things. She went home, slipped quietly into her room, took her bank book out of the desk, and looked through the fashion magazine Mrs. Abbott had given her. The girl with the coronet braids was wearing a pleated jersey skirt and blouse. "Separates," the magazine called them, and they seemed very popular now, though in her cynical opinion "separates" was just an expensive name for a skirt and blouse.

Well, she would go down to the Avenue Shoppe and look them over. It was good-by typewriter, of course, but what good was a typewriter without an editor behind it?

A little later, standing before the triple mirrors in heather-gray jersey separates, Jan couldn't help being pleased. The style was so new, the material so soft and comfortable.

"They're beautiful and I like them," she said, "but I don't look quite right. I'm too short or something."

"It's your shoes," the salesgirl decided. "If you had higher heels you'd look tall enough. Let me try some."

She returned with matching gray suede pumps and the minute Jan put them on she knew this was it. Tall, poised, and neat she faced herself in the mirror and a strange new feeling of delight quivered all through her. Oh, it was fun to be well dressed! It was wonderfully satisfying. But alas, much as she would like an outfit like this for Sundays and special occasions—"I couldn't wear pumps to school," she said mournfully.

"How about wedgies?" the girl suggested. "They can be as tailored as oxfords and still give you the height you need."

In the end Jan took both pairs of shoes, the separates in gray, an extra jersey top in yellow, a plaid skirt, two white blouses, and a gay silk scarf. She was loaded down like a pack mule and her bank account was flatter than the top of Table Mountain, but she felt fine.

She wore her new outfit, shoes and all, out of the shop so she could stop by and show Pete. "You did better than I expected," he said bluntly. "Sometimes I think you'll come in out of the rain after all."

As she crossed the bridge she met Andrew on his way down town. He clutched the railing and pretended to faint. "Wow, you look nice," he yelped. "Practically human," he added as she smiled in gratitude. Jan walked on with great confidence. Andrew never bothered to go through the motions of being polite. He must have meant it.

Stepping lightly in spite of all her bundles, getting accustomed to the new way of walking in heels, Jan made her way home. As she entered the house she dropped the packages on the davenport and called her mother. "Come and see my new clothes," she invited.

Mrs. Morgan rushed in from the kitchen, a look of dismay

on her face. "Janice, you didn't go buy clothes without telling me a thing about it! I hope . . ." Then she stopped and stared. Amazement and pleasure were in her look. "Why, Janice, you look so nice—so smart and attractive." She came closer, fingered the material and inspected the labels.

"How did I do?" Jan lifted her arms and whirled around to show her outfit to its best advantage.

"Very well indeed. But you can't blame me for being surprised and upset. You've shown so little interest in clothes the last few years, and seemed to have no idea of what was becoming to you. How were you able to choose so wisely?"

"I studied," Jan replied, and even to herself she had to admit that she sounded smug and supercilious, but then Mother shouldn't intimate that she was too dumb to know red from blue. "Mrs. Abbott gave me a fashion magazine and I read it carefully and picked out the type of clothes I should wear. You can learn anything if you're willing to study."

All her mother's pleased surprise vanished. "Isn't that just dandy! You'd run around in a barrel and get a crew cut if Elsie Abbott or Pete suggested it. I've been trying to persuade you to dress well and do your hair attractively for a long time and you haven't paid any attention to me at all. I put your hair up in coronet braids once and you pulled them out and said they made your head ache, but I guess you've forgotten all about that."

Jan looked at her mother, taken aback. She couldn't remember anything like that at all.

"As for your clothes, I've read more fashion magazines than you've ever seen. Sometimes I think the happiest part of my life was when I went to Seattle and studied fashion designing. I might have had a career, but instead I married a lumberjack and got stuck in a little town in the hills where I don't get to see a new dress from one year to the next."

"I'm sorry," Jan said hesitantly. She did feel suddenly humble and ashamed. Her mother didn't ever get any new clothes for herself when you stopped to think about it, and maybe the way she had been nagging Jan to buy pretty things meant that she would have enjoyed even buying them for somebody else.

"I would have asked you to go along if I had thought about it," Jan explained. "The thing is I've become accustomed to doing everything by myself . . . and I was in a hurry. . . ."

This half-hearted apology didn't placate her mother. "Of course you didn't think—you never do; not of your brother, or your parents, or anyone but your own selfish self. You're absolutely self-centered and jealous of everyone who isn't just like you. You think a mother is just a convenience to cook meals and keep house."

This was unjust. There was nothing she wanted more than to share her world with her family, and they were the ones who had cast her out. But she hung her head silently.

"You think you have so much talent because you write for the paper," her mother continued bitterly. "Try designing a dress sometime. That takes brains, too. As for those fancy separates of yours, I could have bought the material and made them for you for nearly half the cost. I used to make you beautiful clothes until you decided it would give you more prestige to buy things out of the mail-order catalogs than to have them home-made."

Mrs. Morgan finished her speech abruptly, sniffled a little, then hurried upstairs and slammed her bedroom door. Jan leaned against the wall, her knees weak. Who would ever have thought buying new clothes would set off a chain reaction like that?

Somewhere in the back of her mind she realized that her mother's unhappiness went a lot deeper than not being asked on a shopping expedition. Her mother had grave troubles to face and it was too bad, but Jan didn't have time to worry about them now. She had her own battle ahead and her mother's outburst certainly hadn't made her feel any more confident and courageous. She took her packages upstairs and put them away.

It was six o'clock when she finished and her mother hadn't come downstairs again. That probably meant she didn't intend to, since her father was on fire patrol and wouldn't be home for the week-end and Andrew had gone to the early movie. "I'll have to get a sandwich downtown," Jan decided.

Suddenly she felt too tired to go to the meeting and face the unpleasantness that was waiting for her. She didn't want to fight for her rights. She didn't want to do anything but flop down on her bed and stay there the rest of her life. Let Danny steal her job. Let Miss Layton despise her. Let her mother scold her for her shortcomings and never see that she needed help and sympathy, too. Did it really matter so much to be editor?

Before this mood could engulf her she conjured up a vision of the *Argus* with its headlines standing out in black-and-white symmetry while on page three was the masthead with its thrilling inscription: Editor-in-Chief, Jan Marie Morgan. Beyond the miracle of the printed word was Pete with his linotype and press. Pete, who counted on her to fight and win. Resolutely Jan started for the meeting.

CHAPTER 7

Vote of Confidence

ALTHOUGH JAN ARRIVED at the Larsens' promptly, as a good reporter should, she found that Miss Layton with conspiratorial skill had been early.

"All the faculty members are inside having a confab," Dotty explained as she made room for Jan on the glider set out in the patio behind the house.

A very pretty and relaxing place it was, too, this patio, for a person in the proper frame of mind. Jan recalled hearing Pete say that Mr. Larsen had laid the flagstones and built the barbecue himself. But thinking in that direction made her remember Danny's talking about the patio he and his father planned to build. She sighed and wondered why, out of all the stops between here and Chicago, the railroad had to transfer the Mallorys to Cascadeville.

"Well, what are they doing at their confab?" she asked Dotty, just as if she didn't know.

"That's a good question." Dotty shrugged elaborately. "Miss Layton flew in like a jet-propelled rocket, yanked all the faculty members off these comfortable chairs, and dragged them off to this top-secret conference, students and peasants not invited. Mmmmmm, that's a sharp outfit you're wearing —but luscious."

"Thanks," Jan replied absently.

"I must admit it irks me," Dotty continued. "The confab, not your clothes," she said in reply to Jan's quick look. "What's the point of having a student government if they go

74

racing off by themselves and don't leave us anything to govern?"

Ben Barton, the student body president, who puzzled everyone by having bright red hair and the mildest temper in the world, left the croquet game at the other end of the yard and came over to them. "Finish your speech, Dotty," he joked. "Jan can use it for her first editorial."

"In spite of the fact that you're being humorous, that isn't a bad idea," Dotty said. "How about it, Jan? In big, big type."

"Dotty, you're a scream," Ben interrupted before Jan could reply. "Sometime you'll realize that when our faculty has a secret discussion it's nothing more or less than an attempt to see if they can't get their lunchtime cup of coffee reduced from seven cents to five."

"You beautiful dreamer, you," was Dotty's opinion.

Jan agreed completely, but fortunately she didn't have to say anything, for just then the back door opened and Mr. Larsen called, "Come on in, gang, let's get organized."

"Carl Graves isn't here yet," Ben called back.

Mr. Larsen sighed. "Somebody had better phone him, he's undoubtedly forgotten. But since we don't have any money in the treasury anyhow, we might as well start without him."

"Look at his face," Dotty whispered, clutching at Jan's arm. "Wow oh wow, is he mad about something!"

Jan swallowed hard, and her knees nearly buckled under her as she went into the living room. Miss Layton was sitting on the davenport, painfully erect, two spots of color burning in her cheeks. The other faculty members looked uneasy.

"Sit here at the desk, Dotty," Mr. Larsen directed. "Janice, you take the chair by the lamp. You may want to take notes, too. The rest of you just sit anywhere and we'll get started."

The look Miss Layton gave her could have barbecued a steer, but Jan sat down and took out her notebook and pencil with all the poise she could muster. She smoothed her skirt and the reassurance of her new clothes was soothing.

Ben called the meeting to order and directed Dotty to read the minutes of the last meeting, which since they were three months old seemed like a page of ancient history to the new council members. They voted to dispense with the report of the absent treasurer.

"What next, Mr. Larsen?" Ben asked, and Jan felt such an air of tension she almost expected to hear the room crackle.

"Ordinarily we have committee reports now," Mr. Larsen said. "But before we do that I think we ought to take up a matter of credentials. Since we don't have any passwords or secret badges, 'most anyone could drift into a council meeting and not be thrown out."

The burly, football-playing sergeant at arms, who had been surreptitiously reading the funnies back in a quiet corner, laid down the paper and began to listen. After all, throwing people out was supposed to be his department.

"We have an interloper tonight," Mr. Larsen continued. Maybe his gently facetious manner was entertaining the rest of the students, but Jan heartily wished he would get to the point—one way or another, get to the point.

He did. "We can't imagine a meeting without our editor sitting here turning every word into potential headlines, and yet the editor is not an official member of the council. I think our first business this evening should take care of this omission."

The students all traded surprised glances. "Imagine that," someone muttered.

"Do I hear a motion?" Ben asked.

"Now, Ben, there really isn't any great rush about this," Miss Layton interrupted. "There wasn't even any need for the editor to be present tonight, since the first *Argus* won't be published for several weeks. So if you want to think it over awhile, I'm sure that will be fine with everyone."

Ben frowned at the Robert's Rules of Order he had been diligently reading. Miss Layton's speech was clearly out of order—and she an English teacher—but Jan couldn't blame him for not feeling inclined to mention it.

"Mr. President, I move the editor be made an official, voting member of the council," Dotty said firmly.

"I second the motion." That was Miss Johnson, the librarian and language teacher.

The motion passed without further discussion. Ben bowed and said, "Janice, I hope you're happy to be official instead of semi-official."

Everyone chuckled and Jan smiled, although she didn't feel let off the hook yet. Not by any means.

Mr. Larsen sighed deeply, and the angry, frustrated look Dotty had noticed on his face returned. "I don't think we're quite through with our discussion about the editorship," he said. "Something unusual, in fact, unprecedented has arisen and Ben, if you don't mind my interrupting your order of business, I think we had better deal with it now."

"Sure, Mr. Larsen," Ben agreed. "Anything you say."

"Very well. I'd like to tell Janice how much we have enjoyed the articles she has written for the Cascadeville *Courier* this summer. They've been a credit to her and to the community. I wonder, Janice, if you would like to tell us about your plans for the first issue of the *Argus*."

Jan tried to swallow her nervousness. She could feel the surprise and bewilderment among the students; customarily the editor was just a piece of furniture at council meetings, not the main topic of conversation. She spoke up bravely. "The only new feature I've planned for the first issue is a hit-and-miss interview with members of the freshman class. I want them to tell us about themselves and what they expect to contribute to our high school. I plan to run this interview in place of that old welcome-to-our-ivy-covered-halls editorial."

"The editorial is one of our traditions," Miss Layton said sternly.

"Yes, but I'm sure that when you think it over you will agree that the interview will start a new and interesting tradition," Mr. Larsen said, valiantly walking a tightrope before his feuding council. "I'm glad Janice belongs to the new school of journalism that puts people before literary genius. Anything else?"

Jan smiled gratefully at him and sent an inward thank you to Pete for his constant hammering about how people like to see their names in the paper.

"The only other news I have to report is that Pete is willing to run a weekly high school column in the *Courier*, which means we will have more complete coverage of school news."

There was a nodding of heads and a murmur of approval. Then Mr. Larsen spoke again. "It seems to me that although Janice is younger than the rest of the seniors—she won't be sixteen till November—she has remarkable ability and we're lucky to have her for our editor. However, there is another point of view which maintains that Janice is too young and untried and should be replaced by Danny Mallory, who also has great journalistic talents, was appointed editor of his high school's weekly paper in Seattle, and will be a senior at Mountain View this year. What do the rest of you think about that?"

The silence surely lasted a year. Jan felt they all had been sitting frozen into their chairs for an eternity before Dotty said in a stage whisper, "I knew they were up to something crooked."

Ben chuckled then and said, "If the chairman can be out of order long enough to make a remark, I would like to say that Danny is a sharp character and I hope we'll find some way to use his many talents, but Janice is our duly chosen editor and well able to do her job and that is that. In my opinion," he added hastily.

"I second the opinion." Carl Graves, the solemn, bespectacled, absent-minded treasurer had arrived at the meeting and promptly made his presence known.

By this time Dotty's wrath had risen to dramatic heights. "I never heard of anything so diabolical in my life," she said. "To imagine that you had even considered such a scheme for a minute! Just suppose some boy transferred up here from Seattle and said he had been student body president. I suppose Ben should step aside and let him be president just because he came from a bigger school. Why, just imagine . . . !"

"Put it to music and you'll win the Academy Award," Ben teased gently.

Miss Layton was poised on the edge of her seat ready to join the battle, so Mr. Larsen spoke up quickly. "Does anyone else want to express an opinion? No? Well, we had to have this out, but I'm very sorry that we were forced to put Janice through such a bad time. I now move that we give her a vote of confidence."

The loud chorus of "ayes" that followed Mr. Larsen's suggestions seemed to come from a long distance. Clutching her pencil tightly, Jan looked at her fellow council members through misty eyes. "Thank you," she said, annoyed that her voice was only a whisper. Painfully she cleared her throat. "I will do my best for the *Argus*," she promised.

"We know you will." Surprisingly enough, it was Miss Travers the physical education teacher who spoke up, the one Jan thought didn't like her. "Even we muscle-bound athletic morons know you're a good writer."

Jan had the grace to blush while the others laughed, but the laughter was so friendly that she decided the time had come to speak up definitely for her name. "Since you are all being so nice, could I make a request?" she asked.

"As I always tell you in class, you can *ask*," Mr. Larsen replied.

"Well, I've never liked the name Janice. It doesn't seem to be me. On our masthead I would like to use the name Pete gave me—Jan Marie Morgan."

"Sounds fine to me." Mr. Larsen was agreeable. "Ladies should always be permitted to pick their own names and their own hats."

"Oh it's really classical," was Dotty's opinion.

"If you're through discussing names we might come to a definite decision about what to do with Danny," Miss Layton said, tight-lipped with anger. It was obvious that she was having a hard time keeping her opinions within the framework of the united front the faculty always presented. Seeing the look on her face, Jan thought of Mrs. Abbott's words—that Danny was the first student in a long time who had been nice to Miss Layton.

Maybe if only one person in the world was nice to her she would try to upset a few applecarts, too, but since it was Jan's particular applecart they were after, she just couldn't be too philosophical about it.

"I have a suggestion which I hope will satisfy everyone," Mr. Larsen said. "Our paper has an editor-in-chief, a feature editor, and a sports editor. Therefore I suggest we create the position of associate editor and offer that to Danny. It will take some of the routine burden from Janice—excuse me, Jan Marie—and give us the benefit of Danny's experience. It will also keep Danny from being too homesick for Seattle, since for reasons that baffle us normal folks, journalism students go into a decline if they aren't within three feet of a typewriter and some blank paper."

His mild joke broke the tension in the room. The other members of the Mountain View school council were now at ease with one another and ready to go to work on the rest of the agenda. Jan, however, was struggling with two very different emotions. The first was gratitude that her fellow officers were so loyal to her. Why, they hadn't even stopped to consider that Danny might well be a better editor. She would do her utmost to show them how grateful she was. On the other hand, she felt jealous at the thought of having Danny on her staff, in the very position next to hers, right beside her on every job and in every decision. It seemed like eons ago, that day in Pete's office when she had said she would be glad to have him on the *Argus* staff. He had looked like a nice ordinary, homesick boy then, before she knew he was scheming and treacherous.

She sighed deeply. She wasn't hearing a thing the others were discussing and she would have to go over Dotty's notes to find out what happened. . . . It wouldn't do any good to refuse to have Danny as associate editor. The students would think she was a poor sport, and truth to tell she was. She didn't want Danny any closer to her paper than the Great Wall of China.

Undoubtedly Danny and Miss Layton would try to cause her so much trouble that she would be glad to quit and turn the paper over to them. But they had a surprise in store. There was an advantage in being pushed around at home, she decided. It gave her experience and fortitude in enduring injustice.

After the meeting Jan, Ben, Dotty, and Carl walked downtown together and stopped at the drugstore for milkshakes. Carl came out of his private cloud long enough to say, "I know an English teacher in California who might like to come and sample our mountain air. If she does we'll have to give her Miss Layton's job."

They all giggled. Ben said thoughtfully, "We all have our troubles and it looks like Miss Layton has appointed herself yours."

"I'll make her wish she had stuck to teaching English," Jan said firmly and they all nodded approvingly. Warm inside her was the thought, Why it's more than just fair play! They are my friends.

Jan and Dotty walked most of the way home together. Dotty waved good-by at the corner and Jan came rapidly up her walk. She was more than anxious to get home and out of her new clothes. Wearing high-heeled shoes for the first time was thrilling, sure enough, but it was tiring, too. She could hardly wait to get back into her canvas sandals. As she reached the porch a voice called out, "Wait a minute."

She whirled around and exclaimed in surprise as Danny crawled out from behind the hydrangea. "Sit down a minute, please, Jan. I want to talk to you."

"We haven't anything to talk about," Jan replied coldly and started up the steps.

"Whoa, there." He scrambled up, grabbed her sleeve, and pulled her back. "I was afraid you would be this way," he said with a sigh. "If you were a boy you'd understand that I wouldn't double-cross a good friend. But you're a girl and girls get upset and don't think straight. I've been following you around all evening trying to tell you that Miss Layton went off her rocker and cooked this up but I wasn't buying it."

"You followed me around?" Jan asked, surprised. She hesitated a moment, then sat down in the porch swing. If Danny wanted to have things out she might as well speak her mind to him here and now.

He perched on the porch rail facing her. "Miss Layton didn't say a thing to me about this," he repeated, and his voice was hoarse and serious. "I didn't know from beans about her brain wave till Pete hauled me in off the street this afternoon and told me I was sitting on a time bomb. I rushed right over here but you weren't home, so then I went over to the Larsens' and waited around outside there. Then you came out with that mob and started downtown so I came back here to wait. Took you long enough to get home, too."

"I didn't ask you to wait," Jan replied huffily. "And I guess you weren't eavesdropping hard enough over at the Larsens' or you wouldn't bother to come around with your phony alibis."

"I wasn't eavesdropping at all," Danny said, beginning to get angry himself. "I only wanted to tell you the truth."

"Oh, fiddle-faddle," Jan snorted. "You have them all feeling so sorry for poor little Danny without a paper to call his own that they've created a new job just for you. You're going to be my associate editor."

"Really?" In the moonglow of the summer night she could see his face light up. "No kidding?" His voice was exultant. "Say, that's really swell of you. Believe me, we'll make that paper hum."

Jan hardened to the joy in his voice. "If you were really a friend you'd turn it down."

He looked at her in amazement. "I don't see why. I'm not taking anything away from you. You're the editor, the big boss. I'll be helping you and I'm good at that. I've worked on school newspapers for years and I know all the ropes, inside out and backwards. We could do wonders together."

"I don't want you on my paper," Jan said bluntly. "You and Miss Layton together—why I couldn't trust you any further than I could throw Pete's linotype."

Once her harsh words were voiced she was ashamed of herself. The council members had been generous and warmhearted to her in her time of trial, and instead of passing these qualities on she was being grudging and nasty to Danny. She wished she could be friendly again and share the experiences of publishing with him, but she was afraid of him now. He was too talented, too friendly, and he was a threat to her and the one thing she wanted most in the world. She couldn't really trust him, couldn't believe that even if he hadn't actively participated in Miss Layton's plot, he hadn't planted the seed of the idea in her lonely, muddled brain. No, it was sad, but she couldn't trust Danny.

He stood up and prepared to leave. "Very well, don't trust me." His voice was cold and unfriendly too. "But you won't be rid of me, either. I'm going to take the job."

She shrugged and opened the door. "I knew you would."

He made one more effort to get her to understand. "I couldn't turn it down. I love newspaper work. It's my whole life—you ought to understand that," he said accusingly. Then he turned and walked rapidly away.

Jan went up the stairs. Her mother called, "Janice?" She groaned softly—she just couldn't endure any more scoldings or explanations. "Who were you talking to outside?"

"Danny," she replied.

"Oh, yes. He came here looking for you soon after you left. But, Janice, you didn't tell me you were going to a meeting. I thought you were to be at Mrs. Abbott's. You mustn't go off without letting me know where you are going to be."

"I'm sorry," Jan said wearily. "It all came up unexpectedly."

"What was Danny doing at a school council meeting?"

Jan sought for an answer that would satisfy her mother. She didn't especially want to tell fibs but she was just too weary for any rebroadcast of the evening. "He's going to help me with the *Argus*," she said and hoped that would be sufficient.

It seemed to satisfy her mother because she dropped the subject. "I'm sorry I lost my temper with you, Janice. I was disappointed not to be able to go along with you to buy your clothes. I guess I had forgotten how girls your age like to be independent. You did a good job. You chose very well. But maybe next time if you would let me know what you wanted I could make it for you."

"Thank you," Jan said, again humbled by being treated kindly when she had expected censure.

"It was a shock when I realized that I didn't know where

you were tonight," her mother continued. "Or that I didn't know why you wanted your new clothes all of a sudden. Did your meeting go well?"

"Yes, very well," Jan replied. "I'm glad I had the new clothes. They made me feel much more self-confident." It was only fair to tell her mother that.

"I hope you will let me share your problems and your fun more, Janice. That's what mothers are for—and we used to have fun together. . . . Well, it's late now. You'd better get to bed. But don't ever go out again without letting me know where you are."

"I won't," Jan promised. Tears, long held back during this hectic day, were welling up in her eyes. Did her mother really want to be friends, to share things?

As she turned to her own room she heard Andrew's door close quietly. She wiped her eyes and sniffed angrily. The little sneak had probably been listening to everything she and Danny said, since his room was right above the porch. He had the nicest bedroom, of course, with big windows looking out on the street. He would be around to taunt her about her quarrel just when it would hurt the most. As for her mother wanting to share things with her, Andrew would see that she was too busy with him to pay any attention to her daughter.

Once she was in bed the triumph of the evening slipped away, and close her eyes and turn her head though she might, she kept seeing the hurt look in Danny's eyes as he said, "It's my whole life—you ought to understand that."

She did, of course. If they had taken her job away tonight she would have been ready to jump off the top of Barren Mountain. But after all it was Danny's bad luck his family moved away from Seattle and the Bayside *Barnacle*. It didn't have anything to do with her and he ought to be able to take it like a man. Clutching this philosophy around her conscience as she pulled the quilts around her shoulders, she finally went to sleep.

CHAPTER 8

Armed Truce

"AN EXCELLENT JOB," Mr. Larsen said as he folded his copy of the September *Argus* and beamed at the editorial staff assembled in his office. "I'm pleased with all of you and I especially liked the freshman feature story."

"Yes, you were right about that feature story, Mr. Larsen," Miss Layton said in a judicious tone. "It was very good reading. I am going to see that the beginning journalism class gets some experience at symposium interviews."

Jan smiled in pleased surprise. It was *her* idea that was being commended and they all knew it, even though Miss Layton gave the credit to the principal.

"Everything went fine," Jan said. "We're all looking forward to next month."

"Fine. Fine," Mr. Larsen continued happily. "You're working together so harmoniously I'm going to call you my ham-and-eggs team."

"I'm a ham for sure," Danny announced, "and Jan's a good egg."

Everyone giggled and Cassie, who was making a fine feature editor since Jan had discovered the trick of assigning her a deadline several days in advance of the real deadline, fluttered her eyelashes at Danny. She greatly admired him. So did nearly everyone else.

Jan clinched her fingers till the pencil she was holding left deep ridges on her hand. She could just imagine the sardonic look on Danny's face and hear the irony in his voice as he labeled her a good egg. Ham-and-eggs team indeed! Scrambled eggs would be more accurate. She still hated the sight of Danny and his outstanding ability didn't make her feel any easier around him.

"Any bright ideas for next month?" Mr. Larsen leaned back in his chair and invited discussion.

Before Jan could focus her eyes on her notes Danny spoke. "Since the *Argus* only comes out once a month, and it's a stinking shame, I think we should have a definite theme for each month and tie in the features and cartoons and all with that theme.

"For instance, we've just finished with the special freshman issue. This month is Halloween, November has Thanksgiving, and so on around the calendar."

"A splendid idea," Miss Layton chimed in immediately, giving Danny a warm, encouraging smile.

Jan closed her mouth abruptly. That was her idea! It was the first item on her list of suggestions, and here was smart-boy Danny stealing it away from her the way he had stolen everything he could possibly wangle. She crossed it off. It would sound more than silly if she said she had thought of it, too.

"You have something there, Danny," Mr. Larsen approved. "What do you think, Jan?"

"We have several special issues now," she replied stiffly. "Our freshman issue in September and the Tulip Festival in April and the seniors in May. We shouldn't have much trouble finding a special theme for the few other months."

There, she had agreed but sounded so work-a-day about it that it should take some of the starch out of Danny-boy.

"Speaking of features, I don't have nearly enough room," Cassie wailed. "Do we have to fill up our precious space with those dull stories about the Latin Club and the Girls' Athletic Association?"

"No, we don't," Jan agreed. "I wonder if we couldn't have

all the club notes under one column. We would waste less space on headlines for one thing. I also thought we might have a little continuity between the individual items."

"I'd like to try that," Danny spoke up quickly. "We had a club column on the *Barnacle* and I think it would do the trick on the *Argus*. I'll get it started and then turn it over to one of the reporters."

If only she could twirl a mustache and hiss, "Curses, foiled again." That was just how she felt. Now Danny was going to supervise *her* club column. Really, he was worse than the smell of onions for infiltrating everything.

Suddenly she pricked up her ears. Miss Layton was laughing. Actually in the flesh laughing. It had a rusty sound, and it should, for Jan didn't recall its ever happening before. "I had that down on my list, too," she explained.

"We seem to be overloaded with active brains today," Mr. Larsen remarked.

"Might as well adjourn," he said finally, when all the ideas had been thoroughly discussed. "Being adviser to the *Argus* is really a cinch this year."

The little group left the principal's office and moved slowly along the halls, so eerily quiet after school hours. Late autumn sunshine slanted through the tall windows and set the dust specks to dancing. Jan stopped at her locker to pick up her jacket and the books she would need for the week-end. On top was the envelope with the high school news notes, to be dropped off at Pete's.

"Want me to take it down for you?" Danny, his jacket over his arm, stood beside her. "I'm stopping by Pete's anyhow and I know you're going to be busy tonight at Mrs. Preston's party. You'll need to save your strength for that."

He was being maddening again. Polite, obliging, every inch the gentleman. Acting as if he had forgotten that she didn't like him and didn't trust him.

"Well, O.K., since you're stopping by anyhow," she replied ungraciously as she handed him the envelope. "Thanks."

"Sure. Any time. What kind of a party is she throwing?"

"A square dance. Seems that's the latest thing. They dance themselves into a frazzle, then eat like horses. I'll be handing out hamburgers and doughnuts with one hand while I write it up for Pete's society notes with the other."

Danny chuckled appreciatively and they walked out of the building together. The Indian summer day was warm and colorful. A day more suited to languid strolling than brisk walking and they, like each other or not, strolled, too. "We ought to start a square dance group at Mountain View," he suggested. "Maybe Mrs. Preston would help us get started."

Jan, who again had been thinking the same thing, stiffened. This was impossible. "Takes too much time and energy," she said shortly. "Everybody has enough activities now."

They reached the corner. Danny turned towards town with a friendly wave, but Jan pretended not to see it. It was Friday night so there would be a big dinner and her dad would be home. He would read the *Argus* and say all the warm, approving things about it that her mother and Andrew neglected to mention—if they read it at all. She hurried home.

The next Wednesday afternoon when the Cascadeville *Courier* arrived, Jan picked it up and plopped comfortably on the davenport to look for her column. She glanced at the paper, then sat up straight with a strangled moan. There was a new column in the middle of the front page. "Passing Through," the box head read, "by Danny Mallory." The words danced in front of her eyes like darting black specks. Shaking it into focus, she began to read.

The Northern Flyer, a famous luxury train, made a twenty-minute stop at Cascadeville every afternoon at four twenty to switch from the electric engine that had hauled it over the mountains to the diesel engine that would take it on to Seattle. Danny had gone aboard the train and obtained short on-the-spot interviews with various celebrities and V.I.P.'s. It was really a terrific trick. It took someone with a pleasing personality to get away with it.

She could just see herself barging in on some travel-weary celebrity, Jan thought as she read through the fast-paced, smoothly written column. She would be thrown out with a clunk. Danny did have personality, she had to admit that. But for Pete to put the column on the front page! Pete, her friend and defender—Pete, who till this minute had been the most wonderful person in the world! So now he was Danny-happy, too, just like Miss Layton and all the rest of them. He probably didn't care if she ever turned in another story for him. "Et tu, Brute," she said poignantly to herself.

Her mother and Andrew came in the back door, she carrying a bag of groceries and he licking an ice-cream cone. "Are you reading the paper?" she asked. "Everybody was looking at it down at the store. Isn't that column Danny wrote exciting? Imagine being able to talk face to face with Senator Perkins and a famous movie star."

"Yellow journalism," Jan said disdainfully. "It's pure and simple sensationalism. I don't consider it good writing at all."

"Well, I do," her mother replied. "I enjoyed it."

"The Cascadeville paper is supposed to print news about Cascadeville people," Jan said heatedly. "Pete always said so himself. If you want to read about Hollywood, go buy a movie magazine."

Andrew swallowed the last bit of the ice-cream cone and smirked at her. "Listen to green eyes. You're just jealous because you didn't think of it first and because everybody wishes Danny was editor instead of you."

"That statement only confirms my previous opinion that you haven't a brain in your head," Jan said bitingly, and turning her back on them walked slowly upstairs and into her room. Safe inside that refuge she huddled on her bed while waves of misery oozed through her. She was wrong about Andrew's brains. He couldn't be dumb when he was so psychic about knowing what would hurt her feelings. Why did everybody like Danny best when she worked so hard? Why did he get all the breaks? There was no justice in this, none at all.

Now that Jan was editor she could assign a reporter the task of taking copy to Pete's office and bringing back galley proofs, so she didn't see so much of the old printer as she had during the summer. After the "Passing Through" column became the biggest thing in town she didn't want to see him, either. But finally it was time for her to read page proofs for the October issue. She could tell Danny to do it, of course, but he was getting so he thought he was the whole universe anyhow.

"No, thanks," she said shortly. "I don't need any help. It only takes a few minutes." She went down to the shop alone.

"Welcome back to the old plantation, Mistress Morgan," Pete said, beaming at her as she came in. Jan hated to admit to herself how good it felt to sit down in the old swivel chair and inhale the familiar odors of ink and lead.

"I've missed you, kid," he said as he put the rough pages in front of her. "It's been too peaceful around here."

"Oh, rats," she replied coldly. "You have Danny-boy. How could you ask for anything more?"

Pete came over and sat on the edge of the desk. "Looks like some specks of green got in your eyes. Cut it out, sis."

"Cut what out?" she asked, trying to sound aloof and dis- interested.

"Being jealous of Danny. It's a great big world. There's

plenty of newsprint for both of you to fill. Besides, you'd be a great team if you ever got together."

"I'm not jealous," Jan insisted. "I just don't trust him. He's even hoodwinked you with his rah-rah personality."

"You're the one who's hoodwinked," Pete said, shaking his head. "I thought you were all set to blossom out this year, but instead you've got some specks of green in your eyes, sis, and that old green-eyed monster is chasing you around and freezing you up till you know what?"

"No. What?" Jan asked, curious in spite of her resentment.

"You're getting to look more like that old sourpuss Miss Layton every day."

Jan gasped and put her hands up to her face. She stared at him, then jumped up and ran to the mirror at the back of the shop and peered at herself intently. After a long scrutiny she dropped down on a pile of old newspapers and started to sniffle.

Up at the desk Pete picked up a pencil and finished the proofs. "I'd sure hate to take any bets on whether or not I'm the meanest man in town," he muttered.

Evidently he hadn't intended to be overheard, but he was. Jan came back to stand at the desk and stare at him somberly. It hadn't meant much when Andrew called her "green eyes," but when Pete did, too, it would bear serious consideration.

"No, you aren't mean," she told him. "And if you say I should be nicer, then I will try to be nicer. But it won't come naturally. It will be entirely artificial."

"Most of the world is artificial," Pete said calmly.

Her self-conscious campaign began the next morning, and every morning thereafter she deliberately smiled and said "Good morning" to Miss Layton. By the end of the week the conversation had enlarged to a brief comment on the weather. It wasn't so hard to be nice to Miss Layton, either. No harder than shoveling all the snow off Barren Mountain with a teaspoon.

Jan's first chance to put Pete's advice into effect with Danny came on the Friday afternoon when they found themselves standing side by side with a group of students waiting to be initiated into the Mountaineers.

It really took some doing to be gracious to him, too, when she considered that here she was a senior and editor of the *Argus* before the service club gave her a bid, while Danny had been voted in promptly even though he had only attended Mountain View a few weeks. They were the only seniors. The rest of the students waiting nervously were sophomores and juniors.

"This ought to be a lot of fun," Danny commented. "The Mountaineers have some terrific plans for the year."

Jan nodded. Almost everything was fun to Danny. "I suppose you want to toss a coin to see which one of us is going to write it up," she said.

Danny laughed. "Pal, quit working so hard. Think of those lazy reporters. Make them do it."

"At least we can give them the inside dope. Provided we ever get inside, that is."

Just then the auditorium door swung open and Ben and Dotty appeared, each looking very solemn and gingerly carrying lighted candles. They motioned for the neophytes to enter.

They walked slowly into the darkened room and took their places before a candle-lit table. Some one was singing, "The World is Waiting for the Sunrise." In the midst of all the solemnity Jan was surprised to find Danny clutching her arm. He was jittery with excitement. "Wait for me afterwards," he whispered. "I've just had an idea."

Jan's curiosity had to go unsatisfied a long time. First the initiation, then the refreshments, then Dotty walking along home with them happily chattering about all the fun they would have together as Mountaineers.

Finally they waved her off at the corner and turned towards Jan's house. "You'd better come in," Jan suggested. "It's too cold to do much talking on the porch."

"We would warm it up if we started fighting," he said with an impish grin, but he accepted her half-hearted invitation. Once the front door was shut Jan regretted asking him, because the whole family took over. Andrew poked his head out of the television, goggled, and said, "Hi, Danny, did you come to see TV?"

"Not this time, squirt," Danny replied, giving him a poke. "I just want to talk to your sis."

"You do?" Andrew was incredulous. "Why?"

"Military secret," was the reply.

Just then Mrs. Morgan came in from the kitchen with her usual Friday night jitters. "Janice, I swear I don't see why all those clubs have to meet on Friday when I need your help. Here's your father home for twenty minutes and I'm still not finished, so you make the coleslaw just as fast as you can— Oh, my!" She saw Danny and stopped in her tracks.

Even nonchalant Danny was getting confused. "Golly, looks like I barged in at the wrong time," he apologized. "Maybe I had better fade out for now."

"We wanted to talk about something," Jan explained rather lamely. She didn't especially want Danny around, but she was mortally curious about his big idea.

The matter was settled by Mr. Morgan coming in from the kitchen happily sampling a French-fried potato. "Stay for dinner and talk afterwards," he suggested. "There's fish and chips and plenty of them."

"Why, yes," Mrs. Morgan seconded the invitation. "We would be glad to have you."

"Thanks a lot," Danny agreed without hesitation. "I'll just phone home."

Finally after dinner when Danny insisted on helping Jan with the dishes, much to Andrew's scorn, he brought up his idea. "The Mountaineers' initiation started me reminiscing about how I miss the National High School Press Club and wondering why we couldn't form a chapter at Mountain View."

Jan clapped her soapy hands together in joy and excitement. How many times she had secretly admired Danny's gold pin in the shape of an open newspaper and how wistfully she'd looked at the Press Club emblem displayed in the mastheads of many of the exchange papers. "Could we?" she asked eagerly.

"Don't see why not. We can ask Mr. Larsen what he thinks and I'll write down to Bayside and ask them how to get organized."

"Write the letter tonight," Jan ordered.

Danny laughed. "Better wait till we talk to Mr. Larsen."

Mr. Larsen thought it was a wonderful idea and wrote to the national organization immediately. Then he discussed the matter of eligibility with Jan and Danny. " 'Prospective members must be in the upper third of their class'—well, that's simple because they have to have a B-plus average in English before they can take journalism."

He muttered to himself as he wrote down names on a scratch pad. "Four on the editorial staff minus one who already belongs, eight reporters who've turned in at least ten inches for each issue of the paper. That's eleven. How about the advertising manager? Do you consider her eligible?"

"That's Della Kludt," Jan said appraisingly. "I haven't been very happy with her performance. Danny has brought in much more advertising than she has."

"That's another example of my butting in where I shouldn't," Danny said soberly. "I'm an awfully bossy character and somebody should put me in my place every now and then. I hang around town a lot more than Della and I just happened to mention advertising to some of the storekeepers. I didn't really give Della a chance to get them herself. I know she would have done it in time. And she did get a nice spread from the Avenue Shoppe, which is one place where my influence doesn't penetrate."

Jan scrutinized Danny carefully. That took real character, to blame himself when he could have sopped up praise. "Della has been very helpful with the typing," Jan said. "And she keeps the records straight. I think she ought to be a member."

"I think so too," Mr. Larsen agreed. "Now we have a dozen. Each prospect has to submit some of his work to national headquarters and once that's done we'll be on our way."

While they were waiting to hear from the national organization, Danny received a letter from Bayside that sent him scurrying to Jan. "They say they are going to be welcoming some new members soon and why don't we go down there and have a joint initiation."

"Oh, wouldn't that be wonderful!" Jan cried. "I haven't been to the city for a long time—not since we were there with Andrew, and then all we saw was the hospital district on First Hill. I'd love to really see Seattle, and go through a big school like Bayside."

"It's worth seeing," Danny assured her. "Our journalism classroom is fixed up like the city desk of a big newspaper with a copy-desk and everything. We have our own printing press in the tech school, but heck, I won't say any more. I'll wait and let you see it."

Armed with the letter, they went bursting into Mr. Larsen's office. He was delighted with the idea, too. "We'll take one of the school buses and have a look around town—see the art museum and the university," he decided rapidly.

"Before we come home we could have dinner at one of the waterfront restaurants," suggested Cassie who had read the letter over Danny's shoulder and followed them in to add her weight to the argument.

"Now wait a minute." Mr. Larsen began to worry. "You

kids are getting out of hand. You'll be taking me on a tour of the night clubs and the skidroad if I don't crack down."

However, no matter how much Mr. Larsen tried to crack down, the trip to Seattle became the biggest news in town and students who'd never put pencil to paper any time they could avoid it began to scheme and try to get themselves into the Press Club somehow or other.

About a week before November 15—D Day—Jan came to her mother, a frown puckering at her face. "I've been upstairs trying on all my clothes," she said. "And I can't decide just what to wear for our trip. My things are all very nice, and they don't look worn and I know I'm being real silly, but I do wish I could have a new dress."

Her mother's face shone with sympathy and amusement. "Of course you should have a new dress," she said warmly. "Since when does a girl have to have a logical reason for wanting a new outfit?"

Behind her happy words Jan could sense the unspoken joy, the hope that at last her strange, bookish daughter would be a girl like other girls—a giggling, confiding companion.

"Then could we go down to the Avenue Shoppe and see what's new and scrumptious?" Jan asked, with hopes high.

Abruptly Mrs. Morgan sat down, her worry wrinkles deepening. "The catch is, what will we use for money? Your father doesn't get paid again before the fifteenth and his last check was utterly used up between the house payment and Andrew's six months' check-up. He had to have a blood test and an X-ray both this time. Not to mention those vitamin pills. Now we'll have to save out something for the trip itself, that dinner you are going to have and all, and that certainly doesn't leave enough for a shopping spree. Maybe you can have a new dress for the holidays. There will probably be some parties then."

"I don't care a thing about any parties in the holidays,"

Jan said bitterly. "If I can't have it now there's no point in having it at all."

Weren't things always that way? Whenever, whatever she wanted Andrew was there ahead of her to snatch it away. Why should he have such a thorough checkup so often anyhow? The doctor hadn't found a thing the matter with him. Obviously he hadn't examined his head.

"I have some money saved," she said with a sigh. "But it isn't enough for a good dress."

Her mother brightened. "I know a way out of this," she said. "Don't you remember that I offered to make something for you. Well, the time has come. The Emporium is having a remnant sale and what do you bet we can find just what you want? Now don't look so disappointed, Janice. You've never realized that I'm really a good seamstress. You won't look home-made. Get your coat—let's go."

Jan was ashamed that her doubts had been read so easily and decided that since her mother was eager to undertake what would undoubtedly be a lot of work, the least she could do was to be agreeable.

Feeling comradely and conspiratorial they went first to the Avenue Shoppe, looked over the racks of smart new dresses, and decided on the general style they wanted. Jan couldn't help feeling a pang. How could anything home-made be as nice as these?

But her mother, undaunted, led the way to the Emporium, marched up to the pattern counter, and soon found a design with the same bat-wing sleeves and full skirt that Jan had admired. Then they moved to the remnant table and discovered just the right length of frosty dark green. "It's a good thing you're so small," her mother commented. "The yardage wouldn't be enough for most people. That's why it's such a bargain."

They were having their parcels wrapped when a voice said, "Now this looks like an interesting project," and there smiling down at them were Mrs. Abbott and Mrs. Preston, their arms full of bundles and their faces lit with the satisfied smiles that go with successful shopping expeditions.

"What did you pick?" Mrs. Abbott asked, and when Jan brought out her pattern and material she nodded approvingly. "Very nice. Bat-wing sleeves will be good on you. Make you more broad-shouldered. But you need some contrast on that dress," she continued, "and I know just the thing. I have a silver coin belt that I bought when I went to South America with the Colonel. I grew right out of it and can't wear it any more. I'd love for you to have it if you would."

"Oh, Mrs. Abbott, that would be wonderful," Jan said gratefully.

"How very nice of you," her mother agreed.

"Elsie, that beautiful belt. I'd been wishing, I . . ." Mrs. Preston caught herself abruptly and stopped talking.

So Mrs. Preston wanted the belt, Jan thought in surprise. But why? She had enough money to buy lots of belts. Anyhow, Mrs. Abbott ignored her. "Come and get it when you finish the dress," she told Jan. "I want to see it on you."

The evening of November 14 Jan wore her new dress over to the Abbotts' and Mrs. Abbott brought out the wide silver belt made of several jingling layers of coins. It was amazing and beautiful, a real conversation piece.

"The gauchos wear them," she explained as Jan touched it cautiously. "The Argentine cowboys. They're a very picturesque sight. Someday when you have time you must see our pictures of South America. Now put on the belt. I think it's going to be just what you need."

It was indeed the right touch. Staring in Mrs. Abbott's mirror, Jan realized that the skilfully made dress and wide, elaborate belt helped give her the added stature and poise she needed. Mountain View would not have to apologize for its editor tomorrow.

"What are you going to do with your braids?" Mrs. Abbott asked.

"I thought I'd loop them up in back and tie them with green ribbons," Jan said hesitantly. "I have some ribbon to match my dress."

"Let's try it," Mrs. Abbott suggested. When the braids were in place she nodded approvingly. "That will do it," she agreed. "I know you're going to have a marvelous time."

Jan thanked Mrs. Abbott for her generous gift and her praise, then went home to show her mother. "It's beautiful," Mrs. Morgan said in awe as she fingered the belt. "It's gorgeous. I don't like to think of what it must have cost. She must be very fond of you to give it away so casually."

"She admired the dress, too, Mother. Said you do beautiful work."

"It's not a bad job," her mother admitted complacently. "And more important, it's becoming to you. Why don't you ask Danny over again some evening?" she suggested, obviously connecting this new interest in clothes with prospects of a gay social life.

Jan was annoyed. "Mother, I've told you and told you that Danny just wanted to talk to me about forming a Press Club chapter that evening he was here. It was you and Dad who kept throwing invitations at him. He's nothing but a business acquaintance and I don't want to talk about him."

Jan turned and fled upstairs in spite of her resolution to spend a pleasant evening with her mother. And she'd forgotten all about Mrs. Abbott's message. Mrs. Abbott wanted to know why her mother didn't come to the Sewing Circle meetings again now that Andrew was better. Well, she would ask her another time. She hung the silver belt on the hook above her mirror.

Jan was too restless and excited to enjoy her usual sound

sleep. She woke, fearful of oversleeping, but it was only five, according to her luminous clock. In the last darkness of the night she could see the belt shining; it seemed to symbolize the glamour and mystery she would find someday in the world beyond the encircling mountains.

CHAPTER 9

Busy Day in Seattle

" 'THERE'S A LONG, long trail a-winding, into the land of our dreams,' " the voices sang in happy disharmony as the big yellow school bus rolled down the main highway towards Seattle.

"We're really winding, no doubt about that," Mr. Larsen remarked to Miss Layton as they twisted down the mountain.

Having Miss Layton along jarred the perfection of the day for Jan, but she tried to be resigned to it. Miss Layton taught the beginning journalism class, even though Mr. Larsen acted as adviser to the *Argus* staff, and Mr. Larsen had decided she would have to be Press Club adviser because he wouldn't have time.

Jan was grimly and faithfully carrying out her program of being nice to Miss Layton. But as she had warned Pete, it still didn't come naturally. It was lots easier, and more fun, too, to be nice to Danny. At least today Miss Layton looked almost cheerful. After all she was getting an afternoon off.

"Look back at the mountains," Danny suggested as he came up by Jan. "I've been watching the snow line. It keeps inching down a little more every day. I suppose I'll wake up some bright morning and find myself under a ten-foot drift."

The rest of the busload hooted at him. "Six feet deep in the streets by Thanksgiving," Don Spencer, the *Argus* sports editor, said with a straight face. "I hope you have some snowshoes."

"No kidding?" Danny asked, his voice scaling upwards in alarm.

Laughter bounced off the walls of the bus. It wasn't often anyone could catch Danny.

"Not by Thanksgiving ordinarily," Mr. Larsen explained after the noise subsided. "But we almost always have a white Christmas, which is something you don't get in Seattle."

"We have roses and carnations for Christmas in Seattle." Danny defended proudly. "Once I went wading in the Sound on New Year's Day."

"It's a wonder the rain didn't wash you away." Ben took up the argument. "Here's a hard-earned quarter that says we won't be able to see any sights in Seattle because it'll be raining too hard."

"I'll take that," Danny challenged.

Ben handed over the quarter with loud moans of, "I've been robbed," for just as the bus passed the ramp of the Lake Washington Floating Bridge the mist hanging over the city began to lift and a pale sun set the water to shimmering.

Much to Mr. Larsen's discomfiture the students were singing and yelling as the bus made its way slowly through the traffic-clogged downtown streets. The girls and Miss Layton looked with such interest at the big department stores that Mr. Larsen shouted to the driver in mock alarm, "Don't let them get the door open or we'll lose half the expedition."

Finally they came to a pleasant residential district rising one hill upon the next. On the topmost hill stood Bayside High School, its windows on the west looking out on the Sound and those to the east getting an occasional glimpse of Mt. Rainier. They all walked around the campus, and much as they hated to give Danny the satisfaction of knowing they were impressed, they could only join with Ben in saying, "Wow."

"That's nothing but scenery," Danny said loftily. "Wait till you see the inside."

They walked in just as the bell rang. Instantly the halls were so jam-packed with hurrying students that the Cascadeville visitors pressed themselves against the walls. "Enrollment is over three thousand," Danny said.

"And each and every one of them dug an elbow into me," Jan retorted.

After the bell rang again and quiet was restored, Danny led the way to the journalism department.

The room was empty and Jan could see at once that it was just as Danny had said. The furniture was arranged to look like the city room of a newspaper, with a horseshoe copy-desk, several typewriters, wire baskets, and big stacks of copy-paper.

"That isn't all," Danny said after everyone had admired the room. "In here we have our morgue."

They walked into an adjoining room where they saw large green filing cases for clippings, bound volumes of past issues of the *Barnacle,* and best of all, in the section for exchange papers the *Mountain View Monthly Argus* right on top of the pile.

The visitors just couldn't admire the department enough and wanted to examine all its features carefully but Danny was impatient to take them on to even more glorious scenes. "Let's go see the printing plant. It's just across the hall in the tech school."

"Just a minute," Mr. Larsen cautioned. "We shouldn't go wandering around without a by-your-leave. We'd better let somebody know we're here."

"Oh, I know where everything is," Danny said with an off-hand shrug, but to Mr. Larsen's relief the door opened and several people came in and instantly surrounded Danny with a loud chorus of greetings.

A white-haired man detached himself from the group and came over to Mr. Larsen, his hand outstretched. "I'm Mr. Jepson, Bayside principal. I've been poking my nose out into the main hall all morning watching for you. Might have known Danny would sneak you in through the side."

"Very happy to meet you," Mr. Larsen responded. "It certainly was a nice gesture on the part of your Press Club to ask us down."

"Glad to have you. We think a lot of Danny and we miss him."

In the meantime Danny was introducing the Bayside group to his Mountain View friends. "This is Miss Grover, our journalism teacher and adviser to the *Barnacle*," he said, referring to an attractive young woman who didn't look much older than the students.

"This bum is Don Hartley," Danny continued happily. "He's a poor excuse for an editor but all they could get after I left, and the lush thrush is Maybelle Warren, society editor, no less . . ."

There were so many names and faces that Jan found herself getting dizzy and hoped she would remember half of them. They were all friendly and anxious to talk newspapers. When they found out she was Mountain View editor they swiftly drew her into their hilarious conversation.

As they moved off down the hall to see the printing plant Jan caught up with Mr. Larsen and Mr. Jepson and said, "Mr. Larsen, I have a wonderful idea."

Mr. Larsen held up his hands and pretended to push her away. "No, we can't have a city room at Mountain View. Poor Miss Layton has to use that room for all her English classes and they far outnumber the journalism class. It's tough, I know, but we just don't have the room."

"Well, no harm in asking," Jan decided philosophically.

"Nice try, Janice." Miss Layton gave her rusty little laugh. "I wish we could be elegant and citified, too."

Jan was startled as always to hear Miss Layton indulge in anything resembling mirth. Pete would say she was beginning to respond to friendliness, but more likely it was just party manners for the benefit of the Bayside people.

"We may have to give ours up, too," Mr. Jepson said. "The enrollment is increasing every year and we have to put the students somewhere."

"How about in the morgue?" Danny suggested.

"Anyone who disturbs our city room would have it coming," Miss Grover agreed.

After touring the printing plant and the school broadcasting station they all went back to the city room, where the rest of the Bayside Press Club members were waiting for the meeting to begin.

When everyone was seated Miss Grover stepped to the front of the room. "We're happy to welcome our guests from the Mountain View High School in Cascadeville not only to our school, but also into membership in the National High School Press Club. We feel that membership in the Press Club is the greatest recognition we can give our journalism students."

They all listened attentively as she outlined the Press Club requirements. Then she turned to a heap of gold pins lying on her desk and called the new members of the Bayside chapter to the front of the room one at a time. After telling of his or her particular accomplishments she pinned on the Press Club emblem.

When all the Bayside group had been "pinned," she turned the floor over to Mr. Larsen. Jan watched breathlessly as he took another heap of pins from his coat pocket and laid them on the table. "Thanks again for your hospitality," he said affably. "I'm sure the charter members of the Mountain View Press Club will always remember this afternoon. It's my pleasure to present them to you now."

He picked up the first pin. "Cassandra Warren, reporter last year and feature editor this year. Cassandra is especially noted for her humorous poetry, which has twice appeared in young people's publications."

Cassie, blush-pink and giggly as always, walked to the front of the room and shook hands with Mr. Larsen and Miss Layton, who fastened the pin on her dress.

"Bet she sticks me clear to the ribs when it's my turn," Jan muttered. Danny overheard and turned away quickly to suppress a laugh. Jan was indignant. As if it wasn't all his fault Miss Layton was so down on her.

"Donald Spencer," Mr. Larsen called, "sports reporter last year and sports editor this year."

It was apparent to Jan that she was going to be called last and she didn't know whether she approved or not. Finally Mr. Larsen was down to one pin—but it looked different from the others. It was bigger and brighter. "Jan Marie Morgan—reporter, proofreader, and all-around flunky last year, editor-in-chief this year."

She came forward and stood facing the group. As Mr. Larsen told about her summer's work on the *Courier* and mentioned that she'd only had her sixteenth birthday a few weeks ago, she stood quietly thinking of how she had felt last spring when she had first faced the student body as the new editor. How many experiences, how many lessons in growing up, had been crowded into that half a year.

"Therefore it's my pleasure to present you with this special editor's pin," Mr. Larsen concluded.

"Thank you," Jan responded automatically, shaking hands with him and Miss Layton.

She looked down at Miss Layton fastening the safety clasp (and it hadn't pricked her at all, so she supposed she should be ashamed of herself for thinking it might). Attached to the pin by two tiny chains was a gold bar with "Editor" on it. "Thank you," she said again and went to her seat while applause and conversation crackled all around.

"Nice surprise, huh?" Danny asked. "May I be the first to shake the hand that shook the hand that shook the hand . . ."

She smiled and squeezed his hand but there just didn't

seem to be anything at all she could say. Miss Grover announced that refreshments were ready in the cafeteria and the enthusiasm over this prospect was so great that no one noticed Jan's thoughtful silence.

"Take it easy, gang," Mr. Larsen cautioned as mounds of sandwiches and cookies and gallons of punch disappeared. "We're supposed to have a big dinner in a few hours."

"Maybe we can survive till then if we have a little snack now," Danny said, and everyone laughed as they surged back for more food.

Finally the Mountain View party was back on the bus yelling out the windows and inviting the city slickers to come see them and get a breath of fresh air. "We haven't much time," Mr. Larsen said as the bus pulled away. "We'll take a quick look at the Art Museum in Volunteer Park, drive through the University campus, and then head for the waterfront."

"In case the bus breaks down we can always take Jan's belt apart and have moola to charter a train," Ben suggested.

"A train to South of the Border, you mean?" Danny asked.

"*Si, si, mañana,*" Ben replied, strumming an imaginary guitar.

Jan smiled absently. Any other time she would have been delighted to be the center of interest with her gaucho belt, but right now she wanted to think. All the while her physical self was trailing through the Art Museum listening to Mr. Larsen and Miss Layton point out the things of interest, her mental self was going through a terrific right-about-face.

She supposed it was hard for anyone to give up a stubborn idea, but for herself, rooted in pride and jealousy as she now admitted she was, it was devastating. But she had to give up her prejudice and face up publicly to what she'd really known deep inside of her for a long time. Danny Mallory was a grand person and she had been very wrong to distrust him. She had stormed at him in private, been cold and sarcastic in public, begrudged him his small position on the paper, and been miserably jealous because his talent was appreciated too.

And how had he treated her all this time? Been kind, polite, and helpful, and paved the way for the honor she had received today. She glanced again at the editor bar dangling from the Press Club pin, its inscription visible to the whole world. He had helped her achieve the honor that he too had earned but could not receive.

She tapped him on the shoulder and the two of them slipped away from the rest of the crowd who were exclaiming over the beauty of the jade collection. "How could you stand to leave Bayside?" she asked. "Couldn't you have boarded somewhere and had your year as editor?"

"I did think of that," Danny admitted, "and the Warrens, Maybelle Warren's parents, even invited me to stay with them. I think the poor, harassed souls felt that with a surly specimen like me around to scare people they wouldn't have to crawl over such a heap of abject admirers every time they wanted to go in or out the door."

"Maybelle?" Jan said. "Oh, that real pretty girl." Suddenly, and for reasons she had no intention of analyzing, she was glad he hadn't stayed with them.

"She's a good reporter, too. Well, my folks have been friends with the Warrens for years, but they went into a tailspin at the idea of my staying down here. This will be my last year at home—next year it'll be college or the army—so they thought I should stay with them as long as I could."

Jan groaned in sympathy. Didn't parents ever want their children to be happy?

"Hey, it's not that bad," Danny said in alarm. "Of course I miss Bayside. It would have been grand to be editor of the *Barnacle,* but I'm having lots of fun at Mountain View, and no matter what high school I attend I'll still wind up editor of the New York *Times.* Let's just take the long view and be happy."

"Pete's right," Jan decided. "You do have character."

"He's the one who ought to know," Danny said with a pleased smile. "Maybe I'll skip the New York *Times* and take over the *Courier* when Pete retires. Might be more fun at that."

They rejoined the group, scrambled aboard the bus, and went on with their tour. Cassie came to sit with Jan and admire her special editor's pin. "Your braids are so cute today," Cassie told her, "and gadzooks, that's a fabulous coin belt. For a nose-in-the-printing-press editor you're looking mighty elegant."

Although Jan brightened and talked to Cassie and the others she was still thinking slowly and painfully about Danny. She was trying to imagine how she would have behaved if her parents had moved suddenly, thrusting her into a strange school and yanking her editorship out from under her. Would she have cheerfully made the best of it?

She squirmed away from the answer. After all, she wasn't very easy to live with under the best of conditions. In a situation like that she would be impossible. Well there, she'd fought it all out now. She had been wrong about Danny. He had more character than she and it was up to her to be extra nice to make up for all her unjust suspicions.

"This is Greek Row," one of the girls said excitedly as the bus turned down a lane of large, ornate houses near the University. "Oh, wouldn't you love to live in one of the sorority houses?"

"Not me, thank you," Danny replied with a poker face while the others laughed.

"I don't suppose we could accidentally see Melanie or any of the kids?" Cassie asked. "I meant to write and tell her we were coming, but I didn't get to it in time."

"Since the University enrollment is more than twice the population of Cascadeville, it isn't likely," Mr. Larsen said.

Jan said nothing during this conversation. Early in the year

Budge had sent her a bunch of University *Dailies* and a scribbled note hoping all was going well with the *Argus*. She had been too shy to answer him until the plans for the trip were underway. Then she managed to procure his address from Mr. Larsen in what she hoped was a casual conversation and wrote a letter about the proposed expedition.

Budge hadn't answered and she had tried not to feel hurt about it. After all, he was living a busy and exciting life. She was so occupied with her thoughts that she didn't pay much attention as the bus moved slowly towards the magnificent Gothic library. "I think we will stop here a minute," Mr. Larsen decided. "Just long enough for you to see the lobby."

They started for the door. Cassie glanced out the window and began to shriek, for coming towards them was the small group of students who comprised Cascadeville's contribution to the University. Heading them were Budge and Melanie, each carrying one end of a home-made banner reading, "Welcome Mountain View Press Club."

"Here we sat like birds in the wilderness all afternoon waiting for you," Budge explained cheerfully as the two groups had a joyous and noisy reunion.

"If we had only known we could have arranged a definite schedule and not kept you waiting," Mr. Larsen said.

"We wanted to surprise you," Melanie explained. "We took a calculated risk and decided you would come by the library. Tourists always do. But you're all stinkers not to write more often. Jan was the only one who let us know about today."

"I intended to write," Cassie began, and when the others laughed she said tartly, "Maybe if you characters would answer letters once in a while we wouldn't be so forgetful up at our end of the mountains."

"Now, now," Budge said paternally. "You'll have to bear with us about that. We think about home lots, but mostly we're too busy to write. But it's not long till the holidays and we'll really visit and catch up on the news then."

While they were talking the famous University chimes began to sound through the clear autumn air. The visitors listened entranced to the sprightly melody.

Budge laughed. "They tell me that on the day exams start he always plays 'Just Before the Battle, Mother.' It will be worth it to hear that. And as you may have gathered from the stampede out of the library, that's our factory whistle. If we don't head for the Row we'll be late for dinner, so I guess we had better break up this delightful party."

The good-bys were said and the group climbed back on the bus thoroughly convinced of the values of a college education.

Everyone was tired, hungry, and happy when they pulled up at the Salt Water Room Restaurant and trooped into the section reserved for them. It was an attractive room decorated with fishnets, glass floats, and tortured shapes of driftwood. Through big windows they could look out at Elliott Bay. The sun was sinking behind Alki Point and the ferry boats chugged busily, handling the rush-hour traffic. "Lots of people commute to Seattle by ferry," Danny explained. "They ride an hour each way sometimes." The young people from the mountains shook their head in amazement.

Mr. Larsen and Miss Layton talked to the head waitress about the menu the group had selected. "Crab cocktail, clam chowder, fish and chips, toasted garlic bread, peppermint ice-cream with chocolate sauce. That's it," Mr. Larsen said.

Miss Layton looked ill at the thought. "Better add bicarbonate of soda to that list," she suggested.

However, everyone, Miss Layton included, waded happily through every course just as if they hadn't gorged themselves at the Press Club party. They sang songs in the intervals between courses.

The waitress was very harassed by the time she brought in

the dessert. "They are so busy in the kitchen I have to dish up here and try to get the sauce on before it all melts," she complained to no one in particular.

The first stirrings of the new and noble character she meant to cultivate led Jan to slip away from the noisy table and offer her services. "I'll dish up the ice-cream and you pour the sauce," she suggested.

She was just finishing when Danny noticed her. "Will you look at that?" he shouted, pointing to the dipper in her hand. "Isn't that Jan a character? She even has to scoop the ice-cream."

The appreciative laughter nearly rustled the fishnet draperies. Jan grabbed a dish and plunked it in front of him. "Here's a scoop for you, too," she said while they all applauded.

He smiled warmly at her. "That's my girl."

"Like poison I am," she retorted, and everyone cheered as she finished serving the ice-cream.

Later, sitting quietly while her own dessert melted away, Jan wished just a little wistfully that Danny had meant those joking words, "That's my girl."

She just didn't fit into her own family at all. They didn't understand her and furthermore didn't want to—and it was a lonely situation. How comforting it would be to have a dependable, always-on-hand relationship with Danny—sort of like Budge and Melanie, only different, because they were different. Of course Danny had always been nice to her. But he was nice to Miss Layton, too. No, he was only joking, calling her his girl. She was doomed to go through life as a lone wolf, but at least from now on she would always be a friend to Danny.

CHAPTER 10

Peace, It's Wonderful

WITH THE RINGING of the morning school bell the first snowflakes slipped out of the sullen clouds and plummeted to the frozen ground. By noon an icy wind was whipping the white swirls with such ferocity that Mr. Larsen ordered the buses brought around and school dismissed so that the country commuters wouldn't be stranded in the storm.

Jan and Danny ignored the suggestion that the town students go straight home. In the spirit of friendly cooperation that had been established between them the day of the Seattle trip they decided to visit Pete. Finally after stumbling windblown the length of Main Street they were safe within the warm, dusty shop.

"No brains," was Pete's comment as they stood dripping in the doorway. "Why do you have to make such a mess for me?" he complained as he hung their coats behind the oil stove.

"A fine welcome to the best editorial assistants you ever had," Danny said.

Pete snorted. "Better get a hot drink," he advised. "I don't want any irate parents accusing me of working their sprouts into pneumonia."

Jan opened a desk drawer and took out the ready-mix cocoa Pete now kept beside his jar of instant coffee since she and Danny had become such permanent fixtures in the shop. A bag of fresh doughnuts stood beside them. "You must have been expecting us," she said, then turned to him with a suspicious frown. "Pete, you're up to something with a spread like this."

"That's the younger generation for you," Pete said sadly. "No faith or trust in anyone. The cocoa and doughnuts have nothing to do with the fact that the folding machine broke down today and the *Courier* has to be mailed out tomorrow."

Jan and Danny both groaned loudly. Danny looked out the window and said, "The sporting thing is to toss a coin. Heads we perish in the snow, tails we fold the papers."

"Here's a nickel," Jan said reaching in her pocket.

"You poor excuses for humanity," Pete said scornfully. "What's wrong with folding papers? Show me an easier way to make money."

"Let's see," Danny said thoughtfully. "There's prospecting in Death Valley in July or harpooning whales or . . ."

"Get to work or get out," was Pete's ultimatum, so they all took their cups over to the big table where the papers were stacked. They worked quietly and rapidly until their concentration was interrupted by loud knocking. Danny opened the door and Dotty, a snow-blown spectacle, nearly fell through it.

"Whoosh," she sighed, and sinking down in a chair untied her soppy scarf. "I had a hunch you'd be here and thought maybe I could rope onto you for the trip home."

"Why didn't you go with the others?" Jan asked as she brought her a cup of the hot, heartening cocoa.

"Thanks. This is wonderful," Dotty said as she sipped her drink. "Oh, the Drama Club was having a hot and heavy meeting and we didn't let a little thing like a blizzard slow us down. We might as well have quit, though, because all we did was fight."

"What's the battle about?" Pete asked. "Anything startling or sensational, I hope? I need something for next week's paper besides the snow."

"Just about the class play next spring. Some of us want to

have *A Midsummer Night's Dream* and the rest want a modern play because they don't think we could get nice enough costumes for a Shakespearean production. Oh, you're all working, aren't you? Well, don't let me interrupt."

"You won't interrupt us, you'll join us," Pete commanded. "Even a drama student can fold papers."

"Why, sure," Dotty agreed, and came over to the table.

An hour passed swiftly with the only noises the scrape of papers, the hum of the oil burner, and the wind blowing through the cracks of the old building. Finally, when the pages of folded papers were stacked high and they didn't need to work so fast, Jan turned to Dotty and asked, "I don't understand why you're so upset about costumes. Aren't there places where you can rent them?"

"Yes, there are. But it takes so many for Shakespearean productions that it would cost too much."

"At Bayside the Drama Club had an auxiliary sewing circle to make their costumes," Danny contributed. "They picked materials that didn't cost much and looked wonderful from behind the footlights."

"I wish we could do that," Dotty said, looking thoughtful. "I know most of the kids wouldn't mind buying a costume if it didn't cost too much. It's always handy to have one around for parties."

"Do you think we could interest some of the home-ec girls in the project?" Jan asked.

"It takes more than interest," Danny cautioned. "First of all you'd have to check to see that historical details were accurate, then there'd be drawings and patterns to make, much less the sewing. It would really be a job for a professional."

"You're too, too right," Dotty admitted. "Our sewing teacher is a good gal, but I doubt if she's very original."

"Don't you imagine she could turn out the costumes if she had something to work from—if someone else did the designing and detail work?" Jan asked with sudden excitement.

"I'm sure she could, but we don't have someone like that. Or do we? Jan, you've got an idea! What's up?"

"Well, it may be nothing at all. It might never, ever work, but my mother studied fashion designing, and I have a feeling she's good at it. If she would do the designing I could take care of the research."

Dotty clasped her hands together and shut her eyes in a pose of pure joy. "Oh, if only she could," she said prayerfully. "Oh, I just know that if I could tell the kids we had costumes lined up they'd quit objecting to *A Midsummer Night's Dream*. Oh, Jan, would she mind doing it?"

"I think she would enjoy it if she feels she has the ability," Jan said slowly. "She really needs something to do besides taking Andrew's temperature six times a day."

"Got everybody figured out, have you?" Pete asked sarcastically as he folded the last paper with a flourish. "Know just what makes them tick, huh?"

The girls ignored him. "How about starting to soften up your mother?" Dotty suggested. "Then in a few days I'll come over and give her the triple whammy, and if it all works out I'll have quite a report to make when the Drama Club meets again after the holidays."

"Maybe a sample design for them," Jan agreed.

They all stood up and stretched. "The wind has let up," Danny announced as he peered around the the door. "We'd better leave while we can."

"Sure. Scram." Pete nodded. "Can't think of a thing more for you to do."

The world outside was an etching in black and white. "Bet there's two feet," Danny said in awe as they took off down the street, arms linked together. "Wow, I'll bet we don't get back to school before the holidays at all. We'll miss the program and the Christmas parties."

The girls laughed at him. "Danny, if we quit school because of the snow we wouldn't be back until March," Dotty explained.

"See, they're cleaning things up already." Jan pointed back at Main Street, where the big orange snowplow was making its ponderous way. "Better do your homework, boy," she advised. " 'Cause unless it gets lots worse tonight there'll be school tomorrow—at least for the town kids."

"Might as well go back to Seattle," he said in disgust.

When Jan arrived home she found her mother and Andrew in the midst of a heated argument. Andrew, dressed for the outdoors, stood just outside the front door, holding it open a crack. His face was puckered with grief. "It isn't time to come in," he protested. "I hardly got to play outside at all. First you wouldn't let me go out till the wind stopped and now you say it's too dark."

"It's dark and damp and cold," his mother said firmly. "You can't take the chance of catching cold. Maybe you can go out awhile tomorrow."

"You're just saying that because you don't want me to have any fun at all. I haven't been sick for ages and ages. The doctor said I was fine."

"You wouldn't be fine if I didn't keep my eye on you. You just don't have any sense at all where your health is concerned. You get right in here and get out of those wet clothes," she said angrily.

Andrew slammed the door and stalked into the hall, where he flung his jacket and hat in the general direction of the hangers, stamped on into the living-room, and turned on the television full-blast. His mother followed quietly, picked up his jacket and put it away. "Andrew and his pleasing personality," Jan said sarcastically as she followed them into the hall.

Mrs. Morgan turned to the kitchen. "Poor boy," she said finally. "I know he feels abused, but there's nothing else I can do. Even if he grows up hating me, I've got to protect his health."

She blinked back tears and said softly to herself, "But I never dreamed raising children could be so unrewarding."

Jan, overhearing the remark, felt stung with hurt. She thought of all the "A" report cards she had brought home to be told her mother didn't believe in grading. She thought of the newspapers with her articles, tossed into the fireplace unread. The only time her mother had been half-way enthusiastic about her was when she wanted a new dress. There was such a thing as an unrewarding parent, too.

She pondered over several biting remarks she could make, but then she remembered that she wanted her mother to do the costume designing for Dotty and had best be diplomatic. It looked like tonight wasn't the psychological time to broach the subject, what with storms within and without, but she'd keep it in mind and wait for an opening. In the meantime it wouldn't hurt to do a little buttering-up.

"Don't fix dinner tonight, Mother," she suggested. "I'll make some toasted sandwiches and we can eat in front of the fireplace."

Mrs. Morgan brightened. "Why, Janice, how nice. An indoor picnic. It should cheer up Andrew."

"Oh, sure," Jan replied with a grimace. Then she thought of the fun she'd had walking in the snow and felt a little ashamed of her thoughts about Andrew. Probably she'd be cranky if she couldn't get out and have fun, too.

While they were eating the snow started falling again and they sat a long time in front of the fireplace, not talking, not even thinking much, just enjoying the security and coziness of being in a warm house while the winter's first snow engulfed them.

The rest of the time before Christmas vacation was a continual rush. There was the program at school, the *Argus* staff party which couldn't have been more hilarious, and of course the December issue of the *Argus*. She and Danny bullied Pete into printing it in green ink and it was such a thing of beauty that even Miss Layton was impressed.

The day the *Argus* came out she was late getting home, and when she came in she found her mother putting dinner on the table while her father sat in his place expectantly. She stood against the door and shook her head. "I really must be going around in circles. I thought it was only Wednesday."

Her father laughed. "You haven't slipped your moorings yet. It is Wednesday. We've had to close down for a while. Deepest snow in twenty years, the old timers say."

"Why, that's wonderful," Jan said happily. "Oh, Dad, it'll be grand to have you home for awhile."

"It's not so wonderful on the budget," her mother grumbled as they sat down to dinner. "This could last two or three months. Then how would we get along? I don't know why you always have to have a lay-off at Christmas time when expenses are so heavy."

"We haven't starved yet," he said cheerfully. "I'll start looking for extra work in town tomorrow."

Thinking things over, Jan decided the time had come to tackle her mother about the costumes. That would really get her mind off the budget. When she mentioned the idea Mrs. Morgan's eyes sparkled, then she became apathetic. "Oh, I don't think I could do it, Janice. It's been too long since I tried anything like that."

"I don't call a month very long," Jan remonstrated. "It's not much more than that since we were working on my dress, and you made so many changes in that printed pattern it wasn't much different than designing an original."

"A little different," she said feebly, but she looked with interest at the book Jan put in front of her.

"Here are some pictures of the Hollywood production of *A Midsummer Night's Dream*. Of course our costumes couldn't be that elaborate, but maybe they could give you some idea."

Her father nodded approvingly and stood up to lean over their shoulders and see the pictures. "Nothing too difficult about those," he decided. "They just used a lot more material in those days and didn't have our modern conveniences for sewing."

"Bring me a pencil and paper," her mother commanded. "I'll at least try."

While Jan did up the dishes and her husband went off to the living-room with Andrew, she sat down at the kitchen table and tried to break a dress of the 1590's into pattern pieces. "Don't hang around and make me nervous," she told Jan.

Since Jan understood that feeling well enough, she picked up a book and started for her room, but just then footsteps clattered on the porch and loud laughter sounded through the door. Her heart turned over. She would know that voice anywhere and she flung open the door before he could knock.

"Budge," she said happily. "Oh, Budge, you did mean it when you said you would come visit. Do come in. I didn't realize the University was out already."

"Missy, when ah say ah'm comin', then ah'm comin'," Budge said gaily. "Now are you going to invite me out of the cold, or aren't you?"

Melanie peeked over his shoulder. "Hello, Jan," she called. "I'm not hiding. I've just been using Budge to keep off the wind."

Jan's smile didn't falter as she greeted Melanie. She'd known long ago that Budge and Melanie were a couple for keeps. It was happiness enough just to talk to Budge for a while. And she liked Melanie, too. She really did.

"Come in, both of you," she invited. "I want to hear everything about the University that you didn't have time to tell us in Seattle."

"We'd better start from scratch," Budge suggested. "I don't think we said much that made sense that day."

Budge stood in front of the fireplace while Jan hung up their coats and hurried out to the kitchen to tell her mother about the unexpected company.

When she returned she found Mr. Morgan gallantly seating Melanie. "Andrew, turn off that thing. We want to talk," he directed.

Andrew's mouth flew open in surprise. "This is one of my favorite programs," he protested.

"Turn it off. Your sister has company."

He spoke so sternly that Andrew obeyed, but stamped out of the room muttering, "I'm going to tell Mother."

Jan sent her father a look of warm gratitude as he began to talk football with Budge. If he lived at home all the time she wouldn't be on the missing end of everything.

"How's everything been?" she asked Melanie hesitantly. "I read in the Seattle paper that you had pledged Theta and Cassie talked about how thrilled you were. It must be wonderful."

Evidently she had chosen the right topic of conversation, because Melanie smiled and rushed into words. "Oh, Jan, it's simply heaven. All the girls are grand and we have so much fun at the house. We have to work hard to keep up our grades, and it isn't any cinch, but it's worth it."

"I hope I get to go," Jan replied wistfully. She'd never put it into words before, but she knew now how much, how very much she wanted to go to college.

"Oh, you must," Melanie said quickly. "If you don't mind I'd like to tell our rush chairman about you. Of course I'm prejudiced but I know you would be happy with the Thetas."

"Me like the Thetas?" Jan croaked in amazement. "I thought the sixty-four-dollar question was would they like me."

"Take a look at your record, pal," Melanie said reassuringly. "Besides, you've grown up this year. Your clothes are chic, your hair looks very nice—in fact, 'most any sorority would be interested."

Jan was flabbergasted. "I just wanted to look old enough to be editor," she said. "I mean, I guess I don't know how I look except that I didn't think it was very good."

To her surprise Melanie laughed. "You should have seen me when I was fourteen. I guess you don't remember me then. I was fat, with freckles, and had braces on my teeth. You just had the bad luck to be slow about shedding your old skin and had so many brains that you were going to school with older kids. Nature handed you a rough deal for a while, but it's sure over now. You look fine."

"Thanks, Melanie," she said. She felt grateful and humble.

"Are you women going to talk about clothes all night?" Budge inquired. "I came to hear about the *Argus*. I hear you've been going great guns."

"Part of the credit should go to Danny," Jan explained. "He's my associate editor and comes from Seattle. I don't think you even met him that day at the University. We were all too excited to remember our manners and he just stayed in the background and let the others visit. Anyhow, we've both been having the same ideas at the same time all year and it really keeps things humming."

"Nuts to him," was Budge's opinion. "I worked with you last year, remember, and I know how sharp you are."

His praise poured over her like warm water. Happiness really can make a person dizzy, she thought to herself. Still, she felt obliged to explain about Danny. "He's very talented," she insisted. "I could call him up if you'd like to meet him. He's going to the University for sure next year."

"Sure. Trot him around. Maybe I'll get me a copy boy all lined up for next year when I'm a lordly sophomore."

Feeling a little shy, Jan called the Mallory number. Danny answered and she invited him over. "Sure, I'll come," he accepted promptly. "I want to get a better look at the fabulous Budge. Ben Barton is over here. We've been playing ping-pong to the death. Can I bring him along?"

"Of course," she replied. "Why don't you stop on the way and see if Dotty would like to come, too? Mother is working on those costume designs for her."

"Will do," Danny said as he hung up.

In a short time the Morgan house was filled with noise and laughter. Dotty went right out to the kitchen to look at the designs and talk about costumes. Melanie went along to tell them about the student theatres at the University.

Ben found Andrew sulking in the dining-room and persuaded him to play checkers. Budge, Danny, and Jan happily talked shop.

Throughout the evening Jan was aware of her father busily but unobtrusively making a pleasant atmosphere for them. He put a stack of records on the phonograph, built up a good fire in the fireplace, and, sitting down beside it, turned out basket after basket of popcorn that quickly vanished while everybody chattered.

Finally they all converged back in the living room. "Your mother is simply brilliant," Dotty exclaimed dramatically. "Imagine hiding talent like that under a kitchen roof all these years! Oh, I can just see Shakespeare looming over the horizon."

Ben flipped through the records. "Christmas carols," he announced, fishing up an album. "Let's sing."

They sat on the floor in front of the fireplace and sang, and Jan watched their faces beautified by the flickering fireplace. They were enjoying themselves. She realized with a feeling almost of awe that this was the first party she had had since the time years ago when her mother would invite little girls over for her birthdays.

About the time she would have been interested in having real parties Andrew had got sick and all the joy had gone from the house. She couldn't even have one friend over because their talk and laughter made Andrew so restless and jealous that he would have an upset. "He isn't old enough to understand," her mother had explained over and over again. As the older one she must make the sacrifices for the time being. Someday she could have friends over again. Someday had stretched into nearly three years, as Jan withdrew into her studies and lost her friendships with the girls she had played with as a child.

Now the day—the night, rather—had come and she was sitting in front of her fireplace with her friends having fun. Without any conscious planning or foresight, it had come.

After a while they finished all the carols they knew and were arguing about the words to "Good King Wenceslaus" when Mr. Morgan reappeared carrying plates of ice-cream and freshly baked cookies.

He must have walked downtown in all the cold to get the ice-cream; and as for the cookies— "How did you ever manage?" she asked her mother, who was passing napkins.

"Ice-box cookies," she replied with a satisfied smile. "I had the dough mixed and in the cooler."

After everyone left, walking off into the frosty night, calling back thanks for the unexpected party, Jan found her parents sitting comfortably in the kitchen eating the leftovers. "Thanks so much," she said sincerely. "It was certainly nice of you to go to all that trouble."

"That wasn't trouble," her mother said in surprise. "It was fun. That is what I've been wanting for you, Janice. Parties and friends. You should have lots of evenings like this instead of burying yourself in schoolwork and newspapers."

"But I didn't intend to have a party," Jan explained. "It all just happened."

Her mother laughed. "You simply don't think like a normal girl. Anybody else would call it a party and scheme a way to have more."

"No, I couldn't scheme and make plans," Jan told them seriously. "I'd be scared silly. If I'm going to have a social life it will have to be this way, informally—accidentally."

"But you must get over being afraid," her mother protested. "Every girl should have party manners . . ."

"You had fun, didn't you, sis?" her father interrupted to ask gently.

"Oh, yes, I had such a good time. But I'm sure I wouldn't have if I had known about it ahead of time."

"Never mind the whys and hows. The plans and party manners will come in their own good time. Hop off to bed. We'll do the dishes. You have school tomorrow."

Jan hummed thoughtfully as she went upstairs. How very comforting were her father's words. If only she could quit fretting and fuming about the things she wanted to do and realize that in time—and maybe unplanned and accidental like the party—they could all happen.

CHAPTER 11

Holiday Crisis

JAN'S FATHER HAD FOUND WORK at the post office, helping with the Christmas rush, but this job would end with the holiday, so on the twenty-third—a gray, blustery day—Mrs. Morgan worried aloud. "What are we going to do the rest of the winter?" she asked. "The deep snow could last till March."

"We always get by," Jan said absently, her mind on her own affairs.

"The older children are the more they cost," her mother continued. "I hope you understand that we can't spend a lot of money for Christmas. You're old enough to realize how hard it is to stay solvent during a lay-off."

"Uh-huh, I know all about it," Jan replied, still not really listening. Her busy fingers were knitting the last half inch of the last sock of a pair of brilliantly colored Argyles. Through much teasing and speculation she had steadfastly refused to tell who was going to find the sock in his stocking. But as she worked she smiled at her mental picture of Pete in his drab work clothes topped off, or should she say bottomed off, with the bright socks. Of course he would fume and sputter and declare he wouldn't wear them but he would be pleased nonetheless.

Her mother gave up trying to impress Jan with their financial troubles and went to the kitchen. Jan bound off the sock with a sigh of relief, shook the cramp out of her fingers, and carried both socks upstairs to wrap.

127

After assembling the papers and ribbons she pulled her gifts out of her bottom dresser drawer and looked them over for the last time. A dress length of sculptured nylon for her mother. She ran her fingers over its puckery folds and felt fervent gratitude to Mrs. Abbott, who had picked it up along with her own order from a Seattle wholesale house. She would not have had enough money for it otherwise. At that it cost more than all the rest of her gifts put together, but that was all right. It was Mother's turn for something special. And maybe if she had a new dress she would go to meetings or visiting and not have so much time to exaggerate all of Andrew's symptoms.

For her father a batch of pocket books to read when he was back in camp. She knew he would appreciate them. Early in the fall she had knitted gloves for Andrew, and she had just added a Boy Scout knife. Her mother would probably have a fit, but Andrew would love it.

It was amazing—and irksome too—how loyal Andrew's old friends were. From Cub Scout days on up they kept faithfully visiting, hoping that he would be well enough to join in their games, and when they received his mother's not always tactful veto they would subdue their own natural energy to play bingo or dominoes or watch TV with Andrew. And every Christmas since the accident they had shown up like so many rag-tail, loud-mouthed Santa Clauses with presents.

While some of the gifts were undoubtedly the result of mothers' ideas of social obligations, others, Jan could tell from the article and the wrapping, were the boys' own kind-hearted tribute of friendship. Oh, much as she hated to admit it, Andrew did have something, some mysterious quality of personality that made friends. If his ill health hadn't intervened he would be a leader now. But that certainly didn't make him any easier to live with—especially in the winter when he wanted to be out in the snow.

Well, that was all the gifts except for the handkerchiefs,

scarves, and bangles for the girls and the little gift for Danny. She chuckled over it—a key chain with a tiny crab embedded in plastic.

"Something to help you remember Seattle," she would tell him. But it had more symbolism than that. If she ever started to act jealous and nasty around him again she would just take a look at that key chain and tell herself, "Don't be such an old crab."

She wrapped and tied them all and decided she might as well take the gifts for Pete, Danny, and the girls down town and leave them. On her way back she could stop off and buy some candy and nuts and the little extras her mother insisted they couldn't afford. That would leave her penniless again. My, what a job it was to save anything towards her typewriter when every time she turned around she needed money for something else. She was beginning to understand why adults had such a time balancing budgets.

"Stay out of my room," Mrs. Morgan called as Jan started downstairs.

"I wasn't anywhere near it," she replied, offended. For goodness' sakes, did her mother think she was some five-year-old to be snooping through closets looking for mysterious packages?

Besides, her mother wasn't very sharp at hiding things, what with leaving tell-tale scraps of flowered quilted chintz lying on the kitchen floor. "I hope it's a new robe," she muttered as she put on her coat and tied her scarf warmly around her head.

The first stop was Dotty's. Cassie was there, too, and they pounced on Jan with squeals of excitement and drew her into the living-room, where with notebook and pencils they were busy making a list. Jan put her package under the tree, accepted one for herself, and inquired, "What are you two plotting?"

"A square-dance party for New Year's Eve," Dotty replied.

"Everybody's been wanting to learn more about it, so I sent for some records with calls and instructions and I thought we'd get two squares together."

"That takes eight couples," Cassie continued, stuttery with excitement. "It ought to be such fun. We have to be sure to have the right number of couples so everyone will have partners."

"You and Danny will be one couple, won't you?" Dotty asked.

"You'd better consult Danny about that," Jan replied, aflame with embarrassment. "I can't accept his dates for him."

"Oh, don't be stuffy, Jan Marie Morgan! Everybody knows Danny follows you around like Mary's little lamb." The girls laughed at her confusion.

"That's because we work together," Jan tried to explain. Suddenly brought up before her, though, it was a strange situation. She and Danny spent a lot of time together but they were always at the shop or over at her own house and they talked newspapers. They hadn't ever gone out on a date and Jan was sure they never would. The most she could expect from a boy was comradely companionship.

"No, you'll have to ask Danny yourselves," she said firmly. "And I don't know if I can come, either. I may get a chance to baby-sit that night and I'd hate to turn down that much money."

"You're so right," Dotty said with a sigh. "That's what we all should be doing. Well, I don't know if I'll be able to get a crowd or not. I suppose most of the kids have something planned by now."

"Oh, no," Cassie wailed. "Don't give up yet. Even if we could only have one square we could learn something."

"You don't have to decide now," Jan said. "Ask around a little more and make up your mind after Christmas."

"That's what I'll do. You always have the most logical

ideas. Well, kids, want to come out to the kitchen and sample my fruitcake?"

"Some other time," Jan said as she reached for her coat. "I have to get down town before the stores close. I'll be seeing you both."

Pete and Danny were sitting with their feet on the stove railing, steaming cups beside them, when Jan entered the shop. "Lazy," she said scornfully.

"Sensible," Pete replied. "Pour yourself a mug if you like. Danny thought you might so he made it."

"How did you know I was coming?" she asked as she poured out the cocoa and perched on top of the desk.

"Stopped by your house and just missed you," Danny replied. "And with a late start I beat you here by twenty minutes. Women are really remarkable."

Jan opened her mouth to protest, then snapped it shut. She should live so long she'd explain all her errands to those gargoyles. "I can't stay," she said as she jumped off the desk. "I just wanted to leave these."

Shyly she took the two packages and handed them to Pete and Danny. Pete held his up to his ear and shook it. "If it's a necktie you're fired."

"My sentiments exactly," Danny echoed as he slipped his

package into his jacket pocket. "I can't fire you now but I will someday when I'm editor of the University *Daily* and you're my cub reporter."

"Don't hold your breath waiting for the day," she advised. Further conversation was forestalled by Pete, who reached in his desk and handed out two identically wrapped packages.

"Mustn't go home empty-handed," he said.

"No, you certainly must not," Danny agreed as he placed a large, sloppily wrapped package in front of her.

"Oh, my," Jan explained. "They look so interesting I can hardly wait."

"You'd better," Danny said sternly, "or I'll fire you when I'm editor of the New York *Times,* too. In fact I'd better walk along with you to see that you don't stop in the first doorway and try to peek."

As they reached the door Pete cleared his throat and produced a wide smile on his worn, furrowed face. "Merry Christmas, kids."

"Merry Christmas, Pete," they echoed wholeheartedly.

On Christmas Eve Jan sang carols as she helped tidy up the house. They were all restless waiting for Mr. Morgan, who had to work till nine. "You shouldn't have wasted your money," her mother grumbled as she selected a chocolate from the box on the living-room table. "I told you we were going to have a very simple Christmas this year."

Jan glanced up, a little disturbed. Her mother had been so cranky the last few days that there was just no pleasing her, and it saddened Jan because she had been enjoying their new-found friendliness. They had become steadily more compatible during the fall—why this sudden freeze now? Probably money worries, Jan decided protectively. So often that made adults fractious.

Determined to be light-hearted this evening, she smiled

and replied, "Have some Christmas spirit, Mother. That's free."

Mrs. Morgan frowned, but before she could scold Jan asked, "Why can't I open my presents from the kids and Pete now and just have the family presents when Dad comes home?"

"Yeah," Andrew agreed. "I want to open mine, too."

"Oh, I suppose so," their mother acquiesced. "Anything at all to keep you from heckling me so much."

Jan looked at her mother sadly, then shrugged her shoulders and dived under the tree for her little stack of presents, noting happily that this year she had nearly as many as Andrew. Maybe Andrew did have a way with people, but she was making friends, too.

She opened the present from Pete first and exclaimed happily. "Look," she said holding up a leather-bound loose-leaf notebook with "Jan Marie Morgan" engraved in gold on the cover.

"It's just perfect for taking notes," she said enthusiastically. "Next to a typewriter it's the most perfect present I could get."

"A typewriter!" her mother said, horrified. "Why don't you ask for a linotype and a rotary press while you're at it?"

Jan rubbed the leather caressingly. "I'm going to put it right to work listing who is due for thank-you notes."

"You'd better open the other packages so you'll know who and what to write down," her mother said dryly.

Andrew pulled a gun out of a box, fired loudly, shouted, "Ride 'em, cowboy," and tore up the stairs firing a roll of caps all the way.

"Andrew, come back here!" Mrs. Morgan started after him. "Why will people give him such excitable toys? They should know better."

"They probably think he's a boy," Jan retorted.

"No sarcasm out of you, young lady," her mother said shortly.

Andrew paused on the landing, leaned over, and drew a bead on the Christmas tree angel. "Yippee-aye-aye," he shouted, and then as Jan caught his eye he smiled so sweetly that for a second his sister could understand why his friends kept coming back. "Thanks, sis," he said. "I want to be a boy," and then just before his mother could reach him he galloped on up the steps.

Jan reached for Danny's package. Fuzzy blue slippers. Delighted, she slipped them on and found them a perfect fit. But goodness, what a magnificent present, and she had only given him a key chain. "How did Danny know the right size?" she asked when her mother came back after failing to confiscate the cap gun.

Her mother put her other problems aside long enough to giggle. "He just pestered me until I told him," she admitted. "Janice, I really didn't know what to do about him. He came over to consult me. Not that he wanted my advice—his mind was already made up—but to get your size and decide which color would be best. I tried to tell him that it wasn't proper for him to give a girl slippers but he said you had talked about your feet being cold and that wasn't proper, either. He's stubborn."

"That he is," Jan agreed with a laugh. Somehow the slippers seemed as warm and comfortable as Danny himself.

"I don't know if I did right or not," her mother worried on —worried with a smile this time, however—"I know my mother would never have permitted such a thing for a minute and I don't suppose I should, either. But he is such a nice boy, Janice."

Before they could philosophize about Danny any further they heard a step and a hearty shout on the porch and there was Father, eager for Christmas and happy to be home with his family. Now was the time out of the whole year when, whatever problems they had, Jan truly felt that they were a family. With all lights turned off except for the tree lights and the fireplace they sat together and sang carols. Then her father went to the bookcase, took out the worn old Bible that Great-grandma Morgan had brought overland with her in a covered wagon, and read the Christmas story. As always, Jan enjoyed the feeling of sharing this occasion with other families all over the world. For there must be others who felt the same shiver of sadness at the words "no room for them in the inn." There must me others—Miss Layton, for instance— what was she doing and thinking tonight?

Mr. Morgan finished reading and they all sat quietly a few minutes, but Andrew soon began to wiggle and ask, "When do we get our presents?"

The lights were turned on again. Mr. Morgan clapped his son on the shoulder and with a loud, "Ho, ho, ho," turned himself into Santa Claus. He went to the hall closet and lifted out two large packages. "Since you children are old enough to have a little sense your mother and I thought you'd appreciate one good present apiece instead of a lot of junk."

"That's fine with me," Jan agreed and tore open her package. It was a quilted robe, just as she had suspected, and made duster-style. She put it on and posed happily. "It's beautiful," she said. "Mother, you sew like a dream."

Her mother nodded in proud agreement. "Yes, it's a good fit," she affirmed.

"Good fit," her father said in amazement. "It doesn't have any fit or style at all. It looks like a tent. Alice, you said it was going to be the latest style."

"This is the latest style and it is pretty!"

Both women turned on him with such vehemence that he slunk over to help Andrew open his package, all the while shaking his head. Jan and her mother laughed and turned to watch Andrew set out a large and complicated mechanical building set.

"It even has a motor," Jan said as she squatted down beside him. "Look at the pictures of all the things you can build. Golly, you're lucky, Andrew. You'll have lots of fun these long winter days."

But the anticipation with which Andrew had opened his package faded away. "I don't want to build things," he protested, his voice ragged and close to tears. "I thought the package was a sled. That's what I wanted."

A quiet sadness sifted through the room. Mr. Morgan laid a hand on Andrew's shoulder but he wrenched it away. "We try to make you happy the best that we can," his mother said humbly, and Jan saw suddenly how hard it must be for her. For if Andrew *was* her favorite she would want him to like her, and very often he didn't because he couldn't understand her restrictions.

"It isn't going to be so long, old buckaroo," Mr. Morgan said gently. "You know what? I had a few words with Dr. Conners this afternoon when I was delivering packages and he said you were doing so well he was sure that when you had your next check-up you'd be healthy enough to pole vault over Barren Mountain. When that day comes we'll get you a sled then and there and hold a special celebration."

"That's a wonderful idea," Jan agreed. "I finished my Christmas shopping today with a grand total of sixty-nine cents which I hereby donate to the sled fund." She pulled the coins from her purse and handed them to her father, who bowed and said, "I accept with thanks. Andrew, you get the catalog and pick out the sled you want and it's yours the day Dr. Conners pronounces you normal."

"But I have my next check-up in May," Andrew protested. "The snow will all be gone."

"Winter is a pretty regular occurrence around here," his father comforted. "You'll really have the drop on the other kids if your sled is all ready ahead of time."

"I guess so," Andrew agreed doubtfully, but he didn't protest anymore.

"Here's my present for you," Jan said as she handed it to him. "You'll be out with the other boys some even this year so I made you some mittens to keep you warm when you throw snowballs and here's a Scout knife so you can whittle."

Andrew ignored the mittens but held the knife lovingly. "That's swell, sis, to get me something I really want. I'll take good care of it so I'll still have it when I get the rest of my Scout equipment."

"That's the idea," she agreed.

"I wish I could have gotten a present for you," he said suddenly.

"Good boy," Mr. Morgan approved. "One of these summers you can work at camp. Then you'll have money of your own." Andrew unconsciously swaggered a little at the idea that he might someday work at the lumber camp.

Mrs. Morgan had slipped out to the kitchen. She returned now carrying two additional packages. There were bright spots of color in her cheeks and she looked angry and a little afraid. She glared defiantly at her husband and daughter as she spoke. "I know we agreed to get the children one present apiece, but I felt all along that Andrew wouldn't be happy with his and after all he's a lot younger than Janice and doesn't get to go places like she does or earn money of his own, so I bought him two more gifts. He really deserved them, the poor boy."

She held the packages out to Andrew but he just stood there open-mouthed, his arms dangling at his sides, and she hurriedly began to open them up herself. "This is a clock-radio," she said, holding the pretty little plastic case out to Andrew. "You're such a sleepyhead in the mornings and you hate the alarm clock so much. Now you can just set this and wake up to music."

"Well, I'll be," Mr. Morgan said, looking as if he'd like to say something else.

"And this is an electric jigsaw. It'll be much more fun

than a Scout knife. You can make real things with it—shelves, brackets and toys. I'll show you how to work it and we'll have a good time together."

So that's why she was so cross and unreasonable to me, Jan thought with sudden, painful clarity. Mother knows this is unfair and it's been bothering her.

Trying to stop her lips from quivering, Jan glared at Andrew. But he didn't look as if he were gloating, he looked as if he didn't know what to think. Maybe a small part of his mind, the part that still belonged to the sick, cranky boy who couldn't do things, was thrilled to receive more presents than Jan and to have his mother champion him so strongly, but even before he spoke Jan realized that the biggest and best part of him wanted to be friends with his father and wanted to be fair and square like his beloved Scouts. Besides, he didn't want a clock-radio and a jigsaw. He wanted a sled, an air rifle, and some boxing gloves and a space suit.

"It's nice of you, Mom," Andrew said after a long, boiling silence. "But I don't want more than anyone else. I don't need them."

Then Jan exploded. She hated herself for the angry tears that kept spilling down her face, but this was just too much. It was the end, the ultimate, the absolute outrage. All this time she had been trying to be nicer to her mother, trying to understand her problems, and her efforts just hadn't mattered at all. "How could you?" she choked. "How could you be so unfair? You spent all that money on things Andrew doesn't need, doesn't even want, when you know how much I need a typewriter."

"What's this?" her father asked. "Do you want a typewriter?"

"I've wanted one for years. I thought you all knew that. That's why I worked so hard all summer, and I had enough money then, too, but I had to buy my own clothes for school and then I had to buy Christmas presents." She snuffled and tried to wipe her eyes but the angry tears kept coming.

"So that's how you were able to get the extra money for those gifts, Alice," he said sternly. "You make Janice pay all her own expenses. Is that being fair?"

His wife tossed her head angrily. "Fairness has nothing to do with it. Almost all the senior girls work and buy their own clothes. Why shouldn't Janice be happy to help out? And she could have saved money for her typewriter if she hadn't spent so much on candy and junk. I was telling her so just this evening."

"I bought that candy for all of us because I thought we ought to have some for Christmas," Jan protested. "It's a wonder you don't try to charge me for the air I breathe."

Suddenly Andrew began to cry, too. "I don't want them," he said. "I don't want anything."

"Here now," Mr. Morgan said swiftly. "No more crying. This isn't doing any of us any good. You children run along to bed now and forget all about this. We'll decide what's to be done later when we can be reasonable about it."

Jan was glad enough to grab her notebook and flee upstairs. For a minute she was tempted to rip off her robe and throw it out the window, but it was warm and comfortable, and in any case it was her father's gift, too.

In a minute Andrew came up, too. She heard his footsteps stop outside her door, heard him clear his throat and say uncertainly, "Good night, sis."

Although she wanted to snap at him, she managed to answer his good night gently—mean he might be, but this certainly wasn't his fault—and he went on to his room. Jan had started to get ready for bed when she was jarred again by the sound of loud, angry voices. Evidently her parents weren't waiting until they were reasonable to discuss the situation. She tried to make out the words and couldn't, so she softly opened her door and tiptoed out to the landing. A nasty, sneaky trick to eavesdrop, no doubt, but she had a right to know how things stood.

"You're going to take them back and give Janice her fair share. I've been worried about your favoritism, but I was hoping that time would cure it—that Andrew would get well and Janice be older and more amenable to your ideas. Lately I thought it was happening, but this episode—well, I don't know what to think except that we can't have it. You're going to treat both children alike if I have to quit my job and stay home to see that you do it."

"You can save your empty threats," Jan's mother replied tearfully. "I'm going to take care of my son to the best of my ability and without interference. If you had ever lived at home and been a father to the children you might have some right to dictate, but you haven't and you don't. If you had been home the day Andrew fell through the ice and could have gotten him—but no, he had to walk all the way home freezing and wet. If you had been home to help me decide when to call the doctor—I didn't know it was serious—I thought all children had earaches, and I hated to call the doctor because you grumbled so about unnecessary expense. Then when I did call him he lectured me for not doing it sooner. And all those months in bed—what do you know about them? How much help have you been?"

After a chilling pause the reply came with a heavy sigh. "You knew the kind of work I did when we were married. You knew I would be away from home most of the time. You can't wish any more than I do that I could help more with the children. I hate leaving you here alone with them. It's not what I wanted for you. I've thought of asking for a transfer to the office here in town, but if I did that I'd be a clerk all my life, and if I stick it out up at camp and do a good job I'll be in line to be manager in a few years and that will mean having things better for all of us. A more modern house, a car probably, and a chance for vacations. Remember when we used to talk about taking trips?"

"Talk!" she said venomously. "That's all our life amounts to—talking about something that may happen someday over the rainbow but probably never will. Now that you mention it, I think I will take a trip. I'll take Andrew to Seattle to see a good doctor, not a backwoods country doctor who thinks he knows all about us."

"Dr. Conners does know all about us, and when you aren't angry you know that's a good thing. I'm sure he shows more understanding of Andrew's problems and your troubles in taking care of him than any stranger possibly could. Certainly he doesn't have the suave manners most people expect doctors to have—we know how terribly outspoken he can be at times. But he is kind and competent—and available, too, which is something."

"Why can't we live in Seattle?" she asked suddenly, her mood still troubled and angry. "As long as you aren't home anyhow, what does it matter where the rest of us live? Seattle wouldn't be so much further for you to come home for the week-end—if you do want to come and see us, that is."

"Now, Alice, you're too tired to be reasonable," Jan heard her father say. "What you ought to do is go down to Seattle for a day or two all by yourself. Have a little vacation—get away from it all. Jan could manage things at home, I'm sure."

"Do you think I'd go away from Andrew?" her mother asked, horrified.

"But that's exactly what you should do," her father insisted. "Get away from all of us and get a better perspective on the family."

Suddenly Jan couldn't hear any more for the roaring in her ears. Her knees trembled and a feeling of nausea swept over her. Her mother was going away—going away and taking Andrew along. She said she wouldn't go any place without him. But she hadn't said a thing about going anywhere without Jan. She didn't want her. She would be glad of an excuse to get rid of her balky daughter.

Fighting down the panic that was threatening to make her sick, Jan tried to think of how it would be. Her dad might think that Mother was just going to Seattle for a little vacation, but once she got down there she'd look around and see if she couldn't get a job sewing, and probably she could, and she'd find a place to live that would be more convenient and comfortable than the house here and she'd put off coming back because of this excuse and that (Andrew's condition could furnish dozens of alibis), and pretty soon there just wouldn't be a Morgan family in Cascadeville any more.

In the meantime, what would her daughter do? Where could she possibly go? There was no place for her in a lumber camp with her father, and she was too young to get much of a job. Maybe Pete would help her, find her a place where she could work for her room and board and finish school. But to be lost like this—abandoned, deserted—oh, it was unbearable!

All her life she had lived secure in the knowledge that she was a member of a family unit. The least member in her mother's estimation—the kicked-around member—but still she had a place in front of the world. Now the world would see the family splitting apart with the sorrow and contempt they showed for such failures in living.

Jan had long since lost the thread of her parents' quarrel. How long they might have continued, or how many bitter arguments might have been brought up, Jan would never know—for they were interrupted by the sound of sobbing from Andrew's room.

Jan realized with dismay that he had heard it all. His room was right above the living-room, so naturally he had heard every word!

Jan ran back up the stairs and reached his room a few

seconds before her parents. He was hunched up, weeping into a soppy pillow. "Don't feel bad," she said timidly. "Everything will be all right."

"I don't want to go to Seattle and be poked at by a lot of strange doctors," he sobbed. "I'm not sick. I want to stay here and be able to have fun with the boys."

"You aren't going anywhere you don't want to go," his father said grimly. "I promise you that."

Their mother, too concerned to offer an argument, reached over to brush Andrew's hair out of the way and feel his forehead. "He's flushed," she said worriedly. "If this business makes him sick . . ."

She left the sentence unfinished while she hurriedly went to the medicine chest to find the mild sedative Dr. Conners prescribed for him. While she was preparing it and their father stood abstractedly in the doorway, Jan busily but unobtrusively washed Andrew's face, straightened his quilts, and put on a fresh pillow case.

"Don't worry," she whispered. "You know Mother always does what you want."

"Now you'll think I'm a no-good baby," he said shamefacedly as he tried to restrain his tears.

"No, I won't," Jan promised. "It makes me want to scream and howl, too, and believe me I have more at stake than you do. I stand to get left in the lurch."

Suddenly Andrew sat up. "Yeah, you complain all the time that you're low man on the totem pole around here, but everybody says you have a future and sometimes I don't think I have any future at all."

Jan was taken aback. "What do you mean?" she asked.

"You wonder why I hate school so much. Well, the main reason is that every teacher I've ever had starts right out by saying, 'My, if you are Janice Morgan's brother, we'll be expecting great things of you,' and then when I turn out to be just an ordinary thick-head they don't mind letting me know that they can't imagine how such a smart girl ever had such a dumb brother. Then I have to come straight home from school and stay in the house. I can't go outside with the other kids. Sometimes they come in and play games with me and watch TV, but it's sure not the same as if I could choose what I want to do. And you think you have things so tough when you can do practically anything you want." His voice had risen to a wail and his mother rushed in with the sedative in a glass of water.

Jan was so surprised at his words that she was incapable of replying. "Don't worry about that or anything else," their father said soothingly, patting Andrew's shoulder. "Take your medicine now and go to sleep. In fact we'll all go to sleep. When we wake up it will be Christmas morning, and that ought to make us think more clearly."

In a few minutes Andrew was drowsy and ready to slide away into peaceful sleep. Jan slipped out and went to her own room before she could be involved in any more talk.

Long after the house was quiet she sat huddled by her bedroom window, miserable and unable to stop thinking. Wasn't life a circle, though? Here she was jealous of Andrew because he was favored at home and he was jealous of her because she was respected at school. That certainly took some thinking about. It was really a sad commentary on two people, each wanting everything.

Jan sat and watched the lights go out one by one in the houses down the street and thought of the family parties that had taken place within their walls, the shared jokes and comforts. "Merry Christmas," she whispered bitterly. Burying her face in her arms, she cried quietly.

CHAPTER 12

Uneasy Peace

CHRISTMAS DAY dawned bright and clear, but the Morgan house was filled with gloom as thick and choking as fog. Mrs. Morgan crept down to the kitchen early and prepared a sumptuous breakfast—some of her canned raspberries with the taste of summer, thick slices of ham, scrambled eggs and muffins. Jan was painfully aware that her mother was ashamed of having broken one of her most adamant rules, never to quarrel in front of the children. With fancy cooking and tremulous, uneasy smiles she was trying to bribe her family into forgetting that last night's ugly scene had ever taken place.

"Aren't you tired, son?" she asked Andrew as he came downstairs tousle-headed and grumpy. "Wouldn't you like your breakfast in bed on a tray?"

"No, I don't care about breakfast on a tray or anywhere else. I want to whittle with my knife."

And indeed, when everyone was gathered around the laden table, the food went begging.

Mr. Morgan, too, tried to be cheerful. Although he couldn't manage anything but coffee, he forced a smile and said, "Wonderful breakfast, Alice."

"Better eat while you have a chance," Mrs. Morgan suggested. "It's a long time till dinner. I just put the chicken on to stew a little while ago. I hope you think fricasseed chicken is good enough for your Christmas dinner. Even if we could throw money around and buy a turkey we don't have a refrigerator to keep the left-overs."

No one answered, so she stopped talking. Jan, looking up from her plate, saw her mother's hand tremble as she lifted her coffee cup. To her further surprise, she saw tears sparkle in her eyes for a minute, then go away.

Of course Mother would be unhappy this Christmas Day. She really worked hard on holidays and liked everything to be as festive as possible. For a minute Jan felt compassion, then, remembering last night, she hardened. There was nothing to feel sorry about. Mother was only reaping the bitter harvest of her own unfairness. Ostentatiously Jan pushed away her half-empty plate, excused herself, took a book, and sat down. She wasn't going to volunteer to do a thing. If Mother wanted her to help she could jolly well come and get her.

But her mother didn't disturb Jan. She cleared the table and did the dishes alone. Then she stayed out in the kitchen working on the dinner.

Andrew found a stick of wood and began to whittle. When his mother finally came in from the kitchen, her face flushed from the heat of the stove, she found the living-room floor covered with shavings. "All over my clean floor," she said angrily. "And the rest of you just sat here and let him do it. I knew that knife was going to be nothing but trouble." Tight-lipped, she brought the broom and dustpan and swept up the floor.

"Come on, son, let's try it over here." His father put down his magazine and steered Andrew over to the hearth, where the shavings would go right into the fireplace.

"I'm going to make a boat," Andrew announced.

"That's fine," his father agreed. "I'll show you how to shape the bow."

Jan closed her book, went upstairs, and stared moodily out of her window. Nothing more was said or even hinted about a move to Seattle but she could not feel that the threat was gone. It seemed to her that behind the bright lights of the Chrismas tree, beyond the surface picture of a family working together, it was like a stealthy tiger, waiting to pounce and devour.

Presently her mother rapped abruptly on the door and said, "Time to get ready for church." Jan was surprised. She had forgotten all about the traditional service held every Christmas mid-morning. It was a good thing she had been too busy to sing in the choir this year—the way she felt right now would sour-note the whole performance.

The family walked to church silently, unspoken tensions and angers almost crackling the air between them. Would this be the last time they would appear together as a family, Jan wondered as they walked up the church steps while the bells pealed out overhead. "Peace on earth, good will to men." A fine idea, she thought, and like charity it should begin at home.

As they took their seats Jan saw Danny across the aisle. He grinned at her and twirled his key chain. Sitting beside him was a remarkably pretty girl. Jan frowned. She had seen that young lady somewhere, sometime. What was she doing here with Danny? Did he have a secret life?

Jan took another, furtive look at the girl. She was adjusting a knitted pixie cap that kept threatening to slip off her springy blond curls. She turned to Danny, giggled and batted her lashes. Jan found it hard to concentrate on the service.

Afterwards the parents hurried home to see to the Christmas dinner, but the young people took their time, jiggling up and down in the frosty air, throwing an occasional snowball and talking excitedly about the "loot" under the tree and plans for the remaining week of vacation.

Danny and the blond girl came up to Jan. "Thanks for the slippers," she said quickly. "You shouldn't have given me such a magnificent present."

"Strictly self-interest," he replied. "If your feet are warm you aren't going to be so rough on your poor associates." He turned to the girl beside him. "Jan, do you remember Maybelle Warren from Bayside? She's spending the holidays with us."

"I knew I had seen you somewhere before," Jan replied truthfully and she hoped cordially. Memories came fast now of the afternoon at Bayside and Maybelle Warren, the *Barnacle* society editor, laughing and dimpling at all the boys. She remembered, too, Danny's saying that the Warrens had wanted him to stay in Seattle and live with them. Apparently they were all a closed corporation.

Maybelle laughed and dimpled now. "I'm recuperating from the 'flu," she explained. "Mother Mallory thought some mountain air would be good for me. It's wonderfully bracing here."

Mother Mallory, huh? Well, she didn't need a diagram. Danny wasn't so special after all. He might be an understanding comrade to her, but it was a dizzy blonde he really wanted. Or maybe he was one of those spineless characters who were content to let their parents arrange their lives for them. In either case she was glad she hadn't wasted many approving sentiments on him.

Andrew, who had been listening to the introduction, shook his head and said, "Wow, I didn't know newspapers grew them so beautiful! I thought they were all creeps like sis."

"Creep yourself," Danny said swiftly, giving Andrew a blow on the shoulders that sent him spinning.

Evidently last night's spell of wanting friendship and understanding, of intimating that there were aspects of her life that he envied as much as she envied his life, was all over. It had been as brief and cold as a day of winter sunshine. Andrew was being his habitual obnoxious self again and Jan gave him a murderous scowl. Maybelle laughed and

said happily, "You mustn't talk that way. Your sister is awfully smart. Everybody says so."

Cradle robber, Jan thought disdainfully. Even has to practice her charms on Andrew. "I'm sure our bracing air is just
what you need," she said coldly, but Maybelle didn't hear
her. She was flirting with someone else.

Danny maneuvered Jan aside. "I was certainly surprised
when Maybelle turned up this morning," he said hastily.
"Our folks have been friends for years and she's had a bad
time and needs a change of scene. You understand, don't
you?"

"Understand?" Jan asked with an artificial lilt to her voice.
"Why, Danny, it's a free country. You can entertain Marilyn
Monroe if you like."

"I'd like, but I doubt if she would," he replied, unperturbed. "However, I've been pondering this square-dance
party at Dotty's. I wanted to call you as soon as Dotty told me
her plans, but I didn't want to disturb your Christmas Eve,
and I knew I would see you this morning. I suppose I'll have
to be a good host and take Maybelle, so why don't I get Carl
Graves to take you? It'll do the old hermit good to get jolted
out of his cave for once."

Shame and anger churned through her. Did he think she
was a geisha girl to be auctioned off to some poor sucker who
couldn't get out of taking her to a party? And did he just
naturally assume that any half-hearted invitation just any
old time would have her jumping with joy?

"Thanks for your kind efforts," she said sarcastically. "But
you don't have to call out the shock troops. I'm going to be
working, baby-sitting, that night. I told Dotty she shouldn't
go around automatically pairing off people, that who you
wanted to take was entirely your own business and you
shouldn't have felt responsible for me at all."

"Well, shucks. I was finding responsibility for you most in-
triguing." To her surprise Danny looked disappointed. She

supposed it delighted his ego to think there would be two
girls competing for him. Well, he would have to find some
other form of indoor recreation, because she just wasn't going to take any interest in fickle-minded boys.

When Jan and Andrew got back home they found dinner
on the table and because of the morning's unhappy fast they
ate hungrily, although the table conversation was still sparse
and cheerless. A few words about how good the choir had
been this year, a remark about the new clothes on exhibition
—and then uneasy silence.

As she rose to serve the pies her mother remarked, "Janice, you certainly haven't spent any time helping me today."

"I'll clear up and do the dishes," Jan offered. That was
only justice.

"And I'll help," her father said emphatically. "You just
settle down in an easy chair with a good book or the TV for
the afternoon."

When they were alone in the kitchen, with the door to
the living-room half shut and Christmas music on television
furnishing sufficient diversion, her father talked to her in
confidence. "Mother and I had a chance to talk things over
on the way home from church," he explained. "And I think
we came to a calm and sensible agreement about those extra
toys. The jigsaw we will keep. It's a handy tool and if we
learn to use it correctly we can all enjoy having it.

"The clock-radio, though it's very cute, isn't necessary and
it will go back. The money from it is to be applied to your
typewriter."

Jan looked up from the dishpan in amazement. If Dad had
wangled that big a concession from Mother he was wasting
his talents up here in the mountains. He should be at the
United Nations. "That's wonderful of you," she told him.

"Mother wants it as much as I do, Janice," he said. "She
wants both of you children to be contented. She doesn't mean
to be unfair. If she seems that way at times you're old enough

and smart enough to understand that she has too much
worry."

"But," she asked bluntly, "what if she goes away?"

"I wish she would if she'd go by herself and get some rest.
But she won't leave you children, and that's that. Janice, you
have an active imagination, and I know what you're thinking, but surely you can see that if your mother is so conscien-
tious she won't leave Andrew long enough to have a little
vacation, she wouldn't be the type to break up a home."

"But she said . . ."

"Haven't you ever said hard things in the heat of anger?"
he asked. "Haven't you ever wanted to run away from life
the way it is? Haven't you dreamed about going away to
school where everyone would like you, nobody would be unfair, and they'd publish newspapers every day and twice on
Sunday?"

"Oh, Dad!" she said softly as understanding came to her.
The thing that was so hard to remember was that parents
were people, too. Actually her mother was only twenty years
older than she was. And she certainly wasn't old enough to
like having all her dreams fade away.

"Now it's up to all of us to convince Mother that running
off and trying something new wouldn't solve anything. Andrew doesn't want to go and that will weigh heavily with her.
But you let her know that you need her and love her, too,
Janice. Sometimes you seem so grown-up and independent it
would be easy for a mother to think her job was about over
with you."

"I could try," she agreed, staring reflectively out the window as she scrubbed a pan.

"I'm going to try, too." Her father put a stack of plates in
the cupboard and turned to smile at her.

"If your mother has made any errors in her treatment of
me it's that she's erred on the good side. When I come home
week-ends she tries to treat me like an honored guest and

doesn't mention the problems she's been facing all alone all week because she wants me to enjoy my little time at home. From now on I'm going to be a problem sleuth and ferret them out and try to take on more of the burdens."

"Oh, Dad," Jan said again. She felt immensely comforted. Then she turned to him excitedly. "Dad, you take part of that typewriter money and get Andrew his sled right away. It doesn't matter if I have to wait a little longer. But if Andrew has his sled, even though he can only use it under strict supervision, wild horses couldn't get him off this snowy mountain and down to where they only have a week of snow every three or four years."

Her father laughed. "Janice, you ought to be a horse-trader. We'll do just that. Only I think I'll wait a few days. Sometimes there are good bargains in the January sales."

"I won't say I'm happy, but I do feel lots better," Jan decided, then she remembered the morning's encounter with Danny and her spirits sagged again.

"What now?" he asked ruefully.

"Hum," was all he replied after Jan, embarrassed, had told him about it.

"One little 'hum' means you think I didn't behave right," she said tartly.

"I'll let you think that one over by yourself," he replied. "But if worst comes to worst, maybe I could find you a job shoveling snow on New Year's Eve—just so your conscience will be clear."

Jan sniffed and emptied the dishpan. But she still wished she hadn't been imprudent enough to commit herself to a job that she didn't have; in a town the size of Cascadeville it would be almost impossible to get away with any such pretense.

During the next few days she kept her ear and eye constantly on the phone. Surely there was someone who needed a baby-sitter. She knew she simply couldn't go back to school if the gang ever found out the truth.

Finally Mrs. Preston called. "Don't suppose there's a chance in the world you're free tomorrow night?" she asked.

Jan's reply, "Yes, I am," was received with joy.

"That's grand! I didn't think there would be a chance in the world. Look, I'd have called before but I didn't know whether John would get home in time. Well, he made it and we're invited to this fabulous party in Seattle. We'll probably stay all night because of the roads. Can you manage?"

"I'm sure I can," Jan affirmed. She turned from the phone and the first thing that met her eye was Andrew's building set and jigsaw tumbled into a corner, dusty and unused.

Andrew spent all the time he could wangle out-of-doors watching the other boys slide and skate and bragging about his prospective sled. Indoors he whittled, leaving a trail of shavings behind him that greatly annoyed his mother. Jan kicked at the box holding the building set and said moodily, "I'm never going to buy anything for anybody again. I'll save all my money for things I want."

Her mother leaned out of the kitchen with an unhappy sigh. "Since you evidently begrudge your poor brother a few comforts, you can take back that fancy material you bought for me and keep the money. It's very pretty but I don't have any occasion to wear a party dress. I don't go out anywhere."

"I can't take it back," Jan explained. "Mrs. Abbott got it at some special place for me. Besides, I wanted you to have a dress-up dress so you could go to parties and forget about Andrew for ten minutes."

"You don't understand how a mother feels," Mrs. Morgan said sadly.

"No, and I don't intend to find out," Jan retorted. "If I ever should have a boy I'll leave him on the orphanage doorstep."

She banged the door and went out before her mother could reply, and headed for the *Courier* office.

Pete had his feet up on the desk, bright Argyles very much in evidence. "I can't stand the awful things," he commented. "They keep me awake afternoons."

Jan knew that was an invitation to an argument, but she didn't feel up to it, so she just smiled sadly and sat in silence awhile.

"How come you aren't with that mob of monsters?" Pete asked presently. "They tore in here like a plague of grasshoppers awhile ago. When they left they were heading first to the drugstore for hot-fudge sundaes, then to the pond to skate."

"They are a mob—and I don't want to be with them," Jan replied. Then before Pete could dispense some of the unwelcome advice to the lovelorn that she saw welling up in him, she abruptly said good-by and left.

Pete was showing his usual ability to make her uncomfortable. Her family was not her only grief during this miserable vacation. There was Maybelle, too. For someone who came to Cascadeville for a rest she was behaving in a strange manner. She was all over town, day and night, with a laughing crowd in tow.

At first they had tried to include Jan in their expeditions, but as Cassie so aptly phrased it, she acted as if she'd crawled into the freezer chest and pulled down the lid.

For instance, there had been the day that Cassie, smartly dressed in a dark-red ski suit that set off her brunette curls, came noisily into the Morgan house. "Get your nose out of there," she commanded, jerking the history book from Jan's hand. "Rise and shine."

Out in the street was a station wagon loaded almost beyond belief with the Cascadeville younger set. "We're going for a ride on the Barren Mountain ski lift. It's fun whether you ski or not, and furthermore you're coming. You can't work all the time."

"Well . . ." Jan hesitated, but she was tempted. She had long wanted to ride the ski lift. "I'm supposed to type up some club notices for Mrs. Abbott this afternoon."

"Do them tonight," Cassie said. "And now go hop into your slacks."

"Yes, go ahead. I'll call Mrs. Abbott and explain," her mother encouraged.

Jan started for the stairs, then glanced out the window again. Maybelle, who was sitting on Danny's lap, leaned out and waved. Then she said something and everyone laughed.

A spasm of pain nearly crumpled Jan. She turned to face Cassie. "I'm not going," she said, spitting out the words. "When I promise to do a job, I do it. Good-by."

She pulled open the door. Cassie blinked in surprise, shrugged, said, "It's your funeral," added the remark about the freezer chest, and left. A minute later the station wagon pulled away.

"Whatever possessed you to act like that?" her mother asked angrily. "Don't you have any manners at all?"

"I'm going over to the Abbotts' and start work right away," Jan declared as she went for her coat. "I'm going to earn some money this afternoon."

"Money isn't everything," her mother said.

"It's just about everything," Jan retorted. "At least it is if you live in this house and don't have any."

On New Year's Eve, Jan walked over to the Prestons' carrying her overnight bag. She wouldn't be back till late tomorrow afternoon, and the day after that school would start. Maybe then she would be so busy she would forget about this nightmarish holiday week. She would never feel the same about Danny again, though. It had been so wonderful to have someone like her for what she was. But he couldn't have liked her very much or he wouldn't run off with Maybelle. No, she must resign herself to the fact that no one in the world would ever like her more than all the rest.

As she passed Dotty's brightly lighted house she turned her eyes away, but her ears couldn't escape, and on the air came the blare of music. A twangy voice called out, "Oh, Allemande left with your left hand and a right to your partner and a right and left grand . . ."

Someone shrieked, "Turn it down!" and the blatant music faded. Jan hurried on down the street.

CHAPTER 13

A Cry in the Night

MRS. PRESTON glided across the room to open the door for Jan, then sailed away again, swishing around the floor, her long silk skirts drifting behind her, her dark hair brushing against her smooth, bare shoulders and her face alight with that special party look. "How about it, Jan?" she asked. "Do I look like a country cousin from the old hick town?"

"Wow, oh, wow," Jan replied in spontaneous admiration. Mrs. Preston was more glamourous than most of the girls Jan saw on television. It was small wonder she felt buried up here behind the mountains. She told Mrs. Preston that with enthusiasm.

She laughed and whirled around again. "Thanks, dear. But wait till you see my stole. John gave it to me for Christmas." She glided out of the room and reappeared with the soft, dark fur wrapped around her shoulders.

"Oh, my!" Words failed Jan but her open-mouthed appreciation seemed to be compliment enough.

Mr. Preston appeared in the doorway buttoning his coat, but unlike his wife he didn't seem a bit eager to go to a party. Ignoring Jan, as usual, he said to his wife, "Better wear a sensible coat, it's cold tonight."

"Nonsense, I wouldn't dream of not wearing my fur. Oh, how I'll gloat over those overstuffed frumps."

"They'll do the gloating if you catch pneumonia."

"Silly, why does the car have a heater? But I'll wear my coat en route if you'll quit grouching."

"I'm not grouching. But I don't feel like going to a party when Johnny is sick, and I don't see why I should pretend anything else. I can't imagine why you would consent to go. I always thought mothers cared more for their children's well-being than for a chance to show off some new clothes."

"You know-it-all men are such fuss-budgets," Mrs. Preston said sharply to him. "You're around home so seldom you don't know how trifling children's upsets can be. If I stayed home every time Johnny had a runny nose I wouldn't get my face out the door all winter."

She laid an arm on Jan's shoulder. "Jan will take better care of him than I would if I were at home anyhow."

"I don't doubt it," Mr. Preston said sarcastically. He stamped out the door and a minute later the car motor started.

Mrs. Preston shrugged. "Men!" she said. "Well, come on, Jan, I'll brief you on the situation."

They went into Johnny's room and Mrs. Preston turned on the star-shaped night light. "He's had a sore throat today and been cranky. I don't think it's his tonsils. Colds often start with a sore throat—at least mine do. If he wakes up and fusses give him half an aspirin."

"All right," Jan agreed.

Mrs. Preston might have said more, but the horn sounded imperiously. "Oh, that character," she said with a sigh. "First he won't go and now he won't give me time to get ready. Well, I'm not going to go get my coat now. That will show him. Take it easy, Jan. We'll be back sometime tomorrow forenoon."

She pulled the stole around her shoulders and clattered down the steps.

After the car drove away Jan took a closer look at Johnny. He was warm and breathing heavily. She touched his neck and he whimpered. Swollen glands, evidently. Well, a sore throat could cause that right enough. She placed the aspirins and water by his bed, then found the vaporizer and readied it for operation, just in case. He'd had croup once before when she had been staying with him and that was what she had used to relieve him.

She read for a while but the house was too quiet and she imagined she could hear noise and gaiety down the street. At eleven she closed her book. If she went to bed now she'd be asleep when the bells rang and the whistles blew and the people who didn't have anything better to do than go to parties started to make fools of themselves. Just as she was leaving the room the phone rang. It was Mrs. Preston calling from Seattle. "Everything all right with Johnny?" she asked.

Jan didn't know what to say. She didn't think things were right by any means, but she didn't have anything but her own worry to guide her and if she hauled Mrs. Preston home from a party for, as she would put it, a little cold, she would be off her list but good. "He seems feverish and uncomfortable," she said finally. "But he's sound asleep. He hasn't fussed at all."

Mrs. Preston didn't respond to the worry in her voice. "That's fine," she said heartily. "A long sleep is what he needs. I knew I could depend on you. Good-by, dear." She hung up.

Jan tiptoed into Johnny's room. Although still asleep he was tossing restlessly. She reached for the aspirin, then dropped her hand. Better not to wake him. But just in case, she wouldn't prepare for bed herself. She kicked off her shoes, settled onto the day-bed in his room, and went to sleep.

She hadn't been able to go to sleep before the noise started after all, because here it was filling the room. But she didn't want to hear all the silly people making a racket so she turned her head and pulled the blanket over her ears. The noise wouldn't go away though, and it was strange because the people weren't laughing and shouting "Happy New Year"—they were crying. Crying, coughing, and sobbing, "Mommy, mommy, mommy!"

As comprehension drove out sleepiness Jan was up and

over to Johnny's crib. She snapped on the overhead light. He lay in a sodden heap, red-faced and choking.

She grabbed the flashlight from the stand and pried open his mouth. His throat was an ugly patchwork of heavy red and gray phlegm. "Mommy," he choked and stiffened, coughing desperately, shaking his head in an effort to cough up the encroaching phlegm.

Terrified, Jan dropped the flashlight, grabbed Johnny, and held him against her, rocking back and forth. "Baby, baby," she whispered in anguish, tears filling her eyes. "What will I do?"

Finally the coughing stopped and Johnny relaxed, sagging down against her shoulder with a little moan.

Afraid to put him down, she wrapped a blanket around him and carried him with her out to the telephone, where she gave her home number in a shaky voice. After a long, long time her mother answered. "Johnny's sick," she said without preamble. "He's coughing and choking."

"Janice, it's two-thirty in the morning. If you go baby-sitting you're supposed to know how to take care of children. It sounds like croup. Give him half an aspirin and steam him awhile."

"No, no, it's worse than croup," she protested. "His throat is all red and gray and he's feverish."

Johnny stiffened again and coughed, the paroxysms shaking his body. Then he sobbed plaintively, his eyes half-open and glazed with pain. "Oh, mother," Jan pleaded, "what can I do?"

"Oh, my goodness, he sounds terrible. I'm going to call Dr. Conners right away." Mrs. Morgan sounded suddenly scared. "The idea of going off and leaving a child that sick! Why, it almost sounds like diphtheria, except that children don't have it any more. They get shots for it. Try to keep him warm and comfortable till the doctor comes."

Still carrying Johnny, Jan walked over and switched on

the porch light. Then she began to pace up and down with him while she worried about taking care of him and worried about Dr. Conners, Melanie's grandfather, who was getting old and apt to be awfully cross about night calls. She would have to phone the Prestons, of course, but maybe it would be better if the doctor talked to them himself.

She went to the hall to find the telephone number Mrs. Preston always left. The pad was blank and for a minute she thought her tired eyes were not focussing. Then she remembered, horrified, that Mr. Preston had honked his horn impatiently and Mrs. Preston had run out to the car in a hurry. She had forgotten to give Jan the necessary information, and had forgotten it again when she called from Seattle. If only she had noticed and asked, Jan mourned.

The doctor arrived in twenty minutes, but to Jan, her arms aching from the weight of the baby and her heart in her mouth with every racking cough, it was an eternity. He came in rumpled and cross—cross that is until he looked at Johnny's throat. Jan saw his face turn grave, heard the quick intake of his breath. Then he grabbed the phone and called the hospital. "Antitoxin," he ordered, "and fast."

"Is—is it really diphtheria, doctor?"

"Yes. First case I've seen in years, but you never forget it. We'll pump him full of antitoxin in a few minutes and throw in some penicillin for good measure and I think he'll be all right. Better get hold of his parents." He was rummaging in his bag for a hypodermic needle.

Jan started to explain her predicament, but just then the messenger from the hospital arrived. Jan quickly took the stuff to Dr. Conners and helped him hold Johnny, who with what little strength he had was fighting against the shots.

When the doctor began to put things back in his bag she blurted out, "I can't locate his parents. They went to a party in Seattle and won't be back till tomorrow. What shall I do?"

The doctor's eyes snapped with anger. Finally he let out

a long, disgusted snort. "This didn't need to happen," he said sternly. "There's no reason in the world for a child to have diphtheria in this day in this town. Gone to Seattle are they, but they couldn't take time to have their baby immunized. They couldn't stay home from a party when he was sick. What kind of parents are they breeding nowadays? Well, can you get somebody to help you? This isn't any job for a young kid."

"I'm more mature than you think," Jan said, but she really didn't want to stay alone. "I'll call Mother," she decided.

Her mother answered on the first ring. She hadn't gone back to bed, but was sitting waiting. "What did the doctor say?" she asked. "Is it diphtheria?"

"Yes, it is," Jan replied. "He's terribly sick and I can't locate the Prestons and . . ."

"Oh, Janice, how awful," her mother interrupted. "Now you had better see that you're protected. You had shots when you were a baby and a booster shot the time they gave them at school, but that's been a long time ago and you may need another by now. Dr. Conners will know. I'm sure he doesn't want any more cases. It can be deadly."

"I'll worry about that later," Jan said. "Right now I want to know if you can come over and help me. You know I don't know much about nursing."

Mrs. Morgan sighed. "Janice, I know it's terrible for you to have to be there alone. It's nothing for a young girl to have to endure, but I can't come. Dr. Conners should understand that. I haven't had either the disease or the immunization and I'd be wide open to getting a first-class case, which wouldn't help you or anyone else. And at best I'd be quarantined right along with you and here would be your dad and Andrew all alone with no one to take care of them. Then if Dad should be called back to work where would Andrew be? Surely the doctor can find someone else."

"That would be a mess," Jan had to admit. "Well, we'll just have to get along the best we can."

"I'll stay up," her mother offered. "I'll be right here at the phone with my home nursing book, so you can call any time you need to know something. Maybe that would help a little."

"Oh, don't do that, Mother. No need of you losing your sleep. I'm sure Dr. Conners will tell me everything I need to know. And I'd better get back there pronto, so I'll hang up now."

"I won't be able to sleep anyhow," she said. "You call if I can help."

Jan went back to Johnny's room and reported her failure to the doctor, who said firmly, "Then you'll have to be it. With the medication I've given him he should sleep for a while but you stay right by him in case he starts to choke. These are sterile swabs. Use them to help pull the phlegm from his throat."

"Oh, I couldn't," Jan protested, her hands trembling at the thought.

"You must," the doctor replied with such sternness that she pulled herself together. "He may cough it up himself, or he may sleep and not cough at all, but you must be prepared."

"He is going to get well, isn't he?" she asked fearfully.

"I have every hope for him, but we can't take chances."

"I'll stay awake," she promised. "I'll watch him every minute."

"You're a good girl," he said. "I'll be back in the morning." Then he glanced at the clock and grinned. "I mean later this morning. Fine way to start the New Year."

Working gently, Jan changed Johnny into clean sleepers, smoothed out his bed, and gave him his panda bear. He was quiet and drowsy. He coughed and she reached for the swabs, but then he dropped into an uneasy, hard-breathing sleep.

Jan was terribly tired and sleepy. At first she tried to stay awake by reciting poetry but all she could think of was "Tomorrow and tomorrow," which only made her feel drearier. Then, remembering what she had heard about coffee, she slipped out to the kitchen and made some, and carried it back to Johnny's room and drank it. It was miserable-tasting stuff and she couldn't imagine why people liked it so well, but it did seem to work. She felt much more alert.

As she watched Johnny in a fever of anxiety she began thinking of the differences in people. Of Mrs. Preston, who would leave her sick son with only a fleeting backwards glimpse, and of her own mother who would sit up all night by the phone just in case she could be helpful. Jan wished she could call and tell her that everything was going, in that time-honored expression, "as well as could be expected," but she didn't want to leave Johnny for that long.

She had always felt that her mother fussed and fluttered around Andrew too much, took his illness too seriously. Maybe she hadn't after all. Maybe it had been her constant nagging care that had brought Andrew out of his sickness successfully. She could see now that good nursing could literally mean the difference between life and death. It was too bad no one had explained those things to her a long time ago.

Just at daybreak, at the dawning of the New Year if you wanted to get poetic, which Jan didn't, Johnny had a choking spell. Some of the phlegm had torn loose. Quietly and without fear she took the swabs and pulled it out. The spots where the membrane had torn loose from the throat were raw and bleeding and Johnny moaned with pain. She held him and walked the floor, trying to soothe him and ease his misery.

When Dr. Conners came back shortly before noon she was nearly swaying with weariness but happy because Johnny was better. Filling up his hypodermic needle, Dr. Conners said impressively, "A generation ago he might not have made it. Small wonder we call them miracle drugs."

Johnny didn't share their enthusiasm. The shots hurt.

"Has he had anything to eat?" the doctor asked.

"I tried to give him some fruit juice but his throat is too sore."

"Ice cream would be good for you, young fellow. I'll run out and get some. You can't go, you're quarantined."

Just as he reached the door the Prestons drove into the garage. Mrs. Preston, still in her long dress and stole, came daintily up the walk until she noticed the doctor's car. "Johnny!" she screamed, and ran frantically towards the house, ripping the hem of her dress in her hurry.

Mr. Preston slammed the car door and rushed in right behind her. "What's wrong?" they asked anxiously.

Mrs. Preston reached out her arms for Johnny, but the doctor waved her away. "He has diphtheria," he said sternly.

"I knew he was sick," Mr. Preston accused in cold anger, "and you said I was a fuss-budget."

"But he wasn't sick when we left. Just a little feverish and cranky." Her eyes appealed to Dr. Conners.

"All children's diseases start that way," he said harshly. "You should never take a chance that it doesn't mean anything. Early treatment is always of the utmost importance."

"Shouldn't he be in the hospital?" Mr. Preston asked anxiously.

Dr. Conners shook his head. "It's best for children to stay at home. They recover much faster in familiar surroundings. Besides, you know our little hospital isn't equipped for isolation cases."

Dr. Conners face darkened and he spoke with the authority that came from living in a small town for forty years and bringing two generations into the world. "What I want to know is why you didn't have him immunized? Why didn't he have the shots to protect him from diphtheria?"

"Didn't he?" Mr. Preston shouted, amazed and horrified.

There were two bright spots of color in Mrs. Preston's face. "I didn't realize it was that important," she protested. "No one around here ever has diphtheria or whooping cough or diseases like that. It's such a chore to take Johnny anywhere. He's so heavy and wiggles so much that I just didn't have the strength to take him up to your office and wait around goodness knows how long for a shot."

"I'm sorry your baby is so much trouble," Dr. Conners said. "Maybe I shouldn't have interfered. If I had just let nature take its course you probably wouldn't have to worry about his wiggles any more."

It took a minute for his bitter sarcasm to penetrate. Then Mrs. Preston gasped and knelt by Johnny's bed. He opened his eyes. "Mommy," he whispered, and tried to move towards her. "Mommy, I hurt."

"Johnny baby," she said, and burst into tears.

"Dry up, dry up," the doctor advised abruptly. "We're going to pull him through." He turned to Jan proudly. "Here is a little girl who's dead on her feet from staying up all night taking care of Johnny. How about seeing that she gets some rest. I'll stay here while you get her fixed up and change into something more suitable for a sickroom than that outfit."

Mrs. Preston turned to Jan, her eyes glittering with re-morseful tears. "We'll never be able to thank you enough."

Jan smiled and brushed back her hair. She was so tired she felt like all her muscles were operating on squeaky hinges. "I was scared stiff," she admitted. "But I'm so glad I was able to help. In a way it makes Johnny my baby, too."

Mrs. Preston put an arm around Jan and said, "Come on. I'll tuck you in before I change."

They walked upstairs together. Mrs. Preston opened the door of her dainty guest room and gasped in surprise at the unrumpled bed. "You didn't go to bed at all last night," she said.

"No, I was worried about Johnny so I just slept in his room," Jan explained.

As soon as the covers were turned back Jan crawled in and sighed contentedly. "I could sleep for a week."

"Go right ahead," Mrs. Preston suggested as she lowered the blinds. "I don't know what the quarantine laws are these days but I suspect we're in for quite a stretch."

Jan sat up abruptly. To be sure the doctor and her mother had both talked about quarantine, but she had been so busy and so frightened the implications just hadn't penetrated. "School starts tomorrow," she protested.

"Not for you it doesn't." Mrs. Preston didn't seem very perturbed. "Don't worry, Jan. A few days, even a few weeks won't make a dent in your scholastic record."

"Oh, grades—they don't matter, I don't care. It's the *Argus!*" Weariness and panic blended together to make Jan feel and sound incoherent. "Now Danny will have the chance Miss Layton always wanted for him. He'll be editor all by himself and he'll be so good that they won't care if I ever come back. He'll wow them. He'll be terrific. I've always been so afraid they would find out he's better than I am . . ."

She started to get up but Mrs. Preston pushed her back into bed. "You're so tired you have battle fatigue. I'd better have the doctor give you a pill."

Jan came to her senses, faced the inevitable, and lay down. "I'll go to sleep," she promised.

There was nothing she could do, Jan reflected in the last split-second before sleep overtook her. Events had been taken out of her hands. Well, it would be a new experience to quit scheming and jockeying for position, to turn off her motor and coast down the hill. "Kismet," she said, and buried her face in the pillow.

CHAPTER 14

Quarantine

RAYS OF PALE WINTER SUNSHINE were slanting through the windows when Jan woke up again. After a long, relaxing stretch she glanced at the bedside clock and sat up in surprise. Only three o'clock! It had been past two when she closed her eyes, and yet she felt so rested.

Embarrassment and alarm flooded through her as she realized that it must be three o'clock tomorrow. She had slept the clock around, snoring away uselessly while Johnny was sick and her help needed. She dressed, hurriedly tied her hair into a pony tail, and went downstairs.

Johnny was better, his breathing easier. "He isn't coughing much at all now," Mrs. Preston explained. "Dr. Conners says the antitoxin makes the membrane dissolve. But we must see that he rests quietly so he doesn't have a relapse or any complications."

To Jan's scrutinizing eyes Mrs. Preston looked different. It wasn't just the dark splotches of weariness under her eyes, either. She looked as if she had finally realized there was a world beyond the small circle of her desires. She looked as if at last Johnny was truly her son. Birth was more than a physical process, Jan thought. It had to happen in the heart, too.

"Why didn't you wake me this morning?" she asked. "I wanted to help."

"You needed your rest, dear. John and I took turns with

Johnny and managed fine. And for all we know Dr. Conners sneaked in some knock-out drops along with your shot."

"With my what?" Jan asked.

"Yes, you're reimmunized. Last night he went up and gave you a booster shot so you wouldn't have to worry about catching this bug. You didn't quiver a muscle."

"Imagine that," Jan said in amazement. Sure enough, there was a sore spot on her right arm. "I must admit that's a relief," she admitted. "I can't remember when I had my last booster shot and I was starting to have visions of being out of school the rest of the year. Did Dr. Conners say how long we'll be quarantined?"

"It depends on how fast Johnny recovers. They take throat swabs and after three in a row are negative they admit he's cured and open the gates. By the way, the doctor will be over this evening and he's going to stop at your house for a suitcase. Your mother is getting some things together for you. She called several times yesterday to see if you were all right and not showing any suspicious symptoms. She was so relieved when I was able to tell her you'd had a booster shot and were sleeping like a log."

"I'm glad about the clothes. I'm beginning to feel grimy," Jan said. "Mother is a terrific worry-wart about health. I'd better let her know I'm my same old alive, disagreeable self."

"Come have breakfast first or you might keel over by the phone and then she would have something to fret about. It's all right to leave Johnny. We can hear from the kitchen."

"Can't you just tell me what to fix?" Jan asked. "I don't want to be any bother while I'm here."

"No bother at all," Mrs. Preston said firmly. "You're part of the family now."

While Jan was consuming her brunch Mrs. Preston made a cup of coffee and sat down with her. Mr. Preston's whereabouts were indicated by a banging and sawing in the basement. Presently he clattered up the stairs and thrust his head through the door. "Where's the wood glue?" he asked. "I'm sure I left it in the cupboard."

"If you did it's still there because I assure you I haven't been using it." Mrs. Preston rummaged through the cupboard, found the bottle, and handed it to him.

"Right in front of me. Good thing it wasn't a sidewinder. Well, hello—so Rip Van Winkle finally woke up." He walked over to Jan, patted her shoulder, and gave her a warm, friendly smile. "How's our heroine today?"

Jan almost said, "Who me?" It was startling to be noticed by Mr. Preston, who had always acted as if she were part of the furniture. "I'm O.K.," she said finally, as he stood there smiling and expecting an answer.

"That's good. We'll have to try and think up some sort of entertainment for you while we're all confined to quarters."

"Cup of coffee, John?" Mrs. Preston invited.

"No, thanks. I'd like to finish these toy shelves so they'll be ready to put in Johnny's room when he's able to be up a little. I'll see you later."

Something had happened to Mr. Preston, too. While Jan had been asleep they had evidently gone through one of those noisy crises married couples seemed to have every so often—the accusations, threats, and bitter words giving way eventually to apologies, mutual forgiveness, and pledges to do better in the future. Maybe the Prestons would make good on their promises. Maybe she wouldn't dash from one party to another, bitter and restless if she had to stay home. Maybe he wouldn't be so fiercely ambitious, so ready to sacrifice his family life to getting ahead in business.

Jan could see they were trying now, and her heart warmed towards them. How she wished something would happen to make her father and mother pull together again—something short of her getting diphtheria of course. That would just make her mother furious. And that reminded her that she had better make her call.

She called her number, assuring the operator that she felt
fine. Andrew answered. "Oh, it's Typhoid Mary," he said
jovially. "I see you're still alive, worse luck. How are all the
little germs?"

"Sorry to disappoint you but I'm probably going to survive," she returned tartly.

"Ah, well, we can't all have everything and I have my sled.
Dad got it this morning."

"That's nice, but what are you doing in the house in that
case?"

"You would ask that." Andrew sounded embarrassed. "I
was zooming down that hill by River Road and I guess I
didn't rightly know how to steer. Anyhow, I went right into
a snowbank. And I didn't know Dad was spying on me,
either, but he was and he jerked me home and Mom had my
clothes hung up to dry before I could even think about
sneezing. She's upstairs now packing your suitcase. Do you
want me to call her?"

"Never mind, thanks. Just tell her I called, I'm fine, and
I'll talk to her later."

Jan had barely put the phone down before it rang. "Probably your dream boat again," Mrs. Preston said as she picked
it up. "He's been calling every hour on the hour. That's the
way to have them, right on a ball and chain."

"I don't have any dream boat," Jan protested indignantly,
but Mrs. Preston didn't pay any attention.

"Hello. Yes, your vigil is rewarded. She's up and feeling
fine, but be careful and don't breathe your sweet nothings
too deeply. They say these germs are very contagious." She
grinned and handed Jan the phone.

"Hello, Danny," Jan said coldly.

"Hello, you schmoo." Danny's voice was derisive and it
didn't take television for her to see the look of amusement
on his face. "I know school is rough, but exposing yourself

to diphtheria just to get more vacation is doing it the hard way."

"I didn't think of that when I sneaked up to the hospital and swiped the culture out of the lab," she retorted.

Mrs. Preston giggled, then slipped past and into Johnny's room.

"It proves I was right all along," Danny went on unperturbed. "Us lilies of the field that toiled not but had a right good time on New Year's Eve are in fine fettle while there you are a broken-down old drone battling it out with the bacteria."

"If you called up just to insult me—" Jan began angrily, but Danny rushed on without giving her a chance to say more.

"And what you missed at that party—wow!—our flirtatious friend Maybelle really got it good and proper."

"What, what, what . . ." she stuttered, excitement beginning to gather in her. Danny had said "our flirtatious friend" as if Maybelle didn't mean a thing extra to him, as if . . . but he was rushing on, so she collected her thoughts and paid attention.

"And Ben Barton, our revered, respected student body president. I have always maintained that his red hair had to cover fire of some sort and I was right. He may not have a fiery temper but he's really engrossed in a fiery romance."

"You mean Ben and Maybelle?"

"Did you think I was talking about Amos and Andy? Ben was out of town all week so he didn't know about our little city chicken and came to Dotty's party all unaware, and suddenly Ben met Maybelle and Maybelle met Ben and every time they looked at each other two feet of snow melted outside the house."

Jan was speechless. Utterly, absolutely speechless.

Danny chuckled gleefully and continued, "Yesterday afternoon she took the train back to Seattle with tears in her big blue eyes and a Mountaineer pin on her sweater. Today Ben floated into school and when Miss Layton asked him if he'd had a nice vacation he practically kissed her."

Jan laughed delightedly. "That you've got to put in the paper."

"Well, I don't know. Tried to write it up this morning and the typewriter keys melted. That sort of thing could be expensive after a while."

"Oh—oh—oh," Jan moaned. "Everything wonderful happening out in the big broad world and I don't suppose I'll be out of here till the Fourth of July."

"I was afraid it would be that way," Danny said with a sigh. "Well, since I'm the associate editor, I'd better start associating, much as it pains me to do an honest day's work."

"I'm sure you and Miss Layton will have a wonderful time putting out the *Argus* together," she said acidly, suddenly feeling hurt and lonely and left out. It was childish to be upset over anything beyond her control, and she was ashamed of her feelings, but some jealous inner turmoil put angry words into her mouth. "Maybe Bayside can send someone up to help you with the paper and repair your wounded ego. Probably not as pretty as Maybelle, you couldn't expect that. But at least something better than the local talent. You could send them a telegram right away."

There was an ominous silence on the wire. Jan felt self-disgust choking her as the terrible phlegm had choked poor Johnny. She wanted to whisper, "I'm sorry," but the words were caught in her throat.

"Made your New Year's resolutions yet?" Danny asked suddenly.

"Why, no," she replied, surprised.

"Then here's a dilly for you. Five times a day you can bow towards Mecca and say quote although I am the dumbest, ugliest, most revolting character on earth, Danny is my friend unquote and good-by."

The phone banged resoundingly.

Jan recoiled from the noise, then slammed down her phone, too, while she struggled to keep back the tears. She didn't know whom she hated most, herself or Danny. It must be Danny. "I do hate him," she insisted. "I do."

"Bet you don't any such thing," Mrs. Preston said soothingly as she came back to the kitchen. "You'll have to tell me about it later and we'll see what we can do to straighten things out. In the meantime if you do feel like sitting with Johnny awhile, I think I'll take a nap."

Jan was glad to flee to the sickroom, sit in the big rocking chair, and hold Johnny, awake now and restless, against her shoulder. She sang softly to him and he sucked his thumb and sighed contentedly.

In the evening Dr. Conners came in carrying Jan's suitcase. He banged it on the floor and gave a disgusted snort. "I'm glad to see you're flourishing, young lady. And you had better stay flourishing, too, because if you show the slightest symptom of anything your mother is sure to have a nervous breakdown and I don't have time to handle that."

Jan was puzzled. "Is something wrong with Mother?" she asked.

"Just a little off her rocker, as you kids would say. She kept that doggone phone of mine busy all day wondering if you were having any reactions to anything, and then when I went by to get your suitcase she came tearing out of the house with it before I could get my foot on the brake. Didn't want my germy old self around, obviously."

"Mother is mighty fussy about exposing Andrew to anything. You know it wouldn't be good for him."

"Expose him! He's as well protected as any human being could be. Furthermore he's perfectly well now and he'll stay that way as long as he leads a sensible life."

"Well, the big trouble in our family seems to be that

Mother's ideas of a sensible life aren't quite like any one else's ideas of a sensible life."

"Is that so?"

"It really is. Mother and Andrew are always in a dither because he wants to play outside and join the Scouts and things like that and she won't let him. On the other hand she spoils him and gives him more than his share of things and attention and Dad is away most of the time and"—she sighed and gave a tired shrug—"and all things considered it's a big mess and I'm glad to be away from home for awhile."

Dr. Conners sighed, too. "Mothers are the most heroic people in the world, but they can certainly be the most troublesome, too. Next time Andrew has a check-up I'll see if I can't straighten her out. Now I'd better see to my patient."

Jan took her suitcase and went upstairs while the others were conferring around Johnny's bedside. It would be wonderful to have clean clothes. Mrs. Preston had offered some of her things, but she was much taller. After a quick shower Jan put on her duster, fastened it in front, and let it flare out in back, peignoir fashion. It made her look very grown-up, she decided. However, as she slid her feet into the fuzzy blue slippers she realized with a guilty pang that she hadn't been acting very grown-up. In fact she was a genuine number-one gold-plated brat! As soon as she could, she would do something about it, but right now she had better get downstairs and see if she could help.

Dr. Conners had gone and Mrs. Preston was making Johnny's bed for the night. "Nothing you can do here," she said, shaking her head. "Go on in the living-room and entertain John. I'm sure he's going to be a worse problem than the baby before this is over."

Jan walked into the other room timidly. Mr. Preston sat in front of a card table shuffling a deck. "Do you like canasta?" he asked.

"I haven't played it," she replied, clamping her tongue

before she could tell him that she regarded card games as silly and infantile.

"Then start studying these rules while we're waiting for Carol. You aren't going to learn any younger."

With a sigh Jan took the folder and sat down. Evidently she was going to play canasta. "I have something else to say to you, Miss Morgan."

She looked up to find Mr. Preston glaring at her. "You don't have to creep around with your eyes on the floor and your voice a whisper just because I'm here. Do I act like Dracula?"

"Is that the way I look to you?" Jan asked, surprised.

"Yes, ma'am, you do. I've read your stories in the paper and they're good and I don't understand how you ever get them if you're always so shy about talking to people."

"Oh, that's different," she said. "Getting information from people is part of my job. I'm not me, Jan Morgan, then, just an impersonal newspaper representative. But when I have to talk to people socially, and especially boys, well, I just feel all shy and stuttery."

"Don't be afraid of boys. They're human beings, too, and probably as shy and uncertain as you."

She looked up with interest. "Do you really think so? Most of the time they make so much noise and act so silly."

"Whistling in the dark," Mr. Preston said with a shrug.

Jan thought about this for a while. "You could be right," she admitted.

"Well, thank you, Miss Morgan. And now I'll give you a tip, all free-for-nothing. When you talk to people, and we'll include boys in that category, just pretend you're taking notes for a front-page interview. If you can show the same intense interest in an everyday conversation that you'd show for a front-page story you'll be the most popular girl in the county."

"Hmmmmm," Jan commented thoughtfully. Then she

looked up mischievously. "Very interesting, Mr. Preston. It's obvious that you're a man of great discernment. You must have some frightfully fascinating hobbies. Would you care to tell me about them?"

"Smarty," he said and pretended to throw the canasta tray at her. She ducked, laughing. She didn't feel shy any more or resentful of his pointed advice.

"Are you learning those rules?" he asked.

"In a minute," she said, slipping from the chair. "Before I settle down I've got to make a phone call."

She pulled the phone into the darkness of the kitchen and called Danny's number. "Sorry I was nasty this afternoon," she said, and the words came easier than she'd thought possible.

"Heck, we all have our moments and you were entitled to yours. I just saw Dr. Conners and he said you'd really had a time."

"Johnny's had the time, poor baby, but he's getting better fast now. I wanted to tell you, I made some notes you might use on this month's *Argus*. They're in the back of my history book and it's in my locker but Mother has an extra key. Just use what you need."

"They will be a help. The New Year is our theme, of course, but no one seems to be burdened with specific ideas."

"As one of your features you could write resolutions for the other students as pertinent as the one you suggested to me."

"Hey, I thought we were going to forget about that. Anyhow, I'd have to leave town aboard a rocket ship if I made them very pertinent."

"Not if they're funny. You could make Cassie resolve to giggle only twenty-three hours out of the twenty-four; have Ben resolve to gaze towards Seattle and sigh only once every five minutes; and suggest that Dotty resolve to quit wringing her hands and moaning like Lady Macbeth every time she gets upset. You know, things like that."

"That ought to be terrific." Danny was caught up in her excitement. "I can really think of some corkers. I'll get at it right away and keep you posted."

"Please do," Jan replied, and went back to the canasta rules at peace with the world.

To her surprise, playing canasta wasn't such a dreadful chore. She really had fun. "I should have learned this years ago," she said enthusiastically as Mr. Preston added up the score.

But her words "years ago" suddenly pushed a button to the hidden recesses of her mind, and clearly pictured before her was the memory of Andrew the year he was in bed. She could see him lying there propped on pillows, his face white and wistful. She heard him asking, "Can't you play Old Maid with me, Janice?"

And in her jealousy she didn't see that he was imprisoned in bed, shut out from the sunshine and the other boys playing in the street. All she could see was that he was getting special food, lots of presents, and all their mother's devotion. "No, I can't," she had replied crossly. "I have to read this book for a history report."

His face sagged as he asked pleadingly, "Then read your book out loud to me."

"You're not smart enough to understand it," had been her retort.

Recalling this scene three years later, Jan was so horrified that she dropped her cards and buried her face in her hands. "Green eyes," Andrew had called her once. "You've got some specks of green in your eyes, sis," wise and kindly Pete had said. Oh, it was true! She did have green eyes and green eyes just didn't see. They couldn't focus. They made the whole world grotesque and unreal.

"What's wrong?" the Prestons asked, dropping their cards

in turn. Mrs. Preston put a hand on Jan's forehead. "You aren't getting sick, are you?" she asked anxiously.

Jan shook her head. She couldn't say that she'd suddenly become very, very sick of Jan Marie Morgan.

"Just tired," Mr. Preston decided. "Better get off to bed."

She was glad to get away from them, to lie in the darkness and remember that she could write stories and edit the paper and get good grades and take care of sick babies. She had lots of qualities on the plus side of the ledger. Then she remembered that long ago someone far wiser than herself had said clearly, "And though I . . . understand all mysteries, and all knowledge . . . and have not charity, I am nothing." She shuddered again.

But she would play games with Andrew if the chance ever came again. She would help him with his studies. Even if it was too late for them to be real friends, she would at least look at him with clear blue eyes, not see him through envy-contorted green eyes.

A few days later Jan was helping Mrs. Preston with some house-cleaning when they noticed the local taxi drive up in front of the door. The driver helped a tiny, muffled woman carrying a large bundle.

"Why, it's Mrs. Parsons!" Jan said.

"Oh, that funny old lady," Mrs. Preston agreed as she peeked out of the window. "Why would she be coming here? Is she a friend of yours?"

"Mother knows her," Jan answered. "They met at church some time or other. We make jokes about how Mrs. Parsons always comes to call at the most inopportune and confusing time possible and there's no getting rid of her. But why she's coming here . . ."

Their speculations were interrupted by the doorbell, and Mrs. Preston signaled for Jan to go. When she opened the door Mrs. Parsons handed her the bundle with a sigh. "Good afternoon, Janice. I'm glad to see you looking so well."

"We're in quarantine here, Mrs. Parsons," Jan returned bluntly.

But the old lady walked on in unperturbed and started unfastening her coat. "Oh, I know all about that. I had diphtheria many, many years ago, so this is no risk to me."

There was nothing to do but take her coat and introduce her to Mrs. Preston, who after seeing that her visitor was seated comfortably excused herself and went down to the basement where her husband was. Jan was stuck, so she sat down and tried to be gracious.

"Look at your bundle, child," Mrs. Parsons advised.

Jan did and to her surprise found schoolbooks and tablets. "Miss Layton is my neighbor," the old lady explained, "and she was telling me that she was worried about the lessons you were missing. You've been first in your class all through high school and she didn't want you to fall behind now. So I volunteered to get these to you."

"It certainly was kind and thoughtful of you," Jan replied. "Very kind of Miss Layton, too, and I hope you'll thank her for me."

Jan couldn't have been more amazed. You'd think from past performances that Miss Layton would celebrate any prospect of Jan's lowering her average. Maybe her campaign of planned civility was paying off—or maybe Miss Layton was following the path of scrupulous justice. In any event the books were very welcome. She would be able to keep up with the others now. She wished she could run right upstairs and start in on them, but her guest looked settled for the afternoon. She sighed and cast about for conversational ideas.

"You said you had diphtheria, Mrs. Parsons. Was that before you came to Cascadeville?"

"No, it was right here. Back in 1910. Cascadeville was just beginning to boom as a logging town. There was a different company then—not like Shorewood—a get-rich-quick outfit with no thought of the future. The housing for the workers wasn't decent, the sanitary facilities were almost nonexistent. And the way they logged in those days—cutting everything down, leaving a barren, miserable mess." She shook her head.

Jan sat back, fascinated. Cascadeville was such a slow, staid town now. It was exciting to think of it as a raw, unruly boom town. Civilization had covered its rawness in much the same way that second growth had covered the hillsides left bare by the pillaging loggers.

"I was the schoolteacher back then," Mrs. Parsons continued. That undoubtedly explained her friendship with Miss Layton.

"I had a room in back of the schoolhouse and my own well, so I was a little better off than most of the others. But it struck so fast that winter! There was supposed to be a company doctor but he always managed to be somewhere else when there was any sickness. Pretty soon I was the only well person left in town and I knew if we didn't get medicine soon there wouldn't be any town. So I went to the telephone office—central was down sick, too—and just kept punching things till I got Seattle. They said they would send up a doctor and some nurses as soon as they could and that the nearest medicine was in the railroad hospital at North Junction, twenty miles down the tracks."

Mrs. Parsons sighed and looked dreamily into the past. Jan stared at her.

Finally she went on, "I suppose I was beginning to get sick myself by then, or I would have acted a little more rationally. It would be a day at least, maybe longer, before the doctor came. I thought if I could get the medicine before then I might be able to save a few. So I went down to the station, helped myself to a handcar, and off I went. After all these years I can still remember how the cold wind burned my face, how my arms went up and down and up and down like scrubbing clothes on a washboard. Well, I got to the Junction all right and got the antitoxin and . . ."

There was a bellow of anguish from the basement. Mr. Preston was heard to shout, "Oh, no! Why didn't you tell me before this? We've got to get her out of here," and the sound of his feet running upstairs.

He came bursting into the living-room. "Mrs. Parsons, you're a dear, sweet, unselfish soul," he said genially, "but I don't think you realize the risk you're taking. Even though you've had diphtheria you could be quarantined here for five days till they decided you weren't a carrier. We couldn't let you make any sacrifice like that. You'd better leave quickly before Dr. Conners finds out about this."

Mrs. Parsons, startled, stood up and looked around for her coat, which Mr. Preston quickly draped around her. "Oh, my," she said, "I didn't know that. Five days—oh, I couldn't leave my fish and my African violets that long. I'll just slip out. Not very many people know about this."

"But, John, should we?" Mrs. Preston asked softly. "What if she should be carrying germs?"

"No," he said. "Johnny's door was closed the whole time she was here. I'm sure there's no danger, but I didn't want her stuck here on a technicality."

Jan was stunned by this sudden interruption. She followed the old lady out to the porch and, standing there shivering and breaking the law herself no doubt, called, "What happened then? Did you get back with the medicine all right?"

"I was most of the way back when I collapsed. The mercy train from Seattle with the doctors and nurses found me folded up over the handbar."

"Oh, my goodness," Jan said. "Were you sick then?"

"Why I ever lived through that I don't know," Mrs. Parsons continued, apparently not hearing Jan's question. "It's a wonder the train saw me in time to stop, and it's a greater wonder that the antitoxin took hold and cured me so fast after all the cold and exposure I had been through. Yes, I had quite a time. Well, I'd best be getting on, Janice."

Jan came back in the house chilled but happy. "Do you mind if I tie up the phone awhile?" she asked the Prestons. "I want to talk to Pete."

"No, go ahead. Too bad we had to cut short your visit."

"I found out everything I needed to know," Jan said cheerfully. When Pete came to the phone he was hurried and disgruntled.

"Listen, kid, I'm glad to know I won't have to buy flowers for you but right now I'm making up the pages for the *Courier*."

"I know you are, Pete, that's why this won't wait. I have a front-page story for you."

"If you're referring to your incarceration in the pest house it's already written."

"Stop it, Pete. This is a dilly. Now here's my idea . . ."

Jan waited for the time of publication two days away with great glee. On that day the phone rang. It was Danny. "Pete has appointed me special circulation manager in charge of seeing that you get your paper," he explained. "So if you'll open the kitchen window when I signal I'll make like a Spanish cavalier, but instead of serenading, I'll toss it to you."

"Fine," Jan agreed. "By the way, have you read it yet?"

"No. Haven't had time."

A few minutes later Jan, watching eagerly, saw Danny arrive and quickly opened the window. He took a large slingshot, fitted in a copy of the *Courier* all folded up and secured with rubber bands—and shot it right into the room. When Jan picked it up she saw that it had been wrapped around a large chocolate bar.

"Thanks," she called, holding it up.

"Flies better with a little ballast," Danny explained.

"I still think you ought to take a look at the front page," she yelled at him.

"O.K., if you insist." He took his own copy from his pocket and shook it out.

Jan leaned further out the window, not even feeling the flesh-cutting cold air as she gleefully watched the look of utter astonishment on his face. She chuckled and looked at her own paper. There was Danny's usual column, "Passing Through," and right next to it a new signed Column, "Here to Stay," by Jan Marie Morgan. It contained Mrs. Parsons' thrilling story.

"And there are lots of pioneers around here," Jan shouted to him. "I won't run out of material till the cows come home."

Danny read the story carefully to the end. Then he looked up, smiled, and saluted her. "My hat is off to you," he said, suiting the action to the words. "If you can scoop me while you're in quarantine, what on earth will you do when you get out? I think I'll quit writing and raise petunias."

He put his hat back on, waved, and started down the path. Jan shut the window contentedly.

"Finally," Mrs. Preston said with a sigh. "Love in bloom is all very well, but it was getting a little chilly in here."

"Hardly love in bloom," Jan protested. "Actually we are rivals."

"Ha, ha, ha," Mrs. Preston said, patting her shoulder. "Incidentally, you'd better give your mother a call. I was chatting with her while you were otherwise occupied. She's in a dither because your father has taken a job with a telephone crew up in the pass and that's dangerous work, and Andrew broke the steering gear on his sled and he's unhappy, and I think they are all missing you badly. I can understand that. You're a real help."

"My goodness," Jan said as she started for the phone. "We may be quarantined to keep our germs from getting out but that certainly doesn't keep everyone else's worries from getting in."

Finally it was time to go home. Johnny's reports were all negative, all their reports were negative. The danger of any more diphtheria was over, at least as far as they were concerned. She fastened her suitcase, came downstairs, and put on her coat. "Jan no go," Johnny protested, and she hugged him.

"I don't know how we're going to get along without you. You're part of the family now," Mrs. Preston said affectionately. "But I do wish you'd let me drive you home."

"After all this time indoors walking is a privilege," Jan replied. "Besides, Dad is coming to carry my suitcase. But I will miss you all."

"Same here, chum, even if you couldn't learn all the finer points of canasta," Mr. Preston said, looking up from his newspaper.

"Come and see us soon," Mrs. Preston added. "Don't wait for a baby-sitting job. Just come."

Steps clattered up on the porch, the door opened, and there to Jan's surprise was Danny.

"Your dad had an unexpected errand so I volunteered," he explained quickly, grabbing her suitcase and leading the way to the Mallory family car. "And may I suggest that you get quarantined more often since the folks regard the occasion as important enough to let me have the car."

"I'll do anything to oblige," she told him.

"Thank you. I'll put in a request for some bubonic plague germs immediately."

"Just look under Miss Layton's pillow," Jan suggested, and Danny let out such an uninhibited guffaw that the car swerved.

"Watch it, pal," she cautioned.

"Quiet. No side-seat drivers, please."

Danny swung around the corner and stopped in front of the Morgan house. Lights were on all over, upstairs and down. "Danny, is something wrong?" she asked in alarm. "Did something happen to Dad? Is that why you came for me? Danny, tell me right now."

"What a suspicious character," he chuckled. "Quit thinking in headlines. Nothing is wrong."

"But why would Mother turn on so many lights?"

"You might go in and find out instead of sitting here fuming."

He opened the car door with a flourish and Jan quickly ran up the steps and into the living-room. "Surprise," shouted a number of voices. They all came rushing out from the dining-room and kitchen where they had been hiding— her parents and Andrew and Pete and the *Argus* staff and the Mountaineers.

"Oh, my," Jan said in complete astonishment. Wordless with happiness and surprise she repeated, "Oh, my."

Danny thrust her notebook into her hands. "Write it all up—big doings at the Morgan house. An end-of-quarantine party."

Dotty cleared her throat ostentatiously. "Do you mean Jan is so old-fashioned she writes with a pencil? How utterly revolting!"

Jan was nonplused as the gang broke into howls of laughter. They all pressed around and dragged her into the dining-room, where a small suitcase lay in state on top of the table.

Only it wasn't a suitcase. There was only one thing it could be. Jan began to tremble. Oh, to want one for so long and to feel that she never would get it! Like the day she became editor, she felt as if the world just couldn't hold this much happiness. "Open it," everyone yelled at her.

Because she just stood there staring at it like an idiot, Danny flipped back the lid, revealing the polished, beautiful machine within. "Like mine," he said, "only the latest model."

Her father laid a hand on her shoulder. "Pete and I were waiting for it at the express office. That's why I couldn't come for you."

Jan looked around the circle of grinning faces. "How come?" she asked. "Who dood it?"

Danny was the spokesman. "Community enterprise," he explained. "Your dad took that job with the line crew with just one intention—raising money for a typewriter. At the same time Pete was lining one up and planning to have you work it out. Then Mrs. Preston called up, said they wanted to do something special for you and thought maybe you'd like a typewriter. Isn't it a good thing I was around to co-ordinate everyone or here we'd sit with three typewriters and even you don't have enough hands for that."

The tightness in Jan came to the top and spilled over. "I don't have any words," she said. "I—there, I just don't know what to say."

"Dotty, will you please put that in the official records?" Ben instructed. "The editor ran out of words."

They all laughed but Jan scarcely heard them. She sat down by her machine, ran her fingers over the keys, and explored every inch of the mechanism, while Danny pointed out all the special features.

"Newspaper people—they are bats," was Dotty's opinion.

"All except Maybelle," Ben agreed with a long sigh.

"Yes, let's us ordinary people get out of the way," Mr. Morgan suggested. He led the way to the living-room and turned on the television.

Andrew hung over their shoulders, breathing hard. "Do you think I can use it sometimes, huh sis?"

Immediately she was repelled by the idea, then she caught hold of herself and remembered, "See him with blue eyes." "I'll try to teach you to type," she said. "We ought to keep that editorship in the family."

"We're all ready to eat," Mrs. Morgan called from the kitchen. "Somebody help me dish up these hamburgers."

Everyone but Jan made a dash for the kitchen. She sat dreamily in front of her typewriter. "Snap out of it, kid," Pete advised as he came up to her munching on a napkin-wrapped burger. "Isn't it penetrating your so-called brain that your mother is throwing you a party even though she thinks a typewriter is nonsense?"

As usual, Pete was right. It was nice of her mother to go to all the trouble and expense of giving her a party. Evidently she had been missed at home and it was nice to know that. As soon as the confusion cleared a little she must tell her mother how grateful she was. "Yes, indeed Pete," she assured him.

She smiled dreamily, started to leave for the kitchen, but was back in an instant to slip in some typing paper and proudly tap out, "Now is the time for all good men to come to the aid of their party."

Pete's laugh was loud and appreciative. "You'll do, kid," he decided. "You'll do."

CHAPTER 15

Looking Ahead

"THAT TYPEWRITER may be a help to you after all," Mrs. Morgan decided.

Jan stretched and rubbed her back. Though last night's party had ended late she had been up since six o'clock practicing speed exercises from the instruction book that came with the machine. "Almost forty words a minute," she said complacently. "And that's without any formal lessons. It's just what I've learned since I started studying journalism."

"You'll pick up speed now that you have a machine at home," her mother agreed. "I wish you knew shorthand, too. That would make things easier."

"Oh, I'll get around to it someday when I don't have so many other things to learn," Jan said. She took yellow globes of grapefruit from the cooler, halved them, and began to flute the edges. "It was a wonderful party, Mother. If you toss a party like that every time I'm exposed to an illness all our guests will probably start collecting germs and dropping them in my milk at school."

Surprisingly enough, her mother didn't respond to the praise about the party. She had something else on her mind and it came out in a rush. "Learning things someday won't help you get a job this summer. Oh, I know you'll find one all right. With your grades you can probably take your pick of either the mill office or the railroad, but if you had shorthand you'd start out at a better salary."

The knife slipped, cutting into the fruit jaggedly. Jan put

189

it down. "I'd hoped . . ." she began. "I'd thought some about college."

"Yes, I imagine you have, but surely you can see that it isn't possible. Your father and I were talking it over while you were at the Prestons', and we both feel heartsick about it, but we think it's best if you start facing the truth about the situation.

"Even if your father made a lot of money, which he doesn't, we wouldn't have enough because sickness has eaten away all our savings. You know that's why we don't have a car or a modern kitchen. Having you work will make things easier for all of us. And I'm sure you'll enjoy working once you're adjusted to it. You are bound to be ambitious. And you're still so young—you may be able to go to college eventually. Look at all those servicemen who went to college when they were older."

This was a long speech for her mother to make. She was very flustered, standing there cutting slice after slice of her home-made bread till she had a pile big enough to make toast for an army.

"I'm ambitious because I enjoy my work," Jan explained gently. She felt sad, of course, but not surprised or angry. She'd really known all along that being a cub reporter on the University *Daily* and maybe living in the Theta house was just wishful thinking.

"You don't have to go to college to be a success," her mother repeated. "We would send you if we possibly could," she muttered.

"I know you would," Jan said mildly. "I'm not mad. I'll look for a job as soon as I graduate, but right now I'd better hop off to school. I have so much to do today."

"You haven't eaten any breakfast," her mother protested. "I'll fix you something as soon as I take a tray to Andrew. He says he feels fine, but he looks feverish to me after all that excitement last night. I think he had better stay in bed this morning."

"No, thanks, Mother. Really, I'm not one bit hungry."

Jan quickly put on her coat, scarf, and boots. Gathering up her books, she slipped out the door. In the middle of the block she was hailed by Dotty, frosty-faced and cheerful.

"What's all the rush?" Dotty asked, pushing back a stray strand of hair with a huge fur mitten. "I'm going to stop and see your mother a few minutes and I thought maybe we could walk to school together."

"Wish I could, Dotty, but I want to see Pete pronto. What's with you and Mother?"

"Oh, we've been going full steam on those costumes while you were incommunicado. Your mother is really swell, so talented and good-looking for her age. I tell you we're going to have the best-dressed class play in forty-nine states. Don't you want to come back and see the designs?"

"Not today, thanks. Let me know when you're ready for some publicity."

Jan waved and went on down the street pondering Dotty's description of her mother. Well, she was good-looking when she wasn't worried and frowning, and evidently she did have talent. Too bad Dotty couldn't have been her daughter. They would have had such a good time making clothes and talking about parties. Besides, Dotty wouldn't care at all about going to college. Jan shuffled her boots along the hard-packed snow and reflected that some people just hadn't been sorted out right.

Pete was sitting sleepily at his desk drinking a cup of strong, black coffee. "Going to mooch a new typewriter ribbon off of me already?" he asked.

Jan hopped up on the counter and looked at him seriously. "Pete, I want you to help me get a job in Seattle," she said.

"Hold on a minute," he protested. "I can't have you and Danny both leave. I'm not accustomed to doing my own work any more."

"I'm not kidding," she said seriously, trying to keep a quaver out of her voice. "I want a job as soon as I graduate.

That business of thinking I might go to college is strictly for the birds."

"What's wrong with getting a job here in town?" he asked.

"No," she reiterated. "In Seattle on one of the newspapers. I can take ads over the phone, or run copy or sweep the floor. Then I'll take night classes at the University and somehow, even if it takes fifteen years, I'll work my way up to a writing job."

Staring somberly into her future, Jan was only half aware of Pete's look of admiration and affection.

"Sure, I have friends on the papers," he said after a while. "They'll give you a job. But it will be mighty poor pickings trying to live in Seattle and go to school on a copy girl's pay. It'll be mostly cold rooms and tea and crackers. Whereas if you worked in town here and lived at home you could be really comfortable."

"What's comfort if you aren't living?" Jan asked disdainfully.

He nodded. "Guess you're right. But how about a nightside job? If you could swing that you could go to the University in the mornings and your credits would pile up faster."

Jan jumped down from the counter excitedly. "Oh, Pete, do you really think I could work it that way?"

"We'll put our minds to it. But I doubt if your folks will like the idea. They'll say the grind is too tough for a girl not quite seventeen."

Jan shook her head. "No, if I work it's my privilege to pick the job."

She put her wraps back on and headed for the door. "Guess I'd better get to school. Mustn't be late my first day back."

Pete scratched his head. "Somehow I thought you'd be winning a college scholarship. You're first in your class, aren't you?"

"I've thought about it, too," Jan admitted. "But most of

the scholarships offered at Mountain View are either for some small college without much of a journalism department or else they don't amount to enough to be any real help."

"How about that big competition the Shorewood Lumber Company has for employees' children? I thought sure you'd be signed up for that one."

"I'd have about as much chance of winning that as I would have of winning the Miss America contest. It covers all the Shorewood employees in Washington, Oregon, Idaho, and northern California," Jan told him. "Besides, it isn't decided on grades alone. They send people out to interview you about your school activities, your service to the community, and all sorts of things. I just don't have the right kind of personality to make a good impression," she said sadly.

"She doesn't have the right kind of personality," Pete said sardonically. "She doesn't have any community activities. She's only the editor of the school paper, works on the town paper, helps teach a Sunday school class, is everybody's favorite baby-sitter, and can handle emergencies like an attack of diphtheria. Yah, no personality at all, poor kid."

"Oh, Pete, you know what I mean. I'm not popular."

"Most social pariahs don't have half the people in town trying to buy them a typewriter. Hand your name in, girl. Let the Shorewood Company decide whether or not you have any personality."

"I suppose it wouldn't hurt to try," Jan speculated wistfully.

"Not a bit."

"Well, I will. I'll see Mr. Larsen as soon as I get to school. But see about that job anyhow, will you, Pete? I don't feel very lucky."

"We'll see," Pete promised. "Now scram."

Not quite so down-hearted now, Jan double-timed up the street to school. Danny was waiting outside the study hall door for her. "I stopped by but you had lit out like a jet-propelled rocket."

"Had to go heckle Pete. I'm weeks behind."

"Well, don't ever do a thing like that to me again. A bunch of giggling females hauled me in and made me look at pictures of pretty costumes."

"How were they?"

"Not bad," he said thoughtfully. "Not bad at all. Your mother is really sharp. Dotty was bleating in my ear all the way down about how the girls are hoping she will design their new formals for them."

"Good night!" Jan said. "She'll have to set up a shop at this rate."

"Why shouldn't she? You'll be going away, your dad isn't home much, and Andrew can't take up all her time even if he is sick and I don't think he is. She might as well have a little business."

She glanced at him sharply as he said, "You'll be going away." Well, of course she would, one way or the other, but it wasn't time to confide any plan to Danny. "I'll talk to you later," she said. "I want to see Mr. Larsen right now."

"There's a Press Club meeting lunch period," he called after her as she turned towards the principal's office. She nodded back at him.

"I was going to speak to you about just that the minute you returned," Mr. Larsen said approvingly when Jan asked about the scholarship. "There are three Shorewood scholarships awarded in the Northwest," he explained. "One covers all expenses for four years and the other two are for tuition and fees for the first year and are renewed each succeeding year if the student maintains a B-plus average."

"Now I'll send in your application with a transcript of your grades, and here, you fill this out, it's a questionnaire about your extracurricular activities. You'll need two character references from people here in town."

"Pete," she suggested, "and Reverend Paulson."

"They'll be fine. I'll ask them for you. The company will send a man out to interview you some time in March or April. You know, Jan, you have about the best chance to win of anyone we've had for a long time. It would be quite an honor for the school, too."

"What would be an honor to the school?" Miss Layton asked as she came into the office to pick up some papers.

"Jan is applying for the Shorewood scholarship," Mr. Larsen explained.

Miss Layton nodded approvingly. "I thought you would. That was one reason I wanted to get those books to you even if I did strain a few laws."

"I was very grateful, Miss Layton," Jan replied. "I've been wanting to thank you."

"Glad I was able to help out," she said brusquely and left the room.

"Did anybody from Mountain View ever win?" Jan asked.

"Just one. Your friend Mrs. Abbott—she was Elsie Danvers then. She had to turn it down because her mother was ill. School had just begun the next fall when Mrs. Danvers died, so you see Elsie missed all around. However, by now she probably thinks it was all for the best. There goes the bell Glad to have you back, Jan."

"Thank you, I'm glad to be back," Jan replied.

As she trotted down the hall to her first class, several things suddenly leaped up in her mind and fused together. First was Elsie Abbott saying to her last summer that Miss Layton had been kind to her at a time when she had been 'way down. Then Mr. Larsen telling her that Mrs. Abbott had been awarded a Shorewood scholarship but had been unable to accept. Jan felt as if she could sense how Elsie Abbott must have felt then—alone in the world, her mother dead, her chance to go to college gone. And the stern, aloof teacher would have come to see her, not with the usual words

of sympathy, but to tell her she could have a chance for education and service both if she joined the WAC, and undoubtedly Miss Layton had stood quietly by in those last
lonely days before she went away. Yes, Miss Layton did have
greatness of soul even if it was hidden under layers of punc-
tuation rules.

Jan wondered suddenly if Mrs. Abbott had anything to do
with Miss Layton's changed attitude to her. It was undoubtedly one of those things she would never know.

Heavens, her woolgathering had made her late to class, but
the teacher only smiled benignly as she slipped into her
place. Tomorrow would be a different story, but today was
apparently welcome-home day.

At lunchtime the Press Club members brought their trays
up to the journalism classroom, where Miss Layton called the
meeting to order to the tune of clashing silverware. "Here's
a memo about the Press Club contest for the best stories
printed in high school papers this year," Miss Layton announced. "Stories may be entered in the following categories
—news, features, sports, editorials or signed columns. So be
looking over your stories and deciding what if anything is
worth sending."

Of all the bad luck! Last year when she had written some
outstanding stories for the *Argus* they hadn't belonged to
the Press Club and this year she had just done executive
work. While the others were busily comparing stories Jan
felt that old green haze coming over her eyes. Jealousy was
not an adversary to be conquered in one session.

Miss Layton passed on to new business. "Although the
Press Club is not primarily a social organization, we've been
asked to join with the Mountaineers for a Valentine week-
end party at the Barren Mountain Ski Lodge."

Noisy expressions of excitement and approval completely
disorganized the meeting until Miss Layton got to her feet
and shouted to restore order.

"I presume we don't need to take a vote," she said dryly.

"And since the date is only three weeks away we'd better appoint committees right away to meet with the Mountaineer committees. Now Mr. and Mrs. Larsen will go along and I'll be there." She sighed and shut her eyes as if anticipating the strength she would need. "We'll need a couple of your mothers also."

"I'm sure Mom would like to go," Danny spoke up quickly. "She's been a Scout den mother and likes camping trips."

"This won't exactly be camping," Miss Layton explained. "We'll be glad to have her, though, and I'll call her this afternoon. Danny, I think I'll put you in charge of transportation."

"Sure thing," Danny promised. "Now our car holds seven and Mr. Larsen has a station wagon and . . ."

"Later, Danny," Miss Layton said. She almost had a smile on her frozen face. "I'm the only one permitted to talk out loud just now."

"Jan, I'd like you and Cassie on the meal-planning committee. We'll arrive in time for dinner Friday night and have three meals on Saturday, and two on Sunday, so you can see you'll have your work cut out."

This was the real accolade of approval from Miss Layton, Jan felt. She wouldn't put anyone she didn't trust on a vital committee. Jan was amazed at how happy it made her to be on civil terms with Miss Layton.

"And what that mountain air will do to our appetites," Danny predicted.

"We'll feed you," Jan promised. "Won't we, Cassie?"

Cassie giggled. "Sure. If we get desperate the boys can trap a bear."

"Now one more committee," Miss Layton said as she looked at her watch and prepared to close the meeting. "Fred and Evelyn, if you will look into the sleeping-bag and cot situation and tell us what we'll need, please."

Miss Layton had started to rise from her desk when Ben Barton spoke. "Miss Layton, I have a suggestion."

She sat down again. "What is it, Ben?"

"The letter from the Lodge said there was room for thirty. Only twenty-four of us will be going because so many kids belong to Mountaineers and Press Club both, so I wondered if we couldn't invite a few guests. A few special people who have the same interests we do." His face was as red as his hair by the time he finished stammering through his speech.

Instantly a howl of laughter went up from the meeting. "Special people!" "Same interests—yah, interested in Ben, he means." "Maybelle oh Maybelle, come back to me now," Don improvised heartily.

Ben clenched his fists, his face now nearly purple. He was about to explode and if he ever did it would probably be wonderful to see, but Jan didn't like to be teased either so she stood up quickly and caught their attention. "I think it would be a fine idea to invite Maybelle," she said. "After all, she is a Press Club member and she and all the Bayside group were nice to us when we visited them."

The clamor subsided and Ben sent her a look of fervent gratitude. "Yes, do invite her," Miss Layton said gently. She was biting her lips to keep from smiling. Evidently Ben's tumultuous romance amused her as much as it did everyone else. "But if anyone else has a suggestion for a guest, better mention it to me later, so we won't have another riot. Meeting adjourned." She left in haste before anyone could bring up another topic for discussion.

The Mountaineers already had most of their plans underway, but the students they had appointed to the food committee hadn't done much but worry about the situation, so Jan and Cassie took over the planning, leaving the others to procure supplies and run errands. It was a big job but the girls faced up to it bravely.

"Don't let it worry you," Danny said soothingly. "I'll ask Mom for some ideas. Weiners the first night, pancakes for breakfast, and for Saturday night ask Mom to make a big kettle of her Irish stew—wow, is it filling."

"Well here," Jan said, holding out her notebook. "Why not take over?"

"Not me, pal. I'm just donating my time."

Soon Jan was so busy she was afraid she was going to meet herself coming around the corner. Thank goodness Danny had the plans for the January *Argus* well organized, and she could devote her time to making up back assignments and planning menus for the week-end party. She also found herself kibitzing on the class-play costumes. Almost every time she came home in the afternoon the house was full of girls enmeshed with colorful fabrics or tissue paper while the sewing machine whirred constantly. Her mother was making the first costume and after that would merely supervise the members of the sewing class while they made the rest.

Since the weather had been cold and clear, her father hadn't been called to work on the line crew again, so when he and Andrew felt too smothered by the bundles of cloth all around they sneaked down to the basement and played cards. Jan joined them for a few hands once in a while, and during these times of fun together discovered that Andrew wasn't quite as obnoxious as she had thought. Not quite.

Another happy result of her mother's preoccupation with the costumes, Jan noticed, was that Dad was able unobtrusively to take Andrew outdoors every day for walks and exercises as well as a little supervised fun on his sled. Working slowly and cautiously, he was giving the boy a chance to recover his strength and Andrew was beginning to get color in his cheeks and a sparkle in his eyes.

Then one day in early February a warm, sweet wind blew through the pass from the west and the whole valley smelled like spring. "It's Chinooking," Jan said as she came out of school.

"Look at the snow melt," Danny marveled. The gutters

were rushing cataracts. "We have Chinook winds in Seattle, too, but they usually bring a warm rain."

"Naturally," Jan agreed as she zipped up her boots and prepared to splash home. "Warm rain, cold rain, in Seattle it's always rain."

"It's a wonderful feeling in the middle of winter, isn't it?" Danny said. "Makes you know that spring is just around the corner. But right now I'm not so thrilled about it. I wanted snow for our week-end."

"There'll be snow," Jan assured him. "This time of year a thaw is only temporary."

"Wonder why they call them Chinooks anyhow?" Danny asked as he undid his jacket collar and breathed in the pleasant, sweet air.

"Oh, the early settlers thought they came from the mouth of the Columbia River, where the Chinook Indians lived," Jan exclaimed. "Actually they come from the mountains, but don't ask me why."

When they reached Jan's house they found the family in a flurry getting Mr. Morgan ready to go back to work. "The speeder's leaving in an hour," he said gaily as he stood on first one foot and the other while his wife rushed around packing.

"You said it would snow again," Danny accused Jan.

"Oh, it will," her father assured him. "But it won't be as deep any more. Anyhow, the timekeeper has to be first on the job when the woods open up again."

"Andrew can walk down with me and carry the other suitcase," he suggested when he was ready to go.

"But it's so slushy outside," his wife protested.

"He'll button up," he said reassuringly, and Andrew got ready in jig time, his face aglow with importance.

"Come straight home," his mother admonished. "No loitering on the way and risking a cold."

After they left she sighed and turned back to the sewing

machine. "Now where was I? Oh, yes, this is Dotty's costume and it's about ready to be fitted. Janice, you try it on. You girls are about the same size."

"Who, me?" Jan protested. "Get into that?" She looked askance at the long, flowing gown of rose damask and satin.

"Yes, you," Danny insisted. "This I've got to see."

Jan picked up the dress and started for the stairs. "O.K. Anything for a laugh, that's me."

But after she fastened the dress and stood smoothing it down in front of the mirror she felt pleased and rather shy. It was a beautiful, stately gown. Holding herself tall and erect, she walked slowly down the stairs.

Danny and her mother came out of the kitchen to watch her. Danny let out a loud, appreciative whistle and Jan was so startled and delighted that she nearly tripped over the train.

"Isn't it lovely?" Mrs. Morgan asked triumphantly. "It's been a real pleasure to help make these costumes. You know, some of the girls have asked me to adapt the costume designs into modern formals and I've half a mind to try it."

"Start a new style," Danny suggested. "Let's put Mountain View on the map. Shakespeare suits you," he went on emphatically to Jan. "Those braids on top of your head are just the thing for a period piece."

"Why, thanks, Danny." Jan felt a strange but sweet knee-buckling warmth at his sincere admiration. "I often think my whole trouble is that I was born in the wrong century. Maybe I'm more fitted for the sixteenth than the twentieth."

"Huh-uh," Danny protested. "They didn't have newspapers then."

"They had gossips and that's how newspapers started, I'm sure."

"Better take the dress off, Janice," her mother interrupted. "I don't want anything happening to my bastings."

She bustled back to her work and Jan turned to go up the

stairs again. She was stopped by the sound of Danny clearing his throat. He was shuffling his feet and looking very uneasy. "What's wrong?" she asked.

"I was just thinking about the play," he replied, his usually candid eyes not meeting hers. "It's going to be out of this world. It's going to be something nobody should miss."

"And that's exactly what we'll say in our editorial," Jan agreed.

"I was being personal, not editorial," Danny explained painfully. "I was thinking of how much I'd like to ask you for a date to go to the play if I weren't afraid you'd snap back that you had to work or you were bored with the whole idea or you wish I'd drop dead or something."

Jan stared at him in amazement. Danny the assured, Danny the confident, was going through a soul-tearing moment. Why, it was just like Mr. Preston said—boys were human beings too and sometimes scared and uncertain. He had every reason to be uncertain about her performance, she reflected. Why, the way she blew hot and cold—one day friendly, the next nasty—she was more capricious than any Chinook wind. It was more than she deserved to have his friendship.

On another day she might have snapped at him, too, and refused his offer because she was embarrassed. Today, wearing the lovely gown, with her hair piled high like a crown, she felt different, feminine, the way beautiful women like Mrs. Preston must feel. Somehow it seemed perfectly natural to lean over the bannister, smile, and say, "I'd love to go to the play with you, Danny."

His face lit up like a Fourth of July sparkler. "Swell. It's a date."

"And only two and a half months to wait for it," she teased.

"Oh, we'll have a few rehearsals for the big event," Danny

said heartily, his self-confidence flowing back. "We can do some skating and bowling to get ourselves into condition."

"Holy cow! Hooooollllyyy cow! Rings of Saturn surround me!" Andrew stood in the doorway staring at them incredulously. "Janice has a boy friend. She's not going to die an old maid after all. Yeow!" He skidded towards the kitchen yelling at the top of his lungs, "Mom, you can quit praying! The miracle has happened! Janice has a boy friend!"

His mother came at a gallop asking, "What's wrong?"

Jan blushed, cringed, and raced upstairs. It had been such a wonderful moment until Andrew ruined it—the way he had ruined everything for her all her life.

As she ran Danny laughed, tossed Andrew a quarter, and said, "O.K., monster, get lost."

Andrew shook his head. "This is better than television. I'll watch."

"Be careful now," her mother admonished Jan as she followed her upstairs. "Don't trip and tear the seams."

Jan banged her door and struggled out of the costume, her face splotched with tears, her hair unpinned and straggling. "Now just what happened?" her mother asked.

"Danny," Jan began, then put her face in her hands and sobbed. "Danny asked me for a date and Andrew heard him and started yelling at the top of his lungs and now I never want to see him again."

"Who don't you want to see?" her mother was still bewildered.

"Neither one of them. Danny won't want to see me, either. Andrew has spoiled the most wonderful thing that ever happened to me in my whole life."

"Oh, for goodness' sakes!" As comprehension came to her mother she folded the dress over her arm and smiled. "Danny wasn't bothered at all. I'll stake my word on it. I know you feel bad, and it was mean of Andrew to make such a scene, but it's been done before. It's one of the major facts of history. I'm sure the lady who first wore a gown like this had a kid brother who made things uncomfortable for the cavalier who came to see her."

Jan blew her nose and looked up with interest. "Do you really think so?"

"I know so. Now wash your face, comb your hair, and get back downstairs. You can ask Danny to supper. We have plenty because I didn't expect Dad to leave today. And just ignore Andrew. I'll try to have a word with him. He ought to know that you are more sensitive than most girls, but don't fret if he does tease a little. I wish you understood more about people and less about books." She shook her head and left the room.

"You don't have to tell me," Jan said wearily. "I've heard it before. I don't have sense enough to come in out of the rain."

Sure enough, when Jan came downstairs Andrew and Danny were sitting companionably over a game of bingo. "I have a fine idea to take the starch out of this brat," Danny suggested.

"What?" she asked eagerly. Andrew looked wary.

"Take him along to Barren Mountain. I guess two important characters like us are entitled to a guest between us. We could really make him sing for his supper."

"Oh, gosh, would you really?" Andrew's eyes bugged out in excitement and his voice slid up and down the scale. "I never get to go anywhere."

If looks could kill, the one Jan gave Danny would have French-fried him. As if it wasn't bad enough to have Andrew around home all the time. "Oh, he couldn't," she said quickly. "He isn't strong enough. Mother would have a fit at the very suggestion."

"Not if I explained it right," he insisted, and forthwith took off for the kitchen, Andrew trailing anxiously along.

Jan was correct about her mother's reaction. "Oh, no," she began, but Danny interrupted.

"Check with Dr. Conners first," he suggested. "Whatever he says will go. I'll watch the kid like a hawk to see that he doesn't overdo. But give him a chance at least. He doesn't have much fun."

"That's fair enough," Andrew pleaded.

His mother finally succumbed to the bright hope in his eyes. "We'll ask Dr. Conners," she agreed.

Jan realized that this could be the opportunity Dr. Conners wanted to tell her mother that Andrew was well enough to lead a normal life, to be a real boy. Maybe this was going to be a good thing, but she still wished he didn't have to go along on their week-end.

Danny stayed for supper and afterwards they all played bingo, getting very loud and excited in their enthusiasm. When Danny finally left Jan walked to the porch with him intending to remark that just because they officially had a date it didn't give him the right to run the Morgan family.

Danny anticipated her and spoke first. "Retract your landing gear, pal. I really did it for you. The kid is well and as soon as the information penetrates through your mother's noggin we'll all have an easier time around here—especially you."

That was logical all right, but . . .

"Furthermore he's a good kid and I'd like to see that he gets a break."

"Don't tempt me or I'll see to the breakage," she responded.

"Control yourself, Scoop. There's a good time coming and you wouldn't want to be in jail."

Danny took off down the road. She stood on the porch waving to him while his words rang in her ears. There's a good time coming . . .

CHAPTER 16

Night on the Mountain

" 'ON TOP OF OLD SMOKEY, all covered with snow,' " the voices sang, " 'I lost my true lover by courtin' too slow. . . .' "

"Keep that in mind, Ben," Danny advised, and they all laughed—Jan, Danny, Ben, and Maybelle sitting in the back of the Mallory car; Mrs. Mallory, Miss Layton, and thrilled, starry-eyed Andrew in front.

"Oh, this is fun," Jan said as she bounced up and down on the seat and rubbed a spot on the frosty window to look out at the white, black, and green-edged landscape. The snow was deep and heavy again; the tire chains clicked slowly along the road and there would be lots of fun skiing at the lodge tomorrow. There would be fun around the roaring fire to-night, too, and even the presence of Miss Layton and Andrew couldn't dampen her enthusiasm.

"Good enough being the advance scouts of the expedition," Danny agreed. They had left at noon, driving triumphantly away from school with most of the students hanging out of the windows shouting an envious, raucous farewell. The others would leave at four and get to the lodge in time for dinner. Of course the advance crew would have to work hard getting things ready this afternoon, but it was more than worth it to play hooky and go for a ride on a snowy afternoon.

Finally they turned off the highway, bounced over the icy ruts leading to the lodge, and drew up at the door with a flourish. Miss Layton took the key out of her purse. "It's going to be nasty cold inside," she said with a shudder.

Miss Layton was right. The lodge was miserably, damply cold and the only way to fight off pneumonia was to keep on all wraps and work hard. Jan and Maybelle dragged the box of groceries from the car and put things away in cupboards and coolers, then checked over the supplies of dishes, silverware, and napkins.

Miss Layton and Mrs. Mallory bustled through the two upstairs dormitories hauling blankets out of cupboards and making up the cots.

Danny and Ben hurried to the woodshed to bring in armloads of wood for the cookstove. Andrew came along with them carrying a large load, his face flushed and triumphant.

"The big logs for the fireplace are down the path," Danny said. "It'll be a job to carry them, but we'd better do that next."

Andrew turned to go with them, but Jan, remembering all her mother's injunctions, pulled him back. "Do you have your knife?" she asked. "We need some kindling the worst way if we're to get this stove perking."

Andrew's face clouded but Danny spoke up in quick agreement. "You go ahead and make the kindling, Andrew. I wish I had a knife like yours."

That settled it. Andrew turned to his task with such a will that soon the big black stove was sending its crackly warmth through the kitchen. Andrew was proud of his achievement. Jan hoped that as a result of Dr. Conners' talk with her mother he would soon be busy with friends his own age.

Then Andrew took more kindling in to the fireplace. Danny and Ben staggered in, each carrying a large log, and soon the front room, too, was agleam with firelight while the comforting warmth stole out into the corners and the little group began to relax and remove a few layers of clothing.

"Now I'll make some cocoa," Jan announced when they had all come together before the fireplace, their major tasks accomplished and nothing left to do now but wait for the others to arrive. "We certainly deserve a little snack after all that work."

"Not for me, thanks," Miss Layton said with a sigh. "I'm allergic to cocoa." She sounded tired and dispirited. Miss Layton always did her duty but they could tell she would rather be home with a good book than chaperoning a horde of students.

"There's tea," Jan suggested. "I saw some in a cupboard."

Miss Layton brightened and started to rise.

"Sit still," Jan said with a smile. "I'll make it."

Miss Layton settled back gratefully. "How thoughtful of you," she said in a surprised tone of voice.

Jan and Maybelle carried the trays of cocoa, tea, and sandwiches into the living room. Miss Layton accepted her cup with a happy sigh. "You're a good girl, Jan," she said abruptly. "I'm glad I had a chance to find it out."

"Why, thank you," Jan said, so surprised she nearly dropped her tray.

Back in the kitchen washing up the dishes Jan said dreamily, "Who would ever think that a cup of tea on a frosty afternoon would finally cancel out my telling her that she diagrammed a sentence wrong."

"So that was it!" Danny, coming in with an armload of blankets from the car, had overheard her. "You really must have been a character in them thar days. I'm glad I didn't meet up with you until you had begun to mellow around the edges." He laughed, shook his head, and went on into the other room. Jan glared after him.

"Character himself," Maybelle sniffed. "How on earth you can endure that egomaniac . . ."

"He gets as good as he gives most times," Jan laughed.

"You really do seem to handle him," Maybelle admitted. "Danny has always been like a brother to me—I've known him so long—and he's every bit as unflattering to me as any real brother could be."

"Honestly?" Jan asked with great interest.

"Oh, yes. When I came up at Christmas time I really had had the 'flu all right, but I'd also had a fight and broken off with my boy friend and I was mad at everbody. Danny just wasn't sympathetic at all. He kept telling me that I should be nicer and more understanding. But he did introduce me to Ben so I guess all I went through was just fate."

"That's it," Jan agreed. "Kismet."

Happiness radiated through Jan like the warm rays of heat from the stove radiated through the room. She was flirting with Danny—she was laughing with Maybelle about the foibles of boys—she was being a girl among girls, no longer a lone wolf. She was one of the gang and it was more than just fun, it was right and satisfying.

Why had she wasted so much of her life in the dismal back alleys of jealousy and misunderstanding? Well, it was over with now, the thing to remember was full-steam ahead and eyes wide open forever after.

Refreshed and invigorated from her tea, Miss Layton undertook the task of lighting the gasoline lanterns. The boys went out again and brought back a bundle of sticks to be carved into roasting forks for the weiners and marshmallows.

"We're building up good coals," Danny said judiciously as he gave the back log a poke that sent sparks showering across the hearth.

"You're a good woodsman, Danny," Miss Layton said. "You ought to get a job with the Forest Service this summer."

"His dad is putting him on one of the railroad crews," Mrs. Mallory explained.

"That's too bad," Ben commented. "I'm going to be a fire lookout this summer and it would be fun to have you along."

"No, thanks," Danny said. "You take the high road and I'll take the railroad."

They all groaned. "Oh, that's awful," Jan said in disgust. "Roll him in the snow till he cools off."

Ben and Andrew made a joyous rush for Danny but just then there was a honking down the road. "They're here," they shouted, and, grabbing the lanterns, ran to the door.

"Saved by the horn," Danny commented as he raced outside with them.

Soon everything was noise and confusion, but pleasant, efficient confusion. Overnight bags were dumped in the dormitories and the girls got busy in the kitchen buttering buns, spearing pickles, and pouring out mounds of crisp potato chips.

The weiners were put in a cauldron to boil at Mrs. Mallory's insistence. "Then no matter what the kids do to them they'll be reasonably sanitary," was her reasoning.

Finally the table was arranged and the fireplace banked with weiner toasters arguing about the degree of crispness that made for the best eating. Everyone was so hungry that they had all eaten at least one weiner and bun before anyone noticed a great lack of mustard. "Fine kitchen committee," Ben sneered. "Stand around gossiping all afternoon and forget to unpack the mustard."

Jan and Maybelle looked at each other with dismay. "Wasn't it in the box we brought from the car?" Jan asked.

"We put it in that box," Maybelle affirmed, "but I can't swear that we took it out again."

"Don't look at me. I wasn't here," Cassie said, defending her part of the kitchen committee.

"I suppose it fell out in the car somewhere," Jan said with an exasperated sigh. "I'll go get it."

"Need any help?"

"No, thanks. If it isn't in plain sight you can just do without."

She grabbed a flashlight and a sweater and slipped out the back door. It was snowing again, swirling wet flakes that tangled in her hair and stung her face.

She stumbled forward, staring beyond the flashlight beam. There was the station wagon and the two other cars that had brought the main group, but the Mallory car was gone. For a minute she was alarmed, then she remembered that when Danny brought in the blankets he'd said he was moving the car up the road so he wouldn't block the driveway. Up the road where was the big question.

The sensible thing to do would be to go back in and tell them to eat their weiners plain or not at all, but she'd gone this far and some mustard would be very tasty. She swung the flashlight around and sure enough up the trail was a snow-covered mound. My, it must have been snowing longer and harder than she had realized to cover the car so completely.

She mushed off towards it, thinking that perhaps they would have a real blizzard and be snowed in like Cassie predicted and the boys would have to go out and trap a bear or something for food, or else they'd all have to go back to town over the ski trail. Golly, imagine Miss Layton if she came face to face with a bear-skinning project. Jan giggled, brushed the snow out of her eyes, and thought, "I hope he didn't lock the door."

She reached out to brush the snow away, stumbled on a patch of ice, and reached groping hands towards the car to steady herself. Her hands touched, gave way, and she screamed in terror as the great pile of logs toppled like a child's tower of blocks, hurtling noisily to the ground and smashing the figure in their path.

At first all Jan felt was the skid of the ice as she slipped and fell. Then she heard the rumble of the log avalanche and felt a flash of pain as a log hit her left leg and pinned her to the ground. The agony was so intense that she felt herself dropping into blackness. She threw her arms around her head to fend off the blows of the other logs that would probably send the racing pains through her until there was nothing of her left to feel pain. She was going to be killed on the happiest day of her life because of a jar of mustard. "No, no," she screamed, and enveloping blackness overcame her.

The blackness of unconsciousness was giving way to the ordinary darkness of a winter night. The pain in her leg was intense and she could not move it from its log prison, but she struggled to a half-sitting position and anxiously felt her body. She wasn't dead after all. Tears of joy and relief made icicles on her face.

She was alive, but trapped in the snow wearing only a thin sweater, and heaven only knew how long it would be before anyone in that wild crowd noticed she was gone and realized she might be lost. The flashlight lay too far away for her to reach, casting a futile circle of light in the snow. How long could she stand this? Numbness and misery were beginning to add themselves to the stabbing pains in her leg.

But she had to stand it. She had to live because she had a date with Danny for the class play. She had a date with the Shorewood Lumber Company to win a scholarship. She had a date with a Seattle newspaper to be its star reporter—a date for all the wonderful things that lay ahead in life.

"Help!" she screamed. "Help!" The wind blew the words back at her and the snow sifted down and covered her with coldness.

Some time later, through half-opened, haze-dimmed eyes, she saw the lights on the back porch of the lodge, saw the lanterns being waved and heard the frantic voices calling her name. "Here I am," she called, but they didn't hear.

Perhaps she hadn't made much noise, anyhow. She couldn't tell for sure. Things kept coming and going as if she were in a hammock swinging back and forth above the world. There was one comfort, though. She wasn't nearly so cold any more. She was beginning to feel quite cozy. She didn't even cry when she saw the lights start off in the other direction. So Danny had parked his car down there. Well, they always said she didn't have sense enough to come in out of the rain. Now she wasn't going to come in out of the snow, either. She would have laughed about it if she hadn't been so sleepy.

She was almost asleep when a snow-covered figure suddenly emerged in front of her. He held his lantern high, looking down at her miserable, huddled form compassionately. With a great effort she tried to sit up, tried to smile. She should have known there was no need to be upset. She should have known that Danny would find her no matter where or when. Danny was always there when she needed him. "Danny," she whispered, "Oh, Danny, you're going to save me."

"Sure I'm going to save you," the voice said bending down to her. "Just take it easy, sis."

Incredulously she opened her eyes wider. It was Andrew.

CHAPTER 17

Rescue

ANDREW DROPPED DOWN in the snow beside her, put his jacket around her, and clamped his cap on her head, pulling it down over her ears. This small comfort immediately heartened Jan. "How did you find me?" she asked in the whisper that seemed to be all that was left of her voice.

Andrew, pulling hard at the big logs as he searched for the one pinning her down, answered impatiently. "Elementary, my dear sister. I've lived with you long enough to know how you tick. I may not be overloaded with brains like you, but I could figure out that if you went to get the mustard you'd wander off in the wrong direction and whang into something. Besides, I noticed these logs this afternoon. The boys just pulled the ones they wanted out of the pile and left it primed for an avalanche."

He heaved and grunted as he tossed the logs aside one by one. As hope began to come back to Jan and her thoughts became clearer she realized it was really Andrew there beside her, Andrew working so hard in the cold and without proper clothing—Andrew who had had rheumatic fever and, even though Dr. Conners had pronounced him well, had been sternly told to avoid exposure and foolhardiness.

"Better call somebody else," she protested. "You'll strain your heart."

"I'm doing fine," he replied, and with a tug that brought sweat to his face he lifted the last log off her leg and knelt to examine the damage. "I know it's broken," she said.

He nodded gravely. "I think the doctor would call it a compound fracture. We'll have to get it immobilized before we move you. I *will* need some help."

Rising to his feet, he sucked in his breath and let out a banshee yell. He waved his lantern and yelled some more. The lights began to waver, coming back towards the lodge. "Here she is!" he shouted triumphantly. "I found her!"

When the others came up, breathless and excited, Andrew was taking her pulse. "It's a compound fracture," he explained. "She hasn't gone into shock but her pulse could be stronger."

"Why, Andrew, I didn't know you were such an expert at First Aid," Mr. Larsen said in surprise as he verified the diagnosis.

"Boy Scout Handbook," Andrew said with a shrug.

Mr. Larsen put his jacket around Jan, too, and began rubbing her hands. She tried to smile her thanks but she was too tired. "Get some end poles from the army cots," Mr. Larsen instructed the boys. "We'll use them for the splint. Tell Miss Layton to find something in the way of a hot drink, and Danny, you get on that Forest Service phone in the shed and pray that they didn't disconnect it this summer."

After the makeshift splint was on her leg Mr. Larsen said gently, "Jan, can you hear me?"

She thought she said yes. Her lips made the movement.

"We're going to have to carry you into the lodge and it may be painful. We'll do the best we can."

There was no doubt that they did the best they could. Jan tried to steel herself, but in spite of her efforts she moaned and fainted long before they laid her down on a cot in front of the fireplace.

From then on consciousness kept coming and going in the same swinging-back-and-forth-above-the-earth feeling she'd had when she was out in the snow. Once she came swinging back to the present and saw Miss Layton poised beside her with a cup of tea and a spoon. Mrs. Mallory said, "No, don't try to feed her while she's semiconscious. She might choke."

Other faces came in and out of the fog. Maybelle seemed to be weeping because she hadn't gone for the mustard, too.

The next time she opened her eyes Danny and Mr. Larsen were conferring. "The phone worked after a fashion," Danny explained. "I talked to the operator and she talked to the others. The roads are bad. They're getting more like a skating rink every minute, and even with chains it would be a long, rough trip."

"But we can't just stay here," Mr. Larsen protested. "The longer the delay the greater the danger from shock or infection. They might even . . ." he glanced at Jan and said nothing more.

Danny nodded. "Uh-huh. Dr. Conners goes along with you there. His idea was that it would be faster and maybe even easier if we could sled her down the ski trail to Black Mountain Junction. He'll send the hospital intern, Dr. Grant, up there on the speeder."

"It's a sound plan if we can manage it. Do we have the right equipment?"

"Yes, I looked," Danny replied. "There's a big sled and a lot of snowshoes out in the shed. The trail is fairly well marked and I know something about it that the doctor doesn't know. It goes near the railroad spur for the Shorewood camp, and if there's a speeder handy there we could get her down to the main tracks and the Junction a lot faster than by mushing."

"It's in your hands, Danny. You organize the expedition."

"You and I and Ben," Danny said promptly. "We'll take turns pulling the sled, holding it back on the steep places and marking trail."

"Get back on the phone and tell Dr. Conners our plans," Mr. Larsen instructed. "Ben and I will get Jan ready."

They put Jan into a mummy-type sleeping bag. She wanted

to joke with them and say she hoped the mummy business wasn't significant but the words just didn't come. Anyhow, she was warm now.

They were tying her on the sled when Mrs. Mallory came up looking worried and upset. "It's that boy, her brother," she said. "He's shaking with chills and fever. I'm worried about him."

The men stopped short. "We'd better take him along," Mr. Larsen decided. "There's room on the sled, and maybe if he gets treatment fast enough it will prevent another attack of rheumatic fever."

Jan felt her eyes fill, and tears froze on her face when Andrew, swathed in another sleeping bag, was put beside her. "Mother will never forgive me," she muttered.

"Oh, shut up," Andrew replied crossly. "I don't know why they had to get all excited because I sneezed a few times. I'm all right."

"I hope we are doing the right thing," Mr. Larsen said quietly as they started down the trail. "I must admit I'm worried. Her leg is badly smashed. I don't see how . . ."

"They do wonderful things these days," Danny interrupted, not letting the principal put his fear into words.

So that was why they were so upset—they thought she might lose her leg. Terror shot through her and for a minute she struggled wildly within the narrow confines of the sleeping bag. She wanted to scream her protests. How could she ever keep that date with life minus a leg?

Then she thought of all the stories she had read of war veterans and other handicapped people who lived gainful lives against bitter odds. She thought again of Andrew, who perhaps had risked his life, at least risked the possibility of another long, dreary illness, to rescue her. No, she must be brave and not complain. She would find a place for herself even if it had to be the rewrite desk instead of an on-the-spot reporter's job.

She tried to put her own worries away and think about Andrew as the sled slipped along smoothly over the hard-packed snow, the tall trees hovering like sentinels over them. Andrew had a date with life, too. He had a date with manhood and had fulfilled it. Even if he did get sick again he wouldn't be an object of pity and condescension any more because he had been so valiant.

"Hey, look over there." Danny straightened up and pointed to the right, where a bright light flashed across the sky and disappeared.

"Is it a comet?" Ben asked.

"Heck, no, I'll bet it's a flare from the Shorewood camp showing us the way. How news does travel in our little backwoods community. See, there's another. Mush on men, we've about made it."

A few minutes later they came in sight of the camp. It was ablaze with lights, even though all the men except the small maintenance crew were gone for the week-end.

The speeder was waiting for them, its motor put-putting. Danny, Ben, and Mr. Larsen gratefully accepted steaming cups of coffee which they drank in hasty gulps while the crew moved the patients from the sled to the speeder. Jan was aware of all that took place but couldn't rouse herself to speak. "How about some coffee for them?" the old watchman asked.

"No, leave them alone," Mr. Larsen replied. "And we'd better be on our way as soon as we can."

The old fellow nodded his head seriously. "If you mind what you're doing you'll have just time enough to get to the Junction and off the tracks before the fast freight goes through. But if you stall along the way you'd better be ready to get out of the way fast."

"Quit being so cheerful," Danny said. "I can run one of these babies in my sleep. But just to save wear and tear on your own nerves, you'd better get at your dot-dash and tell the train to take it easy."

"Tell the fast freight to slow down? They won't like it!"

"They'd be delayed even longer if they had to sweep us off the tracks," Danny replied as he took his place by the lever.

"I'll try," the watchman promised. "Both of Morgan's kids in one night," he muttered, turning back toward the camp. "Sometimes you wonder what life is all about."

"Cold but fast," Danny muttered as he pushed the little vehicle for all the speed it could muster.

It was like the rushing of wings through the night, Jan decided, a beautiful thought that she wouldn't bother to share with them. "Not far now," Danny said as he eased the speeder onto the main tracks. "The Junction is straight ahead."

After a while Mr. Larsen spoke uneasily. "Danny, there's a funny vibration in the rails. You don't suppose . . ."

"Oh, yes," Danny said, nodding his head. "That's old 420 rolling her wheels, but don't worry. We're going to make it. We'll hit the side track in a minute. You can see the signal blocks for the Junction up ahead now."

The signals were flashing and the rails humming when Danny finally reached Black Mountain Junction and hurriedly ran the speeder off the main track and around behind the little station house. "Whew," said Mr. Larsen. "I hope my knees aren't too wobbly to walk. I'll never make fun of those tie-poor-little-Nell-on-the-railroad-tracks melodramas any more. I know just how they feel."

"Oh, brother, yes," Ben agreed fervently.

The station door opened and the doctor and the local telegrapher came over to the speeder. "Don't bother to unload," the telegrapher said. "The train will be here in a minute."

"We know all about that train," Danny said. "It's been breathing down our necks ever since we left the spur."

"It's going to help us now," Dr. Grant said. He came towards Jan, then started in surprise. "I didn't know there would be two of them. I was only prepared for a girl with a broken leg."

Mr. Larsen and Danny glanced at each other in dismay. "Are those folks at the Lodge so rattled they didn't think to call back and tell them we were bringing Andrew, too?" Mr. Larsen asked.

"Maybe the phone isn't working at all by now. It was very temperamental when I was trying to get through," Danny said.

They explained as best they could about Andrew's condition and the worry that had prompted them to bring him along.

"Hmmmmm," he replied. "I'll look him over when we get on the train."

While he was checking Jan's pulse the two diesel-electric engines came into view, slowed down, and crept quietly past the station. It was a long, long train and the engines were out of sight by the time the caboose finally came along, but in answer to a couple of beep-beeps, it slowed down and stopped. The crew scrambled out of the caboose and ran towards them.

"Those the kids?" the brakeman asked. "Let's get them aboard, 420 hasn't been late all winter and we don't want to start now."

"You mean you're taking us?" Mr. Larsen asked, surprised.

"Sure. We'll get to Cascadeville in twenty-five minutes. It would be considerably longer in the speeder."

Surprisingly enough, the warmth of the caboose made the pain more intense for Jan. The cold must have provided a sort of anesthesia, she thought briefly. The flow of conversation around her seemed as disjointed as the voices on a radio being flipped from station to station. The doctor was hovering around, but she couldn't concentrate on him either.

"I don't know about you young folks," Mr. Larsen said as he stood warming his hands by the stove. "You're accustomed to miracles in everyday life, but I never thought I'd get a ride in a caboose and if the circumstances were different I'd be quite thrilled."

"If the circumstances were different we wouldn't be here," Danny reminded him. "Railroads are almost as strict about keeping strangers out of the caboose as they are about keeping the cars on the rails."

"What's in the yellow bottle?" Ben asked the doctor.

"Plasma," he replied. "Wonderful protection against shock."

They are giving me plasma, Jan thought, I've read about that. But she just didn't care enough to look around and see how it was done.

"I never tended patients in a caboose before, but this whole evening reminds me of my army service," the doctor remarked.

After doing all he could for Jan at the moment he turned his attention to Andrew. "Your temperature is up," he said, "but your heart sounds fine. I don't think you need to expect any trouble, young man."

"I should hope not," Andrew growled, and Jan smiled a little to herself. Well, he had a right to be surly. . . .

"What about Jan?" Mr. Larsen asked.

"We'll need a much more extensive examination before we can say anything about her. But she is strong and healthy and that will help a lot."

"Hey, there's Cascadeville coming up now," Danny said as he looked through the window. "We're slowing down, and wow, it looks as if the whole town is waiting for us."

"Tell them to bring the stretcher around," Dr. Grant instructed.

The others were hardly off the train before Dr. Conners came aboard, looking as cross as Jan had ever seen him. The two doctors conferred in low voices. Then Dr. Conners came over and smiled reassuringly. "You have a lot of stamina, Jan. You're holding up fine. And what do you know, the fanciest orthopedic man in Seattle is flying up here in the Forest Service helicopter just to fix that leg."

Jan, strengthened by the plasma transfusion, roused herself to ask, "Where is Mother?"

"In the station having hysterics. You'd think no one ever had an injured child before. Well, Dr. Grant, you've done fine, and now I think we might have our patient take a little nap." He reached for a syringe.

Jan shook her head. "No. No. Please. Mother doesn't know about Andrew, and when she finds out it will be such a terrible blow. Do what you can for him right away so that maybe things won't be so hard on him. He got sick saving my life."

"We'll pull every trick in the book to see that he doesn't get rheumatic fever again," the young doctor said soothingly.

"Of course I'm all right," Andrew croaked. "Let me out of here and I'll go home under my own power."

"You'll go along with us for the ride," Dr. Conners said firmly, and signalled to his helpers.

Swiftly they bundled the two patients into stretchers and wheeled them over to the waiting ambulance. Mrs. Morgan was standing there, her face contorted with worry. "Oh, Janice dear, your poor leg," she said while she gently pushed a stray hair from Jan's forehead. "Are you in much pain?"

Then, before Jan could answer or anyone could warn her of what to expect, she saw Andrew. She screamed and would have fallen but for her husband's arm. Why, it's still Friday night, Jan thought. Dad's here.

"Don't be upset. I hope and believe Andrew is not seriously ill." Dr. Conners' gruff voice was quiet and reassuring. "And this I do know for certain. He is a hero!"

"You say he's going to be all right?" Mr. Morgan asked.

"He's righter than he's been for a long time. I told your wife when this trip to the mountains first came up that his need to be like the other boys far outweighed the risk he ran of getting sick again.

"Mrs. Morgan, you needed to consider him fully and completely well so you could see your family in the right perspective. You were so overprotective of Andrew that Jan felt pushed clear out of the family circle, and that's something that could have ruined her life far more effectively than being smashed up like this. But for heaven's sake, I don't have time to deliver lectures in philosophy, I've got a mighty sick girl on my hands."

Any other time Jan supposed she would have felt triumphant, but now she just felt confusedly sorry for Mother, for Andrew, for the whole world.

"How long do you have to live here before you can tell off the populace?" Dr. Grant asked in an awed voice.

"You have to be here long enough to really care what happens to them," was the reply.

But Mrs. Morgan, hearing everything and comprehending none of it, wept over Andrew. "My poor little boy," she said, over and over.

"Not any more," Mr. Morgan said proudly. "He's a man now." He gave his son an approving pat and came over to Jan. "You're a brave girl. You're going to be fine, dear."

"Daddy," she said, and clung to his hand.

"Ready for your hypo now, Miss Morgan?" Dr. Conners asked, and then didn't wait for her to reply.

Jan was content to feel the warm drowsiness come over her. Andrew was home and safe so she could relax and let someone else do the worrying. She was scared, scared about just how much of her would be left when she woke up again, but there was nothing she could do about that. Might as well just float with the tide. She smiled sleepily as Danny came to say good-by. Then from the edge of consciousness she became aware of an argument. "But you're taking Janice away and I didn't get a chance to tell her good-by."

"Listen, this isn't the time or place for family arguments. Jan has all she can do right now. You can weep over her when the operation is safely over. Run along now, we'll see you at the hospital."

"But I ought to go with you. These are my children."

"They are my patients, and right now I'm the boss."

Jan could hear the grief and protest in her mother's voice and wished she could say something to comfort her. In the last few blurry minutes before giving up entirely to the drowsiness, she began to think that maybe Mother didn't necessarily like Andrew the best after all. Maybe she was just the worry-wart type who got all steamed up over illness and forgot everything else. And if that was the way Mother was constituted it was something she couldn't help, and she shouldn't be scolded about it. They would just have to learn to live with it. What if it had been she instead of Andrew who had got rheumatic fever? . . .

The last she heard was her father's voice. "Come on, Alice, we'd better get over to the hospital."

CHAPTER 18

Just Like a Turtle

"I SAID YOU LOOK just like a turtle upside down in the sunshine," Danny remarked. "No matter how much you wiggle you aren't going any place."

Jan shook her head, trying to force open her heavy-lidded eyes. She was in bed in the hospital. She tried to sit up but couldn't because of the heavy cast on her leg. She was exactly like a turtle in the sunshine. "Very funny," she muttered. "Don't ever try to win a prize with that one."

Danny turned to the nurse. "Told you I could wake her up," he said. He came over to Jan and smiled gently. "I have to go now, Scoop. They won't let me stay. But I'll be back for a visit when you aren't all hung-over from dope. I know you'll be around. You aren't going to walk away from this situation."

The nurse washed Jan's face and the fog receded a little further. "How do you feel?"

"I haven't any idea," Jan replied. "Is this tomorrow?"

"Yes. It's late afternoon. Would you like some lunch?"

"I don't think so. How's my brother?"

"Fine. He went home at noon. Your father and the Scoutmaster came in this morning with a whole Scout uniform and a Tenderfoot badge. That Andrew was the happiest kid I've seen in many a day."

"But he was so sick," Jan protested.

The nurse, busy making the bed, smiled at her. "No, he wasn't really sick. According to Dr. Conners, he'd just been told so often that if he overexerted he'd have heart trouble that when he did pull a wing-ding like rescuing you out in the snow it frightened him. It was the scare that made him sick."

"Oh," Jan said. "I didn't want him hurt on my account."

"If he uses a little common sense he shouldn't ever have any trouble," the nurse assured her.

She went out and came back in a few minutes with a tray of food. Jan picked at it a bit but finally pushed it away. Her eyelids were still heavy and it was too much work to eat. There was pain somewhere but she wasn't quite focusing on it. "I just want to sleep," she said.

Sometime during the day a group of doctors held a consultation around her cast but Jan just ignored them.

The fog was all gone the next day when Jan woke up to the busy morning routine of the hospital. Aside from the discomfort of her cast she felt fine. She rather suspected that from now on she would struggle against being in bed as much and as futilely as the poor turtle upside down in the sunshine.

Jan was just finishing a hearty breakfast when she heard voices out in the hall. "But it's not visiting hours," the nurse protested.

"That's why we came," a gay voice answered. "You can tell Dr. Conners to go climb a tree if he objects."

The door opened and Mrs. Abbott and Mrs. Preston came in with big smiles and armloads of packages. "Hello, Jan," they chorused. "Oh, look at the size of that cast, will you!"

"How nice of you to come to see me," Jan said.

Mrs. Preston shrugged. "We know this hospital inside out. The nurse is about due to come in here and give you a bath with laundry soap and stuff you into another of those muslin strait-jackets, so we thought we'd get here the firstest with the mostest."

Mrs. Abbott pulled out a short red sleep coat and some

red ribbons. "Let's get out of that hospital glamour gown and into something pretty," she suggested.

In a short time Jan was clean, comfortable, and cheerful. The sleep coat was warm and soft, her hair was neatly braided into two pigtails, the ends tied with ribbons, and a carnation was tucked into her collar so she could smell it instead of the hospital.

Mrs. Abbott placed magazines, writing paper, and knitting equipment within easy reach. "You're both so good to me I just don't know how to say thanks," Jan said, choking.

The women smiled at her affectionately. "We'll be back again," they promised. "Can't stay long today because we have all the children in the car outside and they're probably tearing it to pieces."

"No baby-sitter," Mrs. Preston said in mock horror. "You think you have troubles—what about us?"

They were gone with a last smile and wave. Jan picked up one of the magazines but had hardly settled to read when the door opened again and her mother entered. "For good-ness' sake," she said in astonishment. "Where did you get that outfit?"

"Mrs. Abbott and Mrs. Preston," she said, and told her mother all about their visit.

"How nice of them to come over when they are so busy. I made you a bed jacket yesterday and I thought surely I would be in time for you to wear it this morning."

She spread the dainty, quilted satin garment on the bed.

"It's beautiful, Mother," Jan said fingering the soft mate-rial. "I'm sure I'll have plenty of opportunity to wear it. As Danny said, I won't be walking away from this situation."

"Oh, has he been over, too? I might have known it."

"He woke me up yesterday," Jan said with a giggle, "by calling me a turtle upside down in the sunshine."

"I tried to wake you up, too," her mother said. "I was wor-ried about you sleeping on and on that way, but Dr. Conners made me go home. I don't know why he feels he has to be so disagreeable."

"Doctor's privilege," Jan said with a shrug.

"It's certainly a shame that you'll be in that cast for so long. The last few months of school are always full of parties —and just as you were coming to enjoy social affairs. Sometimes life gets rather confusing."

Jan smiled gently at her mother, who looked very tired and bewildered. The week-end's events had been shattering for her. Immobilized with a broken leg she might be, but today Jan felt older and stronger than her mother. It seemed as if for the first time she could see beyond herself and could see how life had been for her mother with one child sick and the other one being as disagreeable as possible.

"Mother, it's wonderful of you to make this for me and bring it down this morning, but you ought to go home and get some rest or Dr. Conners will have the whole Morgan family on his list. How's Andrew? Did he go to school today? It is Monday, isn't it?"

Her mother sighed deeply and sank down in the chair. Jan could see her trying to blink back tears. "You can't imagine what Dr. Conners and your father have been saying to me," she said. "Acting as if I was trying to ruin Andrew's life when I would have done anything, anything at all to keep him happy and healthy. They didn't have to take care of him day after day when he was in bed. It's little they know about it. Now they've signed him up with the Scouts and are planning all sorts of camping trips. I—I did the best I could," she finished sadly.

"Of course you did," Jan agreed. "It was a difficult job and none of us helped much. Don't let them hurt your feelings. Men don't understand those things."

"No, they don't," her mother affirmed. "And I do appreciate your talent, Jan. It's just that—well, I don't even like to write letters and I guess I can't understand anyone who wants to find out all about everything and then write about it. . . ."

She called me Jan! Jan said to herself happily. She finally called me Jan! She accepts me just the way I am. Jan looked at her mother and felt a great wave of affection. Her mother did love her, and was trying to understand her, and from now on she would try to understand her, too.

"Don't worry about Andrew," she said aloud. "He may go wild about the Scouts for a while, but he'll soon simmer down to normal—if boys are ever normal. Besides, you're going to be so busy with all your sewing and designing that you won't have time to worry so much about him."

"Yes, that's true," her mother said, brightening considerably. "I do have the sewing."

"Bring some down here," Jan suggested. "I'm not very sharp at it but I could baste or something and you could keep me up on all the news around town."

Her mother was pleased. "I'll do that. Now I think I'll go home and take a nap. Dad will be down to see you later. He didn't go back to work this morning."

"I'll chase him back up to camp," Jan said. "He doesn't need to miss work because of me."

Alone again, Jan chuckled to herself. "We're probably all making so many good resolutions that the atmosphere at home will be too sweet for us to endure," she murmured happily. "I'm never going to distrust my family again. Life is so wonderful that I don't want to waste it quarreling."

"Giving lectures in philosophy?" Danny inquired sardonically from the doorway.

"Is this a hospital or Grand Central Station?" Jan asked. "That poor nurse must be going batty."

"She is," Danny admitted. He pulled a manila envelope out of his pocket. "What I came to say is, I'm getting a little weary of the way you try to get out of your bounden duties by getting banged up. At least you aren't quarantined this time, so you can do a little work. Here's Pete's news—copyread it, write some headlines, and he'll pick it up later."

"Is that any way to treat a sick woman?" she asked.

"Sick!" Danny hooted. "You gold-bricking fake! You're not going to get out of editing this month's *Argus* if I have to bring the printing press to your bedside."

"Speaking of the *Argus,* what are you doing down here in the middle of a morning on a school day?"

Danny grimaced. "That's a good question and I have a feeling Mr. Larsen will be asking it, too. All right, I'll go quietly, but something else I want you to know is that breaking a leg doesn't excuse you from our date either. I'll be over in a wheelchair to get you, honey, better be ready 'bout half past eight . . ."

Whistling impudently, he tossed the package on the bed and left.

Jan lay back on her pillows laughing. Then she opened the envelope and laughed even harder. There besides the typewritten copy and soft lead pencil was a napkin-wrapped hamburger, still warm and juicy.

It wasn't long until lunch but she ate it eagerly, thinking that the whole performance was just like Danny. Tease her, insult her, dump a lot of work on her, then bring her a hamburger in the middle of the morning and skip school to do it!

Budge wouldn't treat his Melanie that way, she was sure, and Ben would be aghast at anyone behaving thus to Maybelle, but Danny was Danny and Jan thought joyfully that she wouldn't trade him and his breezy companionship for any other fellow in the country—not for ten others.

She didn't settle down to her copy-reading until after lunch, and she was still busy with it when the clock chimed for visiting hours and there at her door was Pete. Obviously he had made some attempt to smooth and polish his habitual work-a-day appearance, for instead of looking inky and dusty all over he just looked inky and dusty in streaky spots. Jan repressed a giggle at the thought of what those germ-conscious nurses must think of him.

He tiptoed across the room and laid a callused hand on her shoulder. "Do you hurt much, kid?" he asked.

"Not much, Pete. But I know I'm going to be awfully bored with lying here before long."

"Terrible," he fumed. "An awful thing to happen."

Jan smiled. It was awful, terrible, and stupid but there wasn't any point in a recapitulation. "Right now I can't get this headline to come out," she told Pete. "I can't decide whether to call Andrew brave or heroic."

Pete blew his nose and sat down hard. "Call him both," he said grandly. "Call him both. We have plenty of paper."

Just then Dr. Conners paid a brief visit, grumbled loudly, and told Jan she had steel pins in her leg and that he hoped she could go home at the end of the week.

After he left Pete settled back in his chair. "Well, as I was about to say before we were interrupted, I'm going to break my professional ethics all to smithereens and tell you that I have it on good authority that you've won a Shorewood scholarship. The only thing left to decide is whether you get the big all-expense package or one of the others. Thought that would cheer you up."

A pain sharper than the one she'd suffered in the accident went through Jan. She leaned against the pillows and closed her eyes. "No, Pete," she said finally. "I can't take it."

"Oh?" Pete's voice was ominously quiet. "How do you figure that?"

"Even though my college expenses might be paid, this silly accident is going to cost my folks so much that it's my duty to go to work as soon as I can and repay them. It's time I started thinking about somebody besides myself."

"Amazing what a brush with the grim reaper can do to a person's disposition," Pete said dryly.

An indignant reply leaped to Jan's lips, but Pete forestalled her. "Don't wave your martyr's crown around me," he said. "I agree it's time you thought of someone besides yourself, and I know you mean well, but you aren't getting away with anything like that. You're going to accept your scholarship and go to college and be the best journalist ever to come

out of Cascadeville. Your folks won't go broke getting you
out of the hospital, either, because I'm going to take care of
you and you can pay me back when you're rich and famous."

"Why, Pete!" Jan cried. "Why, Pete!"

Pete didn't meet her eyes. "And you don't have to start
getting all overcome with gratitude, either. I'm just making
a wise investment against my old age because I know you're
going to be successful. Now I suppose I'll have to go up to
your house and fight with your father about this."

"Fight with me about what?" Her father, dressed for his
return to camp, walked in quietly. "I just stopped in to tell
sis good-by. I'd better get back to making a living now that
I know she's going to be O.K. What's troubling you, Pete?"

"This daughter of yours." Pete's tone was venomous.
"Sometimes I can't figure out why folks think she's so
smart. I tell her she's going to win one of the Shorewood
scholarships and she screws up her face and starts saying she
has to get a job to pay her hospital bills. I'm not going to
have her short-circuit her future for a small debt like that.
I want to take care of it. I have a little saved—any kid in
town will tell you that I don't eat or drink anything but
printer's ink."

Her father gave him a smile and a comradely pat on the
shoulder. "Pete, you're a grand guy. You've been such a
friend to Jan, helping her learn newspaper work, printing all
those columns . . ."

"That isn't friendship," Pete hastened to deny. "I have to
put something in the paper every week and folks in Cascadeville would rather read about themselves than anything else."

"Maybe so," Mr. Morgan agreed, "but it's obvious that
neither of you reads anything in the paper that you don't
write yourselves, and of course at home we know that Jan
floats around in her private cloud and doesn't listen to family discussions about dull things like Shorewood's new employee benefits."

There had been some talk around town about a new plan at Shorewood, only just as her father said she'd been too busy to consider anything that didn't concern her. But maybe it did, after all?

"Employee benefits?" Pete asked suspiciously. "Every time the Shorewood company signs a new contract with the union they send me a release and I set it up and print it, but why should I bother to read it? What are you getting at?"

"As of last month the hospitalization insurance the company carries on its employees has been extended to their families. The policy will take care of most of Jan's expenses. You couldn't have picked a better time to break your leg, sis."

"How perfectly wonderful!" Jan said softly. She squirmed and twisted on her pillows. Oh, it was wonderful, but it was terrible, too, to lie here helpless. She ought to be up and busy and getting things done, now that she knew she wouldn't be carrying around an obligation as heavy and burdensome as her cast.

Pete wasn't ready to quit arguing, however. "Are you sure you can handle it all? There are always lots of extras in an emergency like this."

"To be sure," Mr. Morgan agreed. "But we'll handle them the way we always have—a little at a time, till they're all cleared up. But, Pete, I'll always remember your offer and the kind heart that prompted it."

"It's just good business sense," Pete insisted irritably. "And you still haven't said what you think about this scholarship. She can easily work for her room and board if she just gets one of the tuition scholarships instead of the all-expense deal. But can't I help with clothes and such things?"

"Her mother and I have been pretty gloomy about college," Mr. Morgan admitted. "We thought for awhile that it was going to be beyond us. You see, these new benefits won't help us with Andrew, because he has what they call a preexisting condition and his check-ups and treatments aren't covered. But on the other hand, we hope now that he won't be needing much more along that line. The way he came through that night on the mountain shows he's in pretty good shape. Pete, we felt that Jan was so young it wouldn't hurt for her to stay out of school a year and work, but if she really wants to go next year, and if she does get any kind of scholarship, we'll do the best we can to help her."

"Well, all right. That's what I've been trying to find out. Now if you'll excuse me I can't be sitting around all day like some ladies' tea-drinking society. I have a newspaper to publish."

Pete got up, shoved his shapeless hat back down on his head, and stamped to the door. "I'm going to do something," he said over his shoulder. "I'll find a way to be included yet."

The Morgans were quiet and thoughtful for a few minutes after he left. Then Mr. Morgan said, "I have to go, too, Jan. One of the bosses is going to camp for an inspection, which is why I'm getting a ride at this peculiar hour. I hope that when I come up this week-end it will be to bring you triumphantly home. Take it easy."

"Nothing else I can do," Jan reminded him. " 'By now, Daddy."

Soon after he left the bell rang for the end of visiting hours. Jan lay still, exhausted by the many emotions of the day. From the clanking and bustling out in the hall Jan knew that soon the nurse would be in to wash her up for dinner, but right now it was pleasant just to lie quietly and think of how richly blessed she was with friends.

Suddenly she laughed. She might indeed be flat on her back, helpless as a turtle upside down in the sunshine, as Danny had so flatteringly remarked, but she was the luckiest girl in the world. Bar none, the luckiest.

CHAPTER 19

A Family Now

"YOU'D BETTER PUT a sign on the door saying, 'Mountain View High School Annex'," Miss Layton suggested, as she came into the Morgan house with an armload of books and papers.

Jan's headquarters was the dining-room. Her bed had been brought down and placed at one side of the room, and the dining-room table, pushed against the wall, held a hodgepodge of books, papers, knitting, puzzles, and other impedimenta.

Danny was crouched on the floor correcting page proofs for the March *Argus*. Dotty, carrying a stack of material, dashed downstairs, grabbed the iron from the kitchen, and raced back up. Now that Jan's room was vacant, her mother was using it for her sewing.

Jan pushed her wheelchair across the room to greet Miss Layton. "It's really wonderful of you to help me keep up with my classes this way," she said as she took the books and put them on one side of the table. "Thanks to you, I'm about caught up. All but that awful term paper for history. It's due next week and I won't have it done."

"Take your time," Miss Layton advised. "Mr. Carter will understand if it's late. By the way, we'll be having a Press Club meeting next week. Too bad you can't be with us because we have some important business to transact. As a regular school organization we have the privilege of choosing a candidate for Tulip Festival Queen."

"Hot dog, I'll put on my wig and be right over," Danny announced.

"Down, Rover!" Jan commanded. "This is a serious business. I wish you would nominate Cassie. She's always wanted to be Tulip Queen."

"So have I," Danny insisted. "And where does it get me?"

"Be serious," Jan protested. "Quit hamming things up."

"I'm very serious. I'm pointing out in my own subtle way that I'm about as suitable for Tulip Queen as Cassie. Oh, I know she is very pretty, but she has about as much dignity as a hurricane, and a queen should have poise."

"That's very astute reasoning, Danny," Miss Layton concurred. "But that is one of your special gifts—insight and perception. No, Cassie just doesn't have quite the right qualities."

Danny would always be Miss Layton's favorite, Jan reflected, but that was fair enough. He deserved to be. But astute reasoning or not, she didn't intend to be talked out of her idea. "Some of you didn't think I had the right qualities to be editor," Jan reminded Miss Layton, and saw her turn faintly rosy at the memory. "Probably I didn't," Jan went on, "but when I had my chance to do what I wanted, I tried hard to develop the qualities I needed. That's what I want for Cassie—a chance."

"Fair enough," Danny agreed. "And after all, a club nomination is only the beginning. She would have to pass the executive board and the whole student body before she could be queen. Like you say, it wouldn't hurt to give her the chance."

"Very well," Miss Layton decided. "It's too bad we don't have absentee ballots, Jan, but you can count on Danny for the nomination, I'm sure. No, thank you, I won't stay for tea today. This place is too much like school. I want to get home to some peace and quiet."

Miss Layton left, but the door had hardly closed before

Andrew and some fellow Scouts streamed in the back way. "We're going to ask Mom if we can build a fire out in back and cook stew in aluminum foil," he said excitedly. "That's something every Scout should know."

"That sounds very edible," Danny commented, folding up the proofs. "I'll just take these down to Pete and then invite myself back to dinner. I'd like some Scout-style stew."

"How to earn the Congressional Medal of Honor the hard way," Jan muttered.

"Some people are just cynics," he retorted as he left.

In a few minutes Andrew and his mother came down the stairs together, she looking stern, and Andrew with the aggrieved pout Jan hadn't seen for several weeks. Evidently he had pushed his mother a fraction of an inch too far on his Scout activities.

"No, you cannot!" she said firmly. "I want you boys to have fun but you've got to be reasonable. In the first place, I don't want you building any fires without adult supervision; in the second, I don't know what you think you'd use for fuel when all the wood outside is soaked through from the snow and rain; and in the third place I can't afford to waste good food."

The faces of all the boys sagged gloomily. "Now here's what you can do and it can be just as much fun," she said brightly. They all looked at her suspiciously as she brought a large kettle out of the cupboard.

"You can make your stew right here in the kitchen. Every good Scout should know how to cook in an emergency, and since this stove has to be stoked with wood it's practically the same as cooking over a campfire. Jan will tell you what ingredients to put in and answer any questions. So get to work and don't bother me about the details. We're fitting the Titania costume and it's really complicated. Is that O.K. with you, Jan?"

"It's fine with me," Jan replied. "I was going to have to cook dinner anyhow. I'll be glad to have some helpers."

"Oh, crumb!" Andrew protested, giving the stove leg a kick. "What's the use of cooking dinner in a kitchen?"

"Come on Andy," Jim Conners said. "Some of the camp grounds have stoves just like this. This is all right for a Scout."

"Yeah, let's get going," one of the others agreed. "Where's the meat? I'll cut it in cubes the way my mom does."

"Tell you what," Jan suggested, "stew takes a long time to cook, and while you're waiting for it to get done I'll teach you how to make fudge."

"Swell," Andrew agreed instantly.

"Fine. First stoke up the stove so it will be hot enough to brown the meat, then go wash your hands thoroughly."

"Wash?" They were aghast.

"Who ever heard of a woodsman washing his hands?" Jim protested.

"Besides, all the germs would get killed in the cooking," was Andrew's solution.

"No wash, no fudge," Jan said, so they all trooped over to the sink.

While they were busy peeling vegetables, Jan took one of the history reference books and started to make notes for her term paper. Last winter it had seemed a wonderful idea to make a special study of the political development of South America, but now it was beginning to be a headache. It was all the fault of her beautiful coin belt, she decided. If it hadn't been so glamourous she wouldn't have wanted to know more about South America.

Everyone was working busily and quietly when the doorbell rang. "I thought everybody in town had already been here today," Jan muttered as she rolled through the house to the door.

A strange man was standing there. "Janice Morgan?" he

asked, and when she nodded introduced himself. "I'm Lyle Everett of the Shorewood Company."

Jan was glad she was sitting down. Here was the long-expected interviewer for the Shorewood scholarship, and oh, brother, what an impression she would make now. Pete had said she was sure to get one of the scholarships, that the interviewer's job would be to determine how much help she deserved. But they could change their minds altogether, she was sure. After all, Pete's rumors were far from binding.

She had so wanted to be at her best when the interviewer came, but now he was here and all she could do was hope that he could see through the confusion of the surroundings to the seriousness of her hopes and ambitions. Before she could think of anything even remotely intelligent to say to Mr. Everett, Andrew came out from the kitchen with streaming eyes and a look of anguish.

"How many more onions?" he asked frantically. "I can't stand this."

"Just a minute," she said. "Don't cut any more till I get there. I'm helping some Boy Scouts cook stew," she explained to Mr. Everett. He might as well know the whole, sad story.

"Go right ahead," he said politely. "I'll come out to the kitchen with you and we can talk there if you don't mind. We have already studied your scholastic record and have an idea of your community activities. This is really just a get-acquainted interview."

Jan was tempted to say that he would get acquainted all right, but she led the way back to the kitchen and helped the boys finish assembling the stew and get it to bubbling on the back of the stove. She introduced them to Mr. Everett and said, "Now all you have to do for a while is keep the fire from going out. You can play a game or something while you're waiting, and we'll make the fudge a little later."

"We'll go in the other room and practice tying knots," Andrew decided. He was being tactful for once, and Jan was surprised and grateful. She and Mr. Everett continued to sit in the kitchen. Amazingly enough, she found that he was very pleasant and easy to chat with. They talked about the Scouts and about her accident, and how she was keeping up with her work. He asked about the books on South America and suddenly she was telling him about her belt and how it had inspired her to study South America.

"That's very interesting," he said. "I've heard of gaucho belts but I haven't seen one. Might I see yours?"

Jan called Andrew and sent him upstairs to get it. When he came back his mother was with him. "I heard the bell, but I thought it was more kids," she explained.

She greeted Mr. Everett pleasantly, then went back upstairs. Jan began to feel her tense muscles relax. He didn't seem at all disapproving. Maybe she would get through this ordeal after all.

Mr. Everett admired the belt, then laid it aside, leaned forward, and asked, "Why do you want to go to college, Janice?"

That was the jackpot question for sure. Jan was so anxious to say the right thing that at first she was utterly tongue-tied. "Ever since I entered high school I've known I wanted to do newspaper work," she began hesitantly, but in a few minutes she warmed to her subject and began to speak happily of her desire to have the best training possible for this career.

He nodded approvingly and was about to reply when the doorbell rang timidly. Before Jan could move to answer, the door was pushed open and a high, elderly voice said, "Whoo, whoo, anybody home?"

The crack widened to show Mrs. Parsons carrying her inevitable knitting bag and beaming with pleasure at finding a house full of people to visit. "Janice, I'm glad to see you looking so bright. I've been worried about you."

"That's very kind of you, Mrs. Parsons," Jan said grimly. "Mother is upstairs working like crazy on the costumes for

the class play, but if you would care to stay down here and
visit with us awhile . . ."

"I'd be delighted," the old lady said, and began fumbling
at her coat buttons. Mr. Everett helped her off with her coat
and assisted her to a chair.

"Wouldn't you both like some tea or coffee?" Jan asked.
"The water is hot."

She was trying to keep a smile on her face, but it was rough
going. Mrs. Parsons would surely outstay Mr. Everett and
she would have no further chance to show him what a seri-
ous-minded, hard-working student she was. All he would see
was a banged-up girl driving her wheelchair around in circles
trying to keep up with her schoolwork in the midst of utter
confusion. And all she'd get out of this would be another
pioneer story from Mrs. Parsons, because now that the old
lady had an outlet for her memories, she just never stopped
talking.

If she failed to win a scholarship she would have to remind
Pete of his promise to get her a newspaper job so she could
go to the University part-time—but oh, she did so much want
to be a regular student enjoying not only her education but
the fun of campus life.

Sure enough, Mr. Everett was reaching for his hat. "I must
go now," he said. "It's been pleasant visiting with you, Janice. You'll hear from our office about your scholarship application soon. In the meantime I hope you'll permit me to
make two observations."

"Yes," Jan said, puzzled.

"The first is that courtesy to all people in every situation
is the mark of the truly educated person. May I compliment
you on that score."

"Oh," Jan said. "Oh." Why, he had seen and appreciated
her struggle to be polite to Mrs. Parsons!

"The second is that all of you have a real spirit of family

cooperation. It's been very nice meeting the Morgans of Cascadeville."

Then he was gone, leaving Jan in a first-class turmoil. We are a family she thought triumphantly. We have become a family. And everything considered, more than fame, more than college, more than anything, she wanted a family.

Mrs. Parsons, knitting needles clicking, talked on and on about the days when people were always breaking their legs up in the woods and dying before they could get back to town. . . . Andrew and the boys came storming in and wanting to know if they should put more water in the stew and when was she going to make the fudge. . . . Dotty whirled through the room in her costume, dancing around, eyes bright, asking and receiving admiration. . . . Danny came stamping back in asking when chow would be ready.

Jan, busy and laughing, loved them all and rejoiced that she was now truly part of the biggest family of all—the human race.

CHAPTER 20

Tulip Time Again

IT JUST HAPPENED THAT WAY, it was strictly coincidental, but Jan graduated from crutches to a cane on Tulip Festival Day, the last day of April. She didn't think she would be any more thrilled three weeks from now when as valedictorian of her class she would graduate from high school.

"A phenomenal recovery," Dr. Conners said as he watched her hobble slowly but triumphantly across the room. "You're an amazing gal, but try not to overdo it."

Jan smiled her thanks. "Why shouldn't I recover? Don't I have a good doctor?"

"Flattery will get you nowhere but downtown. Would you like a ride to the Playfield? I suppose you're going to that hocus-pocus."

"No, thank you, I want to walk. Now don't get excited," she added quickly as the doctor's face grew wrathful. "I'll go slowly and carefully, but really the greatest thrill I could possibly have today is to feel the ground under my feet."

"Feel it all you like but don't blame me if you fold up." And Dr. Conners was off on his busy rounds.

Jan turned to her mother, who had been watching the scene from behind a stack of fabrics. "Want to change your mind and come along?"

She shook her head. "Just can't today, Jan. I'm swamped." She had been over to the Playfield that morning to check the fittings of the gowns the queen and princesses were wearing.

Jan hobbled slowly out of the house, thinking happily

about her mother's metamorphosis. Mrs. Morgan was now the official Cascadeville designer and dress creator. At the class play last month the costumes had won such universal admiration that she now had more business than she could comfortably handle. Her earnings were going to pay for a new electric sewing machine that did everything but cut out the material, and in all probability a lifetime business had been established.

The family fit themselves around her new life with little grumbling. Jan was so delighted to have her mother busy and happy that she didn't mind doing more of the housework, and although Andrew kept protesting that Scouts were supposed to cook and keep clean out in the woods, not at home, still he was doing his share. On week-ends Dad couldn't do enough to show his pleasure at being part of a busy, alert, affectionate family.

Jan chuckled as she thought of Andrew's efforts to catch up with the other Scouts his age. The Scoutmaster said that in all probability he was going to set a record for earning his Second-Class Badge. He was even skipping the festival this afternoon to go for a hike and look for trail-blazing signs. It was grand to see him so happy and healthy. Seemed like he'd grown inches the last few months.

Well, this walking business was turning out to be more difficult than she had expected. She hadn't realized how far it was to school. She sat down on the bridge a few minutes and watched the river, high and noisy from the spring run-off.

"Waiting for a street car on a bus line, no doubt," Danny commented as he came up beside her. "Since it will be a good fifty years before our thriving metropolis expands enough to need a bus, hadn't you better let me go get the jalopy?"

Jan stood up and leaned on her cane. "No, thanks. I'm doing fine. I'm sure you'd like to trundle me into the Playfield in a wheelchair the way you did to the play, but I'm steaming under my own power today."

"Then," he said agreeably, "more power to you."

They walked slowly across the bridge together. "The school year is like the river," Jan philosophized. "We're running downstream hard and fast, and pretty soon we'll graduate and be spilled into the ocean."

"Since you're getting spilled onto the biggest raft in said ocean, it isn't such a bad simile," Danny said.

Jan could feel herself churning with pride—or was it only the feeling of eating lunch in too big a hurry? Anyhow, she had won the Shorewood all-expense scholarship.

Sometimes it didn't seem as if she could possibly be the most deserving senior in the Northwest. Sometimes she wondered if Mr. Everett had been prejudiced in her favor by her politeness to Mrs. Parsons and the Boy Scouts that harried afternoon. She would never know, of course, but she was convinced that the course of a life could pivot on such small incidents. Everyone else seemed to feel she deserved the award and would be a credit to the town, and that she was determined to be.

"You managed to spear a pretty big fish yourself," she retorted, "with that feature story on New Year's resolutions taking first place in the Press Club contest."

"I'll get by," he admitted modestly.

They turned into the Playfield and made their way to the grandstand, where Danny left her to go backstage and put on his costume of Court Jester. People called to Jan and eager hands helped her down the steep stairs to a seat by Dotty and Maybelle Warren.

"Nice to see you again, Maybelle. And thanks for the flowers from your Press Club. They were beautiful."

"I had a terrible time getting here," Maybelle confided. "When I asked to be excused for today Mr. Jepson asked me why I just didn't get my diploma up here and be done with it —the old sourpuss."

All three shook their heads over the unreasonable attitudes of principals.

"But he knew he couldn't make me stay there today. I'd tear up my diploma and throw it in his face before I'd miss the chance to see Ben in his Prime Minister's robes. He's noble—simply noble."

Dotty and Jan exchanged amused glances. "Where's your notebook?" Dotty asked. "Aren't you writing this up?"

"Not today," Jan said. "With the queen herself on our staff, we'll really get an inside story, because Cassie is going to write it herself. How it feels to be queen from one who knows. Our next year's editor Freddy Carter is handling the other angles, so this is my day of leisure."

"Here they come now," Maybelle said excitedly.

The band began the coronation march and the procession came across the field towards the throne banked with bright layers of tulips. Cassie walked slowly and proudly, followed by two kindergarten girls who in stumbling admiration were carrying her train.

Jan would always be glad she had helped engineer this. Just as she had predicted, the chance to be queen had changed Cassie from a pretty but giggly high school girl into a poised beauty. Jan had missed the assembly where the candidates were presented to the school but Danny had told her about it in an awe-struck voice. "She was a wow! Simply terrific! How did you know she would be like that?"

"I didn't," Jan explained. "I only hoped. People ought to have their dreams come true. It's good for them."

"If Cassie is any example you can say that again."

The procession halted. Cassie walked forward alone and knelt on the velvet cushion. The trumpets sounded and Ben stepped forward with the crown. Maybelle was right. He did look noble. He was indeed worth a seventy-two-mile trip. He raised Cassie and led her back to the throne. The trumpets rang out again and the audience sank back with a long sigh while the field was cleared for the maypole dance.

Jan couldn't take her eyes away from the radiant happiness in Cassie's face. It would be wonderful to be Tulip Queen. No doubt about it. It had been a thrilling moment indeed for Cassie, for Melanie, for Mrs. Preston and all the girls who had shared this magic hour.

But life was full of wonderful things, as she had discovered this last year, and perhaps the most wonderful discovery of all was that it was silly to be jealous of anyone. Never again would anybody call Jan Morgan "Green Eyes." She had blue eyes that were wide open to the beauty and wonder of the world, and they were going to stay that way.

She joined in the applause for Cassie heartily and sincerely, and when the show was over sat quietly waiting for the stands to empty, not wanting to slow anyone with her ponderous walk. Pete stopped by for a minute. "You and Danny be by tomorrow?" he asked.

"Yes, we'll be there," she promised.

She just couldn't look at the old printer without her throat choking and her eyes clouding over. Since his help wasn't needed with her hospital or college expenses he was grimly determined to contribute to her college wardrobe, a gift that her parents had accepted as much for his sake as their own.

He had carried his determination to the point of accompanying Mrs. Morgan on a fabric-buying expedition, and that trip was going to be a source of family amusement for many years. "You should have seen him," Mrs. Morgan laughed, as home again and surrounded with bundles she recounted her adventures to Jan and Andrew. "He stuck out his chin with that army-mule look and headed straight for the velvets and brocaded satins and even, heaven help us, the gold lamé, and he just wasn't going to move from the spot. None of the clerks could convince him that wasn't what the well-dressed college girl wore."

"Oh, my, what did you end up with?" Jan asked, giggling.

Mrs. Morgan sighed. "I finally persuaded him that if he made you go to class in gold lamé you'd be so concerned with keeping it clean that you wouldn't hear a thing the professor said—you'd flunk the course and lose your scholarship. That worked. He let me lead him over to the washable woolens without a murmur. But he did insist on a dark red velvet for your best dress, and it is beautiful, Jan. I know you'll love it."

"I know I will, too," Jan said happily, as she eagerly went through the packages.

Now, watching Pete move off with the crowd, she was glad she wouldn't be able to take a regular job this summer. She wanted to spend these last months before she went away working in the old shop alongside Pete.

Presently Danny appeared at her side in the nearly deserted stadium. "You were a wonderful jester," she said.

"Happy to oblige. Jest any old time at all."

"I'm going home," she groaned. "Even your mother's cooking would be indigestible after that." Jan was invited to the Mallory house for dinner, and in the evening she and Danny would go to a party Ben was having for the festival participants.

Danny laughed and helped her up the stairs. At the top of the grandstand they paused and looked out over the field and beyond it to the encircling mountains. "When we pulled in here last summer I thought I'd just be putting in a year at hard labor. I didn't dream a hick town in the hills could be so rewarding."

"A small town like Cascadeville is nice," Jan agreed. "The world in nucleus. What more could you ask of life than good people, bad people, and a newspaper to tell about them?"

"That from a girl who probably has a University catalog under her pillow."

They laughed and made their slow way out of the Playfield

to the street. "Mom left the car for us," Danny explained. "One walk today is plenty for you."

"Of course we have to go away." Danny settled Jan in the car, got in beside her, and continued their discussion. "If you stay in a small town all your life you're stuck, but if you go away and choose to come back, then you've really found the secret of living."

"I imagine a lot of people feel that way," Jan said. "But they don't come back. There are so many jobs to do, new friends to meet, places to go that somewhere in the circle of the world they put down new roots and never do get back to the old town."

"We will," Danny promised. "We'll do the jobs, and meet the people and see the places, but someday maybe five, maybe ten, maybe twenty years from now you'll be interviewing an archeologist in Iran and I'll be covering a revolution in Argentina and all of a sudden an alarm clock will go *ding,* and we'll drop our notebooks in our tracks and head back to Cascadeville and make the *Courier* the biggest thing since the Emporia *Gazette.*"

"Sounds feasible, but what about Pete?"

"He'll wait for us. He won't retire till we get back."

"Maybe he'll wait, but I'll bet dinner won't. Crank up your rocket ship and point us towards this brave new world."

Danny turned to her with an amused, tender smile. "Here's something else for you to remember. I won't want any back-seat drivers on my rocket ship, either."

Bending over, he kissed her, then quickly put the car in gear and rolled off down the street.

Jan, her face flaming and her heart beating rapidly, was content to sit and say nothing. He shouldn't have done it, of course, but she didn't reprimand him because her whole being was flooded with delight at the knowledge that love, when it was time for love, would be only a deepening and fulfilling of the wonderful comradeship she had known thus far.

As the car turned the corner Jan saw the sun poised on the edge of Barren Mountain before its descent to the west. Long rays of light slanted towards them. The school children were told that on these ladders of light the dew ascended to be turned into rain. But today Jan wanted to believe that she could catch hold of these ladders and they would carry her out of the valley and down to the city, to all the cities all over the world where she would go in her quest for news.

She turned to Danny to share her fancy with him. Then she stopped. No, not now. Someday, if as he predicted they left freely and returned gladly together—if, *when* that day came she would tell him.